Petra

The Prison World Revolt, Book One

Matthew S. Rotundo

This novel is a work of fiction. All characters, places, and incidents described in this publication are used fictitiously, or are entirely fictional.

Cover design by Ryan Malm (http://twitter.com/ryanmalm).

If you would like to be notified about new releases and other news of interest from Matthew S. Rotundo, please sign up for his mailing list at http://www.matthewsrotundo.com. Your email address will never be shared and you can unsubscribe at any time.

ISBN: 978-1523447640

For my wife, Tracy, who makes all things possible.

ACKNOWLEDGMENTS

Thanks to my first readers and beta readers: Laurel Amberdine, Mark Boeder, Erica Hildebrand, Michele Korri, Jay Lake (I miss you, brother), and Shara White. Your honesty, sagacity, and bravery have been indispensable.

Thanks also to Tamara Blain, copy editor *par excellence*, for making me look good. Believe me, I know how difficult that job is.

My deepest appreciation goes to the incredible Annie Bellet for her unflagging encouragement and hand-holding throughout the indie publishing process.

To Jeanne Cavelos and everyone involved with Odyssey, know that those six weeks in New Hampshire changed my life and set me on the course that led to this book. Class of '98 rulez!

Finally, to my wife, Tracy—words like *thanks* and *love* seem far too facile to encompass how much your constant support means to me. But thanks, and I love you.

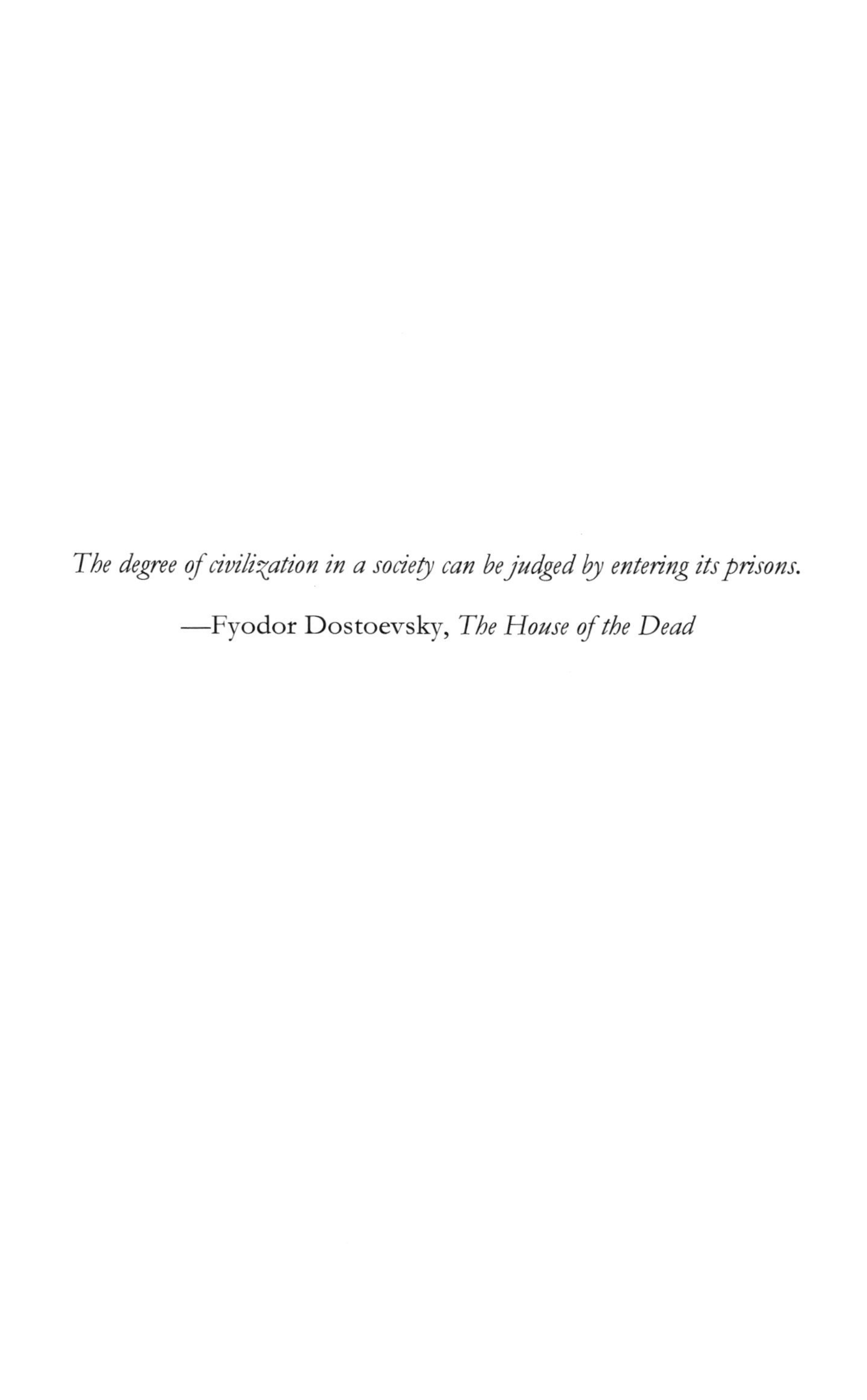

The degree of civilization in a society can be judged by entering its prisons.

—Fyodor Dostoevsky, *The House of the Dead*

PART ONE

CONTROL

CHAPTER ONE

From above, he almost felt he liked the place.

As Kane Pythen piloted the lander through its final leg, he marveled at the glittering deep blue of ocean beneath him and the arching pale blue of sky above. His destination, the island called Control, was still over the horizon, so nothing disturbed the near-perfect serenity of the view. It was easy to forget, for a few moments at least, that he was landing in the biggest prison humanity had ever known.

The lander hurtled west-east. Kane banked it north, following the vector transmitted from Control, positioning the craft for final approach. He glimpsed the faintest discoloration in the east, a trace of gray that marred the perfect sky—the furthest edge of a weather system, according to his readouts, large and headed slowly southwest, but too distant to affect his flight plan.

He pulled his gaze away from the horizon and focused on his instruments, descending and decelerating while maintaining a graceful arc. He spoke into the lander's radio: "Petra Control, this is JUR 6267, requesting landing clearance."

A female voice responded in a monotone: "JUR 6267 acknowledged. Please validate."

That was Kane's cue to give the final clearance code, the one that had been transmitted to the orbiting Portship upon its arrival. The code had to be given orally so that Control could verify Kane's voiceprint. He glanced at the display of his allcomm, docked atop his array. "Acknowledged, Petra Control. SK9-4YN-8C7. Repeat, SK9-4YN-8C7."

"JUR 6267 acknowledged. Welcome to Petra, Director Pythen. You are cleared to land."

"Petra Control acknowledged, and thank you."

Smooth on the yoke, he completed another ninety-degree arc, bearing zero-nine-one, still decelerating and descending.

The idyllic moment was gone. Already, his mind was on business, noting the handling of security procedures, alert for any lapse or corner cutting. This was, after all, a scheduled flight, planned months in advance. The lander was small and, like the Portship still in orbit, unarmed. It carried no prisoners, just one government functionary. Some on the Petra staff might be tempted to let down their guard a little. But so far, Control had followed the manual step by step.

Kane had expected no less. But part of him couldn't help feeling…disappointed.

He clamped down hard on the thought. He had a job to do. Hoping for signs of lax security—that was no way for an Assistant Director of Corrections to behave. A lot of people back on his homeworld of Juris were counting on him.

Correction: they were counting on *Petra* to deliver them from the mess they were in. They needed Kane to bring them good news. That he personally found the concept of a prison world disturbing, even repellent, had little bearing. He would do what they sent him here to do and take a modicum of comfort in knowing it was the last time.

He thought of Tayla and of what she had said to him that last evening before he left: *What have they turned you into, Kane?*

That night had not ended well. And now here he was, on the wrong side of an interplanetary Portal, far removed from everything familiar and comfortable, on a planet reserved for the worst of society's worst—no appeal, no parole, no escape. Those sentenced to Petra never came back. It was either the last word in penal systems or an inhumane hellhole, depending on whom you asked.

Still, for a few moments at least, he had almost felt he liked the place.

A hazy silhouette, elongated and irregular, came into focus on the southern horizon—Control. Kane put aside his discomfiture and focused on getting the lander down.

* * *

Halleck Ellum waited behind the cover of rocks as the surveillance skimmer headed into the trap.

The bait—an old transport Hal and his people had acquired during a raid last year—waited in a shallow depression dotted with thin Petran grasses. Multimodal, its wings were retractable; its suspension system allowed for limited ground travel when necessary. Thirty meters long, with a twenty-five-meter wingspan when airborne, its white body was covered in a layer of grime. Even so, the rock-and-eagle insignia of Petra, done in black and gold, still showed through in a couple of places.

A transport long thought either lost or destroyed, turning up intact in northern Mainland, where it had originally disappeared. The skimmer would have no choice but to investigate.

It circled, about a hundred meters up, a compact black craft, wingless, repulsor powered. Its engines buzzed and thrummed, a vibration Hal could feel whenever it passed directly overhead. It would be scanning the area for hostiles, he knew. The black outcroppings surrounding the hollow would make that difficult.

The day was sunny, with unseasonably warm winds out of the south, from the direction of the Fracture. As good a day as any for the start of a revolution, he supposed. It had been a long time coming—fifteen years since the bastards had dumped him on Petra. Justice delayed, but not denied.

He glanced toward another outcropping five meters to his left, where Cromberg crouched, concussion gun at the ready. Miga was on the other side of the hollow. The rest of the strike team—twenty-one of them in all—were scattered throughout the rocks.

The skimmer continued circling. The crew—three of them, per Petran SOP—would be radioing back to Control for instructions. It seemed to be taking a long time.

Cromberg called out to him, his gravelly voice unmistakable: "They're not goin' for it."

Hal kept his attention on the circling skimmer, but put up a hand. "Hold."

"What if they fly off? Decide to come back later, with friends?"

Hal focused on Cromberg. The man's dark, craggy features seemed swallowed up by his mane of hair and long, bristly beard. A black-and-white striped heelocat pelt draped his shoulders, covering tattered and stained clothes gone gray with wear. Even at this distance, Hal could see the tension in the set of the man's body, as if he were about to spring.

"I'm gonna draw them down," Cromberg said.

"Hold."

"Damn it, Hal, we—"

"*Hold.* If you break cover, they'll just gun you down. And *then* they'll go get backup. Keep your position and keep quiet." Hal turned his attention skyward once more.

Cromberg grumbled something unintelligible in reply. But he held.

The tenor of the skimmer's repulsors dropped. It began descending.

It came down, struts extended, on the north side of the hollow, closest to Miga's position. It settled into the stony soil, the struts automatically compensating for the uneven terrain. The repulsors modulated to a deep rumble, idling, ready to be powered up on a moment's notice, if need be.

Hal signaled a thumbs-up to Cromberg—his authorization to proceed. Cromberg passed it on to Orem, the next member of the strike team. The go-ahead order would complete the circuit in a matter of seconds.

They'd done guerilla raids in the past, God knew. The concussion guns his people carried had come from just such excursions. But this was a different animal altogether—more of a precision operation. Their typical *strike fast, strike hard* approach, which guys like Cromberg were so skilled at, would avail them little. Any misstep could ruin the entire plan. They would never get an opportunity like this again, and Hal had an old friend to meet.

The skimmer's top hatch hissed open. A Petran guard, dressed in bulky black body armor, head encased in a helmet with dark blastproof shielding the face, emerged and stood atop the craft, holding what looked like a rifle-length pulse emitter. Unlike handheld models, which were built to incapacitate, the weapon this one carried could deliver lethal jolts. He—or she—it was impossible to tell in that armor—swung the emitter in a quick circle, searching the rocks.

Another head appeared in the hatchway—a second guard, similarly armored and armed. The two of them scuttled down a set of rungs on the side of the skimmer and flattened themselves against the ship. The hatchway resealed with a hiss.

They proceeded toward the transport, one taking point and the other hanging back five meters, watching the rocks. Neither of them would be visible from the skimmer's forward viewport.

It had to be now, or never. Hal scooped up a handful of pebbles and flung them into the grass three meters away.

"Wait." A man's voice, muffled by the helmet. He held up one hand.

The point person stopped, turned. "What?" Another male voice, clipped, impatient.

The cover man pointed with his emitter. "Something over there. By the rocks."

"Did you see anything?"

The cover man shook his helmeted head.

"Fuck it." The point man opened fire, sending pulse after pulse into the grass Hal had disturbed. Hal kept low, peeking through a narrow gap in the rocks that formed his cover, steeling himself. As the blasts slammed into the ground, every instinct screamed at him to bolt. He'd been shot at too many times.

The point man stopped firing. Smoke and the smell of burnt grass rose on the wind.

"All right," the point man said. "Let's check it out."

The two of them headed in Hal's direction.

A figure emerged from the rocks aft of the skimmer—Fallon, the youngest of their number, born on Petra, fair-haired and wiry, shirtless and barefoot, carrying a bone knife in one hand. He came up behind the guards, swift and silent. He got to the cover man and reached around to jam the knife into a vulnerable spot in the armor, the join between the helmet and the body, getting the guy in the throat. No chance to cry out. Fallon caught the sagging body before it hit the ground.

The point man kept coming, for the moment unaware that his comrade had fallen. He got close enough. Cromberg had the best angle. Hal signaled at him.

Cromberg took aim and fired. The blast from the concussion gun knocked the emitter from the point man's hands. A moment later, Fallon tackled him from behind.

Hal and Cromberg moved.

The point man had fallen face-first. Fallon was on his back, pinning his arms behind him. The guy flailed in his armor, bucking.

Fallon flew off, but by that time, Hal and Cromberg stood over the guard, both with concussion guns pointed at his face. The guard saw the two of them and stilled his flailing, hands raised.

Fallon was back on his feet in a flash, standing next to Cromberg and Hal, breathing hard, eyes wild. Hal could only imagine how they looked from the guard's perspective.

Hal bent closer, tapping the barrel of his weapon on the man's faceplate. The helmet would keep him from getting killed—probably—but a shot at this range would still hurt. A lot.

"Tell your pilot to open the hatch, and we'll let you live."

The guard remained still and silent.

"Or," Cromberg said, "we'll let your pilot watch as we beat you to death with the butt ends of these things." He jabbed at the guard's armored chest.

"Kelso," the guard said. "Open the hatch. Right now. There's…been an accident."

Hal glanced back at the skimmer, straining to hear the hiss of the hatch unsealing. He heard only the breeze. He looked back to the downed guard.

"Kelso, damn it, don't argue with me! Just open the frigging hatch, will you?"

The hiss came.

"Good boy," Hal said. "On your feet now. Nice and easy." As he spoke, he looked again toward the skimmer. Miga Bronn, identifiable at this distance by her thick, matted hair, had emerged from her hiding place. She slung her concussion gun, scaled the rungs, and clambered atop the craft. She dropped out of sight through the top hatch.

Cromberg grabbed for the guard's chinstraps and unbuckled the catches. He ripped the helmet off and cast it away.

The guard was a young man—a kid, really. Couldn't have been much older than Fallon. A clean, pretty face, smooth. Pale blue eyes. His mouth had drawn into a tight moue, cinched like a drawstring bag.

Hal said, "Just take it easy, and you don't get hurt. That's the deal. Got me?"

The guard's eyes lighted on the body of his partner.

Fallon interposed himself in the guard's line of sight, brandishing the knife. "That's right, asshole. And more where that came from. So don't be stupid."

Hal touched Fallon's arm, easing him back. "Let's walk. No sudden moves."

They headed toward the skimmer. Hal had no way of knowing what was going on in there. His heart hammered. So much depended on the next few moments.

A figure emerged from the hatch, hands upraised. No armor for this one, just a black Petran uniform. Miga came next, weapon trained on the skimmer pilot—Kelso, one assumed.

The two of them descended, meeting Hal, Cromberg, Fallon, and the taken guard. Kelso was a middle-aged man, small, with thinning, straw-colored hair and a baby face. Miga stood half a head taller than him. He appeared calm, displaying none of the agitation and chagrin of the guard.

Hal glanced at Miga, who nodded. Her face was bony and weathered. Scars marked her jawline and her left cheek, just below the eye. Up close, the streaks of gray in her matted hair became apparent.

"How did it go?" Hal said. He watched her carefully for any sign of slippage. Her outbursts could be damnably difficult to see coming.

"Easy." Miga's mouth twitched in a thin-lipped smile. "I've searched him already. And I checked the radio logs. He didn't have time to send a distress call. We're clean."

Hal resisted the urge to close his eyes and allow himself a moment's relaxation. Cromberg, however, let out a whoop and a yell at the sky, holding his concussion gun overhead. Fallon joined him.

The rest of the strike team emerged from the hiding places, cheering, laughing, and slapping each other on the back as they gathered near the skimmer. They passed the slain Petran guard without a second glance.

Kelso stared at Hal. "You kill us, and Control will firebomb this entire sector. You know it."

"True enough," Hal said. "Wouldn't be the first time, either."

Cromberg, his grin obvious even through the mass of his beard, stepped up to the young guard. "Hey, you're pretty good with that pulse emitter, kid. Nice weapon. I think I'll take it. And your friend's too. We'll—"

The guard lunged, lowering a shoulder and barreling into Cromberg's chest. Cromberg fell, and the guard was on him. With a faint *snick*, a dagger, hidden up one armored sleeve, slid into the guard's hand.

Hal was ready for the move. He kicked, sending the knife flying. He kicked again, catching the guard in the face. The kid tumbled off Cromberg before the others even knew what was happening.

The guard lay supine, groaning, blood pouring from a broken nose—not so pretty anymore.

Cromberg scrambled to his feet, snarling. Hal held him back. "No! *No*! Keep your head. It's over."

Cromberg struggled for a moment longer before backing off. The others had stopped congratulating themselves and were tense once again, some pointing weapons at the guard.

When he was certain Cromberg was back under control, Hal released him, then addressed the rest of them: "Strip the armor off this one. Make sure he's not carrying anything else. And let's be a little more careful from now on. We have a long way to go yet."

Somber, Fallon and some of the others moved to obey. The guard did not resist. The fight had gone out of him.

Hal turned his attention back to Kelso. At the first sign of trouble, Miga had armlocked him. He still appeared serene. He said, "Kill us, then, if that's what you have to do."

"Hey." Miga grabbed a handful of the man's thinning hair and jerked his head back. "You don't give the fucking orders around here. Not anymore."

Hal put up a hand. "All right, relax. We don't want to kill anybody. I'm sorry about your friend back there"—he gestured in the direction of the body—"but that was self-defense." A bald-faced lie, but Kelso wouldn't know any better.

"If you're not going to kill us, then—"

Hal pointed to the transport. "We need you to fly that for us."

Kelso laughed. "*That*? You can't be serious. I doubt it would even get off the ground."

"It will fly, trust me. It has plenty of fuel and has been unused since we took it."

Kelso shook his head. "If you need to fly, you'll be better off in the skimmer. I wouldn't trust that crate any further than I could throw it. Not after it's been sitting for a year."

Miga tightened her armlock on him, making him wince.

"The skimmer's too small to carry all of us," Hal said. "The transport will fly. And you're going to fly it for us. Or I'll leave the two of you to my friends here. One way's easier for everyone."

Kelso glanced over Hal's shoulder, toward the body. "And, ah…where do you want to go?"

Hal smiled. "Control."

Kelso started to laugh, but stopped when Miga hiked up his arm a little higher.

"You…" He grimaced. "You can't be serious. You wouldn't get within ten kilometers. The security—"

Hal stepped forward, still smiling, bringing his face within inches of Kelso's. "You let me worry about the security. Just get us to Control."

CHAPTER TWO

On approach, Control resembled any number of military bases Kane had known, albeit larger than most. He had time for a few glimpses as he brought in the lander. Steel and concrete and dark glass seemed to grow out of the surrounding vegetation, lush greens sprouting industrial grays and blacks, with the island's mountainous spine, dotted by the complex's comm arrays, forming the backdrop.

Kane knew the rest of the island from his research: forty-five kilometers along its length, from northwest to southeast, and twenty kilometers at its widest point. Heavy forest on its southern side, marshes on its northernmost tip. The largest of a small chain of islands, about four thousand kilometers from Petra's biggest landmass, Mainland. There were two other continents: Southland—somewhat smaller, but with a roughly equal inmate population—and Farside, the smallest and, as its name implied, the most remote and uninhabited.

Two spotter skimmers, painted gleaming black, escorted him in, each riding a wing. They kept a respectful distance, careful not to interfere with his flight pattern but close enough to take quick action in the event of a security situation.

The landing was uneventful. The runway was in good repair, its concrete smooth and unpitted, its markings brightly painted. Kane taxied past Petran craft parked on the tarmac—landers, transports, and skimmers—pulled the lander into a cavernous, well-lit hangar, parked, and shut down. Maintenance crew members approached. He acknowledged them with a wave.

Several minutes later, Kane emerged from the lander via the debarkation ramp. The sun shone a dazzling yellow-white; he shielded his eyes against the glare. The heat and humidity would have been oppressive if not for a faint breeze. He caught mingled scents of lander exhaust and ocean tang. Petra's gravity, a little stronger than Juris's, tugged at his limbs. A case packed with personals slung over one shoulder, he picked his way carefully down the ramp. Though he hadn't been offworld in a long time, Kane remembered what getting acclimated to a foreign gravity field could be like.

Two uniformed figures awaited him on the tarmac: a tall man, broad through the shoulders, with clean-shaven features and deeply tanned skin, and a woman with cropped red hair. She stood shorter than the man by a head and a half. Both waited with their hands behind their backs. The uniforms were black with gold trim, adorned with the Petran rock and eagle.

The man extended a hand to Kane. "Director Pythen. I'm Chief Tomas Mehr."

Kane recognized him from the personnel dossiers he had stored on his allcomm. Mehr was second-in-command on Petra. His hands were callused, his grip strong.

Mehr turned to the woman. "This is Emma Goring, my executive assistant."

She smiled. "Welcome to Petra." They shook.

"The trip was good, I trust," Mehr said. "No troubles Porting? Or with reentry?"

"Everything went very well, thanks."

Emma peered over Kane's shoulder, looking up the debarkation ramp. "Where's your pilot, Mr. Pythen? And the crew?"

"The Portship crew is still in orbit," Kane said. "Security was easier to arrange for one. As for the pilot, you're looking at him. I used to fly reentry vehicles in the military."

"Oh, yes, of course. I knew that."

Kane cocked his head. "Really?"

Mehr glanced at her, too.

"I've followed your career somewhat. You flew during the Cassean War, didn't you?"

Kane was surprised. "Are you Jurisian? Or Cassean?" He prayed the latter wasn't true.

"Oh, no. Neither. I'm from Adriana. But I studied the Cassean War in school."

That stuck Kane as a little odd. Adriana was on the other side of Ported Space from Juris and Cassea. He hadn't realized the conflict had been that well known. "I'm long since retired, but I still like to fly. The Ministry of Enforcement indulges me."

Mehr flashed a perfunctory smile. "Emma will be your personal liaison for your stay. Feel free to ask her for whatever you need."

"Thanks."

"Warden Ankledge regrets that he couldn't be here to greet you personally," Mehr said. "He's looking forward to seeing you at dinner. Meanwhile, we'll get you settled." He gestured toward the waiting tramcar, white with all rounded edges and large tinted windows. They went to it and clambered inside—cushioned seating, climate-controlled. Once the doors sealed, the tramcar hummed to life and accelerated down the rail, running from the hangar to the complex of structures that housed Control's command facilities, and, at the center of it all, the Hub,. Kane watched the passing scenery, such as it was. Seen up close, the smooth, aesthetically balanced architectural lines resembled a modern business center more than a military base, much less a prison.

"Feel free to rest as long as you want," Mehr said. "The trip must have been tiring."

Kane shook his head. "I'm fine. I'd rather just drop off my things and begin the tour right away."

"Well..." Mehr removed his own allcomm from a uniform pocket and tapped a few keys. "I'm managing an inventory at the armory this afternoon. Can't be put off, I'm afraid. It's been scheduled for months. Better to start the tour tomorrow, I think. Tonight, you can—"

"We can start the tour with the armory, then." The armory wasn't high on Kane's list of priorities, truth be told. But he wanted to establish the tenor of his visit right away: shake them up, make them uncomfortable. They might even expect it of him.

A trace of a frown creased Mehr's well-tanned forehead. "The inventory will take several hours. You might get bored."

"I'll be more bored sitting in my room, watching the view."

Mehr and Kane stared at each other across the small cabin. The chief's features twitched. The tramcar rounded a bend and fell under the shadows of the taller buildings in the center of the complex.

Mehr returned his allcomm to its pocket. "Well, fine. If you like. I'll make the security arrangements." But the trace of frown remained.

"There's an alternative, Chief," Emma Goring said.

They turned to her.

"I mean, if you'd like to get started right away, Director, I can clear my schedule for this afternoon and take you wherever you need to go."

Mehr said, "You can? I thought you had to—"

"It's no problem at all. I'm happy to help." She smiled.

The tramcar slowed. A large steel door blocked the railway ahead. It rolled back as the car approached, disclosing the entrance to a tunnel. The car passed inside, and the door closed behind them.

Kane glanced from Mehr to Emma. "What I'd really like to see is inmate processing, from the moment they land at Control all the way through to the drop sites. Can you help me with that, Ms. Goring?"

"We won't be able to do it all in one afternoon, but we can at least get you started. And it would be a much more productive use of your time than the inventory at the armory."

The tramcar slowed further, came to a stop at a concrete platform.

Kane had to admit she had a point. "That…sounds fine to me."

Mehr's forehead smoothed. He stood. "Good. I have to catch a connecting tramcar here. I'm sure we'll talk more later." He shook Kane's hand without looking him in the face. The doors unsealed, and Mehr stepped onto the platform. The tramcar continued on its way.

"Nice work, Ms. Goring," Kane said. "Resourceful. The chief relies a lot on you, I assume."

"I suppose he does. It's all part of the job." Her smile slipped away. "You can call me Emma. Let's get you to your quarters."

The guest suites were situated in the hills. Kane's featured a lovely view of the local foliage and the harbor to the north—a long expanse of white sand, broken by three great piers, at which were moored a small fleet of patrol ships. He watched dusk settle over Control as he dressed for his dinner with Rolf Ankledge.

The fat, reddened sun blazed in the west, casting the island in ruddy-orange light. The storm system he had observed while landing loomed to the north, a spreading purplish-black that would soon blot out the last of the sunset. Flashes of lightning stabbed at the darkness. From his window, Kane observed tree branches swaying as the wind increased; the storm was headed for the island.

If he looked down, he could see the squat, cylindrical structure called the Hub—the heart of Control. Security, communications, and air traffic control were all run from there. Emma had taken him through it earlier in the day. Inside was a giant open space, perhaps fifty meters across, with a ceiling ten meters high. Monitors covered the walls, flickering with constant scrolls of new data, giving off enough illumination to obviate the need for overhead lighting. The monitors displayed satellite tracking, graphics for every conceivable measure of security for the island, and video from surveillance flights. Long rows of consoles were manned by staffers wearing headsets, all so intent on their own displays that they had hardly noticed Kane walking among them.

He had been impressed. He had seen military HQs that weren't as well equipped.

During his tour, he had asked Emma if it wouldn't be easier—and more secure—to have orbital facilities only, with nothing on the Petran surface. She'd pointed out that prisoner processing would be much harder in orbit. The consequences of any mechanical failure would be greater than on the ground. The constant need for provisions and oxygen would be expensive. And an orbital facility would be difficult to expand; Petra was a growth industry.

She had proven a knowledgeable guide, and quite a forthcoming one, too. By the time they had wrapped up in the Holding Area, he felt better prepared for his dinner with the warden.

Kane donned his best formals—white with red accents at the collar and cuffs, adorned with the silver hand insignia—not a military uniform, but unmistakably Jurisian. It struck him as absurd, something an ambassador would wear to an official reception. In a very real sense, that was an accurate description of this dinner. Despite his title, Ankledge could not be considered merely the warden of a very large prison. His position as the founder of the

Petra Compact made him something analogous to a head of state; he should be treated as such. Or so Kane's superiors back on Juris had insisted.

Diplomacy and politics were not Kane's strong suits. He was a senior administrator in his world's penal system, but he was also Kane Pythen, distinguished veteran of the Cassean War. He held no illusions about why the Director of Corrections, his superior, had selected him for this job: Kane was to bring some *gravitas* to this meeting with the warden. It was important that Ankledge be impressed with him; it would aid immeasurably in setting the terms of Juris joining the Compact.

For the Jurisian Ministry of Enforcement, that conclusion was foregone, regardless of any report Kane might make on this visit. But they couldn't let Ankledge see that.

It was a role, then, for Kane—but he was well suited to playing it. His testimony before Parliament during the war had earned him a reputation for contrariness. He would play the heavy, get them the deal they wanted, then collect the special duty bonus he'd wrangled from them and leave Juris forever.

He had tried explaining as much to Tayla, his wife, when he'd told her of the assignment. She'd only shaken her head and turned away. *Petra*, she'd said. *They're seriously considering Petra.*

It's not decided yet, he'd said—lied, actually. *That's what this trip is all about.*

You're going to leave me and Shamlyn here…for what? Porting hundreds of light years away—why? Just to come back and tell them what they want to hear?

The thought of Tayla and Shamlyn, his baby daughter, made his chest ache. He pushed them out of his mind; he had to focus on the task at hand. He was doing this for them, after all. Shamlyn would not grow up on Juris if he could help it.

Dinner was in a special dining room in the guest wing of the complex; Emma had transferred the relevant floor plans to his allcomm so he could find his own way.

The guest wing was appointed like a resort hotel—painted in tones of rust and green, soft carpeting underfoot, hidden lightbars casting a friendly ambience. On his way to the dining room, he passed a member of the cleaning staff, dressed in a pale blue uniform instead of the ubiquitous Petra black and gold, stocking an electric cart with supplies. The staffer acknowledged him with a polite smile and wished him a good evening.

Following the directions on his allcomm, he took the stairs down one floor and crossed an open reception area—catching the savory scents of spices and breads as he did so—to a set of carved wooden doors that marked the entrance to the dining room. The doors opened inward as he approached.

The interior was more intimate than Kane expected. He'd pictured a grand banquet hall. Instead, he found a room with a single round table, big enough for eight, covered in white cloth, complete with a floral centerpiece and two place settings. In one corner stood a pair of padded chairs in front of a faux brick fireplace—artificially lit, casting a flickering glow but giving off no heat.

He was alone. He had arrived a few minutes late deliberately, hoping that Ankledge would already be there. With a shrug, Kane went to the table. A name card—*Assistant Director Kane Pythen, Republic of Juris*—marked his place. He pulled out a chair and sat. Kane sipped at a stem glass filled with ice water while he waited.

Ten minutes later, the wooden doors opened again, and in strode Rolf Ankledge.

The warden was a balding man with a white mustache, lined features, and narrow eyes that gave him the appearance of a perpetual squint. He wore a resplendent all-black uniform, with none of the usual gold trim, only a Petra insignia sewn on the right breast.

Kane rose to meet him. He and Ankledge were much of a height; their gazes met squarely. Ankledge's handshake was firm. Though he was in his seventies, his stance was erect, his steps quick and assured, his eyes clear.

"Director Pythen." Age had roughened his voice, but left it strong. He smiled wide enough to show bright white teeth. "A genuine pleasure to have you here on Petra."

"Thank you, Warden." Kane allowed only a slight upturn of the lips. He held the handshake just long enough for Ankledge to feel it. "Nice to be here."

"Sorry to keep you waiting; it's been a very busy day. Please sit."

They took their places across from each other. Moments later, two staffers in blue uniforms brought in the first course—salads in glass bowls.

"Made from the local vegetation," Ankledge said. "Garnished with berries from Mainland."

The salad leaves were large, dark green; the berries white, pebble-like.

Ankledge dug in. Kane followed suit.

The salad was crisp, fresh, a tad bitter. The berries were sweeter than Kane had first supposed, a nice counterpoint to the leaves.

"We had a bit of excitement," the warden said between forkfuls. "One of our surveillance flights returning to Control had a transponder malfunction; we couldn't identify it on radar. We had to go on heightened alert."

Kane paused in his eating. "Everything's all right?"

"A transponder malfunction, like I said. The crew identified with the proper clearance codes for today. We have multiple backup systems for just such occurrences. They'll be back on the ground within the hour."

One of the staffers brought a carafe of reddish-brown wine and poured each of them a glass. Finished, the staffers left the carafe and a bowl with the remainder of the salad on the table and exited the room.

"So between that and preparations for the storm that's coming in...well, that's why I was late."

"I noticed the storm. How bad will it be?"

"It's a Category Two—typical for Petra. Ocean currents bring down cooler water from the north, so tropical storms rarely get enough heat to spin up any worse than that. Still, they can be disruptive. This one's big and pretty slow moving. It will be with us for most of the night, I'm afraid." Ankledge set down his fork and raised his glass of wine. "I'd like to offer a toast, if I may. To Juris."

Kane covered his distaste and raised his own glass. "To Juris." They drank.

The wine was thick, syrupy, and very sweet. "Delicious," Kane said. He preferred dry wines.

"Imported from Land's End. A little taste of home."

They finished the salad course, discussing pleasantries. Ankledge asked after Kane's family, how long he'd been in Corrections, about his military service—all information he probably already knew, assuming he had prepared at all for this visit.

Rolf Ankledge, Kane had learned from his own research, was a widower. He'd lost his wife decades ago, prior to his arrival on Petra, and had no children. In the early days of the planet's settlement, he had come from Land's End to explore the feasibility of setting up a prison farm. His world was largely ocean, with only a handful of sizeable islands—no landmasses that could be considered continents. Real estate was at a premium on Land's End, far too valuable to be wasted on prisons.

The rest of the settlers had more grandiose ideas.

The first surveys of Petra had been promising, but the system was too far removed from the rest of Ported Space to make sublight expeditions feasible. A Portal had been built in orbit in the hope that future riches would justify the initial expense—a calculated risk, but one that had paid off in settlements past.

Petra proved to be the exception.

It was, in the parlance of interplanetary exploration, *resource poor*. An unlucky freak of planetary formation, its ores and metals were locked in its core, far too deeply buried to be profitably extracted. Fossil fuels were next to nonexistent. Despite ample evidence of tectonic activity in its past—the most striking example being the Fracture on Mainland, a continent-spanning rift formed by a single cataclysmic event millions of years ago—Petra had long since gone tectonically dead. Its mountain ranges may have been mighty in past eons, but only a handful of its peaks now rose above the treeline. Its continents were slowly but inexorably eroding into its oceans. Its strong magnetic field was weakening. Petra was an old, old world, and it was dying.

One by one, the colonies failed, and the settlers went back to their homeworlds. The Petra Portal became an extravagantly expensive boondoggle. The Interplanetary Settlement Council began to debate the feasibility of dismantling it and reassembling it elsewhere.

But Rolf Ankledge's prison farm, efficient and escape-proof, had done well. The government of Land's End petitioned the ISC to keep the Portal in place. The ISC agreed to allow it, on one condition—that Land's End assume the debt for the Portal's construction costs.

Such an arrangement would have broken most planetary economies. But Ankledge, devoted to his brainchild, had submitted a counterproposal, a way of spreading the costs to several worlds. And so the Petra Compact had been born. It encompassed ten worlds in Ported Space—eleven, if Juris decided to join.

Polite conversation continued through the main course—blackened filet of bluedragon, a native marine creature, with generous helpings of mixed vegetables and a variegated grain Ankledge called Petran rice. A small loaf of soft, warm bread and a dish of sweet butter came on the side.

Occasional rumbles of thunder filtered through to the dining room. Chimes from Ankledge's allcomm kept interrupting their conversation. He received regular updates from the Hub concerning the surveillance skimmer with the broken transponder.

After the third such update, Ankledge set his allcomm aside and said, "I'm such an admirer of Juris, Mr. Pythen."

"Thank you."

"I mean that. You're the envy of anyone who's made a career out of Corrections. Swift trials, limited appeals, no horrendous backlog of cases—I can't stress enough what a blessing that is for your society. Justice delayed is justice denied. I've always said that citizens of Juris are the luckiest in Ported Space."

"You're very kind." Kane ate another piece of bluedragon, noting with surprise that he had nearly cleared his plate. Normally, he didn't care for seafood, but the savory filet had been cooked to perfection, moist and tender.

"So much luckier than those damned Casseans, eh? You would know that better than most."

Kane kept his expression neutral. "I'm afraid I never saw Cassea at its best."

"Maybe you did."

"Cassea is part of the Compact, isn't it?"

Ankledge wiped his mouth with a cloth napkin. "I do business with them, but to be quite honest, I've never had much respect for them."

Kane remained silent. He couldn't help but wonder what Ankledge said when he spoke to the Casseans about Juris.

"But Juris, on the other hand…I'm honored that you want to join the Compact. I'm really looking forward to working with you."

Another rumble of thunder sounded. The storm was still distant but growing louder.

Kane gave his best diplomatic smile. "Nothing's decided yet, Warden. I'm simply here to record my observations and report them to the people who will make the call."

"To be sure. But your recommendation will carry a great deal of weight, yes?"

"Some."

"And I intend to do everything in my power to make sure I get that recommendation. How's your dinner?"

Kane held up the last forkful of his filet. "Quite good," he said, and ate.

Ankledge spread his hands. "And what do you think of our facilities?"

Kane washed down the filet with water; the wine proved too sweet for him. "Impressive, so far. Expensive, too, I'm sure."

"Price is a concern for you, of course."

"I didn't mean—"

"For your government, I mean. That's only prudent. I would expect no less from Juris. And I can assure you, Mr. Pythen, we do not spend money extravagantly here."

Kane glanced around the room and at the table in front of him.

Ankledge caught the look. "Oh, we're not Spartans, no. But this"—he made an all-encompassing gesture—"is an infinitesimal fraction of the budget. A well-deserved reward for one of the hardest, most thankless jobs in this or any society. As I'm sure you know all too well."

"I suppose I do."

Ankledge's allcomm chimed again. He offered an apologetic smile and picked it up. He glanced at the display, nodded, and set it down again. "The skimmer's landed safely. Just ahead of the storm."

"Good news."

"Yes." Ankledge set his plate aside and folded his hands in front of him. "So. Let's discuss the rest of your agenda. I understand from Chief Mehr that you're interested in observing the entire prisoner intake process."

Kane took another drink of water, inwardly bracing himself. "Yes."

"I'm not sure how much more there is to see. You've already toured the landing field and the Holding Area."

There hadn't been much to see at either one. The Holding Area had been empty of incoming inmates, clean and clinical, more like a hospital than a jail, the air scented with fresh disinfectant. "I haven't been to a drop site yet."

"Ah." Ankledge stroked his mustache. "Well, that might be difficult to arrange. We have a regular schedule of surveillance flights to maintain. And there are no prisoners to be processed at this time. We're between deliveries."

"That's unfortunate."

"No, the scheduling was deliberate. Standard procedure when we have visitors. Makes the security arrangements easier."

The two staffers entered the room and began clearing the table, loading the dirty dishes on a cart.

"I think you'll enjoy dessert," Ankledge said. "We've imported—"

"Warden, I really need to see the drop sites."

"Of course." Ankledge glanced sidelong at the staffers. "As I said, it will be difficult to arrange, at least on this trip. Especially with the storm coming in."

"I can wait out the storm."

"And the schedule of surveillance flights can't be disrupted. It's an important security measure for the members of the Compact. None of them would want it compromised, even for a day or two. They expect regular reports."

The staffers finished loading the cart and wheeled it out of the room. Kane pursed his lips and tapped a finger on the table. "No, I wouldn't want to take up a skimmer. Your fleet is small enough already. Especially if some of your skimmers are out of commission at the moment."

Ankledge's perpetual squint narrowed even further. "What do you mean?"

Kane hesitated before responding. "You just had a transponder malfunction on one of them. And all those flights have to take a toll, don't they? I would imagine your maintenance crews have their hands full keeping the fleet operational."

It was more than mere supposition on Kane's part. Emma Goring had intimated the skimmer fleet's flight readiness at about seventy-five percent. "Some have been damaged in raids," she'd told him. "A couple have either gone missing or been destroyed outright."

Kane had been surprised by the admission, so at odds with the image of complete security and order that Petra liked to project to the rest of Ported Space. But he'd appreciated her candor.

Ankledge studied him. Long moments passed in silence.

At last, the warden said, "Yes, it can take a toll. Some of our skimmers are grounded at the moment. What are you insinuating, Mr. Pythen?"

Kane had to suppress a smile. "Not a thing, Warden. It's just an observation. That's what I'm here for."

"So this is to be a true inspection, is it? Not just some perfunctory visit, a chance to be wined and dined for a few days?"

"I'm afraid not."

Ankledge's features relaxed. "Well, good. It's nice to meet someone who takes this business as seriously as I do."

"It's my job."

"Yes." Ankledge picked up his wine glass and swirled its remaining contents, looking into its depths. "And for Juris, it's a very serious job, indeed, given the situation you find yourselves in."

Kane tensed. "What situation is that, Warden?"

Still swirling his wine, Ankledge said, "One keeps abreast of the news, learns to read between the lines. One can even do a little digging. The Enforcement system on Juris works wonders on the crime rate, but it doesn't come cheap, does it? And it requires a rather large ratio of inmates to citizens. Some estimates put Jurisian incarceration numbers at two percent of the total population. Maybe more." He glanced across the table.

Kane didn't give him the satisfaction of a reaction.

The warden went on: "If those numbers are anywhere close to correct, one can only imagine the strain it puts on the entire prison infrastructure. Overcrowding becomes more than a humanitarian concern; it becomes a genuine security threat. It forces some compromises, some unpleasant choices. There are only so many prisons you can build, even on Juris. Your prosecutors have to decide which cases are worth pursuing and which ones can be plea bargained away. Parole boards feel pressure to exercise leniency in borderline cases. Not pretty." Ankledge swallowed the last of his wine. "One might suggest that Juris *needs* Petra. Badly. It would certainly explain your presence here, Mr. Pythen. You Jurisians are a proud people. One would suspect the situation to be pretty desperate if you're asking for help." He tipped the empty glass Kane's way in a mock salute, then set it down.

Kane settled back in his chair with his arms crossed. "A small skimmer fleet, over-reliance on satellite data, and a control structure entirely contained on one small island, vulnerable to tropical storms and who knows what other hazards—one might suggest that you face some difficult choices, too. Petra needs an infusion of capital. You can either raise your rates—something the members of your Compact would certainly object to—or you can bring in another signatory."

Ankledge's deep laugh shook his entire frame. "This will be a very interesting negotiation."

"Let me state my position clearly. Juris is far from desperate, Warden. We're just exploring our options at this point."

"Excellent. Wouldn't have it any other way."

"I *will* see the drop sites before I leave, yes?"

"I'm sure we can work something out. Are you ready for dessert?"

Kane put up a hand. "I don't think I could eat another—"

A new rumble cut him off. This one was different from the others—much nearer, much more immediate. Kane felt it in his seat; his remaining wine rippled in its glass.

His eyes went wide. "Jesus. Was that a lightning strike?"

Ankledge sat bolt upright in his chair. "I—"

An emergency siren blared, loud enough to hurt Kane's ears. He started as if struck.

Ankledge winced. He grabbed his allcomm, stabbed a button, and held the unit to his ear. "What the hell is—" He stopped, listening, holding one hand over his other ear to blot out the alarm. His mouth drew into a taut line. "Is anyone hurt?" he said over the siren's wail, and paused again. "Give me regular reports. What? No, I'm not in the Hub right now. I'm at dinner. Yes. Yes. And someone shut off that goddamned alarm!"

Kane's head hurt. He gritted his teeth, certain his ears would start bleeding if it went on much longer.

A moment later, the siren cut off. Kane shook himself, blessing the silence.

Ankledge clipped his allcomm to his belt. "I've just spoken with Chief Mehr. There's been an explosion at the armory."

"My God." Kane thought of asking how big of an explosion, then realized how stupid that would be. The armory, he knew from his notes, was near the barracks to the northwest, about a kilometer distant. And it had sounded much closer than that. "Casualties?"

"Too soon to tell. Fire crews and medics are on their way."

"Any idea what caused it? Was it a lightning strike?"

"The storm hasn't come ashore yet."

"Do you need to go? I understand if—"

"No." Ankledge gripped the edge of the table with both hands. The white tablecloth wrinkled and smoothed as he clenched and unclenched, clenched and unclenched. His features were stony. "No, we'll let the emergency teams handle it. We'll know more soon."

"Wasn't Chief Mehr doing an inventory at the armory today? Was he injured?"

Ankledge shook his head once. "The inventory would have been over with by now. He was most likely going over the reports with the duty sergeant. Damned lucky for him that he wasn't inside." The warden breathed hard, as if he'd just run a race. His hands kept clenching and unclenching. Sweat beaded on his brow, gleamed on his bald pate. "Son of a *bitch*."

From beyond the doors came muffled shouts and hurried footfalls. Warning sirens from other parts of the base, faint with distance, rose and fell.

Kane said, "Warden, please. You don't have to stay here on my account. I can go back to my—"

Ankledge raised a hand. "No. My people are trained to handle this. The situation is under control. The fire will be contained in a few minutes; then we'll sort out—"

A fusillade of explosions shook the base. Warden Ankledge jerked at each one.

"Some of the weaponry going off?" Kane asked.

"Undoubtedly." Ankledge's breathing became a kind of growl with each exhale.

His allcomm chimed again. He snatched it off his belt. "Tell me." He listened, nodded. "How long until it's contained? Right. Give me a preliminary damage report." He was silent again for a few moments. "You're sure? What about casualties? All right. I want to know the minute it's out." He disconnected and reclipped the allcomm. Without looking up, he said, "Three fire crews are on site and working. They should have it contained within ten minutes. The armory is a free-standing structure, so there's little danger of the fire spreading to other areas. Medics are treating some burn victims, a few people hit with shrapnel. The chief doesn't think anyone was inside the armory went it went up."

"Thank God."

"Yes." Ankledge's gaze was still distant. "I think—"

The sirens sounded again.

Ankledge got on his allcomm, bellowing: "What? What are you—Where? Repeat! Where are—Maintain channel discipline, goddamn it! One at a time! Who is—" He stopped, his mouth forming silent syllables, then dissolving into a gape.

Kane couldn't stand it anymore; he put his hands over his ears. He would have crawled under the table if he thought it would do any good.

"God *damn* it!" Ankledge snatched the allcomm away from his ear is if it had burned him. He pointed at Kane. "Stay here! That's an order!" He ran for the doors and slammed them shut behind him.

Kane sat in the unbearable din with his hands clapped to the sides of his head. He'd be damned if he was going to just sit here like a child. He went to the door, opened it, and stepped into the reception area. The sirens were more bearable here, but still loud and incessant. Small light panels, spaced at regular intervals near the ceiling, strobed bright red.

A uniformed man with square features and a lantern jaw ran past, carrying a sidearm. He noticed Kane and stopped. "Who are you?"

"I…" For a moment, Kane had no idea how to answer. "A guest of the warden's. We were at dinner."

The guard frowned, as if having difficulty processing this information. Then he said, "You'd better go back to the dining room. For your own safety."

"Has the fire spread?"

"Fire, hell. We're under attack."

Incomprehension and shock settled over Kane. From somewhere nearby came the unmistakable reports of rifle fire…and then a scream.

The guard nodded toward the double doors. "Get under cover!" He ran in the direction of the shots.

Kane retreated to the dining room, hands still over his ears.

CHAPTER THREE

Kane's military training reasserted itself. Sitting at the table would make him an easy target should the assailants penetrate this far. So far as he knew, the double doors were the only way in or out. His gaze fell on the two chairs and the fireplace in the corner. A set of black accessories stood by the hearth, including a poker. Blocking out the sirens as best as he could, he darted to the fireplace and grabbed the poker. Though only decorative, the implement was iron, with satisfying heft.

Kane looked toward the door. Thanks to the sirens, he could hear none of the goings-on outside the dining room. It made him nervous.

He moved from the fireplace to the doors, standing to one side, one ear pressed against the wall, the poker held at the ready. He heard only the alarm.

He settled against the wall and allowed himself to wonder how in the hell this had happened.

Under attack, the guard had said. The gunfire Kane had heard told him that whoever they were, they were already inside the complex. He leaned the poker against the wall and took out his allcomm. He brought up the floor plans Emma had given him, looking for escape routes, ways to the landing field.

Even as he worked the control pad, part of him nagged that it was futile. His lander still needed to be refueled and prepped for launch, and a tropical storm was bearing down on the island.

Thinking of the lander brought to mind the Portship in orbit, and its crew. He cleared the floor plans from his display and placed a call to the ship to let them know what was happening here. The familiar *Establishing Connection* message popped up, along with a miniature Jurisian coat of arms that slowly rotated, indicating the allcomm was processing the request.

The message hung on the display. The sirens continued to wail. Kane's head throbbed in counterpoint. He shook the allcomm, came within an ace of banging it against the wall.

The *Establishing Connection* message vanished, replaced with another:

Emergency Allcomm Blackout
All unauthorized signals are BLOCKED
By the authority of Petra Control

"Shit," Kane said.

The lights went out. The sirens cut off.

Kane's ears rang. His breathing slowed; it burned in his throat. Faint illumination came in through a crack under the doors. Staring in that direction, he shoved the allcomm in his pocket and groped for the poker. His fingers closed around the handle.

In the corner opposite the darkened fireplace, emergency lights flickered to life, dispelling some of the shadows. New sounds filtered back to him: shouts, footfalls. Coming nearer. Kane brandished the poker.

One of the door handles turned. The door creaked open. A flashlight beam stabbed into the room, sweeping left and right. Kane tensed, edging closer to the door.

The figure holding the flashlight stepped into the room—a man, about Kane's height. Kane stepped forward to strike.

"Pythen? Where are you?"

Kane lowered the poker. It was Ankledge.

"Right here," Kane said.

The warden shone the flashlight on him. "Anyone else?"

"No."

Ankledge swung the beam right and left again, then snapped off the flashlight and tucked it into a pocket. He spoke over his shoulder: "All clear."

Two guards, dressed in body armor and smartvisor helmets, entered. Each carried a huge assault rifle.

Ankledge put a hand on Kane's shoulder. "Are you hurt?"

Kane shook his head. "I heard some shooting earlier, down the hall. But nothing's happened here."

"Good." He ran a hand over his scalp. "I won't lie to you, Pythen. We have a serious situation here."

"Inmates have attacked the island?"

"The explosion at the armory was a diversion. They came in on a hijacked transport—what we thought was a skimmer."

Kane thought about it. "They disabled the transponder. So you couldn't tell on radar that it wasn't a skimmer."

"Your pilot training shows."

"But...I thought that flight had the proper clearance code."

"It did. We don't know how."

"How many of them are there?"

"Unknown. Thirty at most; that's all a transport can carry."

"*Thirty*? Against the entire base? That's suicide."

"Excuse me, Warden," one of the armed guards said. His uniform bore sergeant's hashes. "We've gotten confirmation that we've been locked down."

Ankledge seemed to deflate. "Damn it. Bastards."

"What does that mean?" Kane asked.

"It means they've succeeded in locking down the Hub. And the Hub is the only way to get to this wing."

Which made sense from a security standpoint. It limited access to the guest suites. But it also meant that they were now effectively cut off from the rest of the base.

"*They* locked it down?" Kane said.

Ankledge gave an exasperated sigh. "In the confusion following the explosion, they managed to occupy the Hub. Now they've activated security features that are intended to keep intruders *out*. Instead, it's locked them in. And us with them. As I said, it's a serious situation." He turned to the guards and spoke to them in a low voice.

Kane considered the implications. The Hub, he knew from his research, was built to withstand all manner of unlikely events, including a revolt of prisoners in the Holding Area, sieges, and even limited bombardment. Every single exit, maintenance accessway, sewer, and air duct could be sealed with plate steel. The Hub had its own generators, air, water, and stockpiles of emergency provisions.

If hostile forces had managed to occupy it, they wouldn't have to take on the entire base. They could simply hole up until they got whatever it was they wanted.

"Can we call for help? At least let someone know where we are?"

"Keep your voice down," Ankledge said. "They may be in the halls."

Kane glanced toward the door.

Ankledge stepped away from his guards. "No, we can't let anyone know where we are. Not without letting *them* know where we are. They're monitoring all our communications. And any unauthorized transmissions—"

"Are blocked. I know. I tried to call my ship."

Ankledge started pacing, slowly, tapping a finger to his lips. "Chief Mehr should know where we are. I told him we were at dinner. But he still has a fire to contain. And he can't get to us, anyway."

"You mean to tell me there are no emergency exits from this wing? Nothing that doesn't go through the Hub?"

"Of course there are. And they're all sealed—correct?" He looked to one of the guards for confirmation. The guard nodded.

Silence fell. Ankledge kept pacing. Kane went back to his place at the table and sat, setting the poker to one side. He could think of nothing better to do.

The sergeant said, "Warden, I'm starting to get casualty reports."

"Let me hear them."

The guard recited data, reading it from his smartvisor: "Two dead, thirty wounded in the explosion at the armory, five critically. One dead at the landing field, where the transport touched down. One wounded at Tramway Platform A. Five men down outside the south entrance to the Control Complex. Four down outside the Hub. They don't…" He trailed off, peering as if he had trouble making out what he was reading. "They don't appear to be wounded, but they're unconscious. Their vitals are very low."

"Were they bludgeoned?" Ankledge asked.

"Unknown, sir. And…correction: two of them *are* wounded by rifle fire. They appear to be prisoners."

Ankledge's perpetual squint made his eyes hard to read, especially in the low light. He paused in his pacing. "Well, that's a nice little overview of the route they took. Appears they ran into a shootout just outside the Hub."

"Yes, sir."

Ankledge stood with his arms at his sides, his brow furrowed, his hands clenching and unclenching.

"Warden," Kane said, "can you establish contact with these attackers?"

"If I do, they'll be able to track us down."

"Shouldn't we find out what they want?"

"If they find me, they'll want my head on the end of a stick. A nice little trophy they can parade around. Goddamned savages."

"Savages?" Kane was stunned. "Warden, what do you think is going on here? Whoever these people are, they have obviously been planning this for a long time. This attack was coordinated, precise, and took you completely by surprise. They have managed to penetrate to the most secure place on Petra while only losing two of their number. Now they're fortifying their position. They must think they're going to be here for a long time." He took a breath. "They're dangerous, but I wouldn't call them savages. It's a standoff."

"You think I don't know that?" Ankledge glared. "Of course it's a standoff. And if they track us down here, we'll all be hostages."

"We're cut off. We already *are* hostages. Warden, you need to talk to them."

"Don't tell me how to run my planet, Mr. Pythen. I know a hell of a lot more about it than you do."

"Fine. Then you tell me what they're up to."

Ankledge swatted in his direction, as if shooing an insect, and resumed his pacing.

Kane massaged his temples. His head still throbbed from the sirens. It made thinking difficult.

None of this made any sense to him. Their attackers had gone to a great deal of trouble to pull off this…stunt. He had seen his share of prison takeovers on Juris. Standoffs like this were geared to attract the attention of those outside the prison. But here on Petra, there *was* no outside—no general population to outrage, no media to provide nonstop, breathless coverage.

Maybe Warden Ankledge was right. Maybe they were just savages hellbent on nothing more than mayhem and vengeance. In which case, if they found the dining room, he and Ankledge—and anyone else unfortunate enough to be caught—would most likely die.

No. It just didn't add up.

Muffled thuds, felt more than heard, reverberated through the room. Ankledge looked to his sergeant.

"Projectile fire, sir. Bravo Squad is trying to blast their way into the Hub."

"Waste of time. And ammo."

"Should I order them to stop?"

"No. Maintain radio silence."

"Warden," Kane said, "if you're not going to talk to them, may I ask what you intend to do?"

Ankledge favored him with a squinty stare. "Avoid detection. Wait until we know more. They'll tip their hand sooner or later."

A knock sounded at the door.

The guards swiveled their weapons in that direction and assumed firing stances.

Ankledge pointed at Kane. "Find cover," he whispered.

Kane was already on his feet. He grabbed the poker and went back to the fireplace. It was tempting to hide under the table, but it would leave him with no vision and no mobility. He crouched behind a chair and waited, watching.

Ankledge went to the doors and flattened himself against the wall, much as Kane had. He looked again to his guards, holding a finger to his lips. The guards nodded and raised their weapons.

The door creaked open.

Something small flew in through the opening. It glinted in the low light. A moment later, a flash flared between the two guards, and grayish smoke erupted from the carpet.

The guards dropped to the floor without firing a shot.

Kane and the warden exchanged glances. Kane held his breath.

The smoke cleared quickly. Two figures entered the room. Bulky gas masks covered their heads, obscuring their faces. What little Kane could see of their clothing appeared tattered. One of them wore what appeared to be some kind of pelt over his shoulders. Each held rifle-length pulse emitters.

When they were fully into the room, Ankledge charged from behind.

They either heard him coming or had expected it. As soon as he moved, they swung the emitters in his direction. Ankledge froze in his tracks.

In a gravelly voice, the masked figure in the pelt said, "Well, I'll be damned." He slowly approached Ankledge, keeping his emitter trained on the warden. Ankledge stood firm, chin outthrust.

"I'd love to fry your fuckin' brains right now," the gravel-voiced man said. "But we got orders." He swung the butt of the emitter, catching Ankledge under the jaw. The warden went down, landing supine, groaning. The masked man stood over him. Over his shoulder, he said, "Miga, get in here."

A third masked figure, smaller than the first two, also carrying an emitter, entered the room. This one looked down at the warden for long moments, then removed his gas mask.

Her gas mask, Kane saw. A shock of dark, matted hair fell as she hooked her mask to her belt. The gas that had taken out the guards had no effect on her. Kane hadn't seen anything so fast acting and so quick to dissipate since his military days.

"I've got this one, Cromberg," Miga said. "Finish the sweep."

The other two moved to obey, heading in opposite directions to search the rest of the dining room.

Kane calculated the odds of overpowering three armed assailants with nothing but a fireplace poker. He set his weapon aside and stood, hands raised.

The gravel-voiced inmate in the pelt, the one Miga had called Cromberg, spotted Kane. "Got him!" The other two turned in his direction.

"I'm the only other one in here," Kane said. "I'm unarmed."

Face still hidden by the gas mask, Cromberg edged closer, gesturing with his emitter. "Come out from behind there. Slow."

Kane obeyed, keeping his hands raised.

"Kneel," Cromberg said. "Hands behind your head."

Kane knelt and laced his fingers as instructed.

The other masked figure crossed the room and stood two meters from him, weapon at the ready, while Cromberg put up his emitter and crudely patted Kane down. He found Kane's allcomm, looked it over, then clipped it back on Kane's belt where he had found it. "He's clean, Miga. Looks like Jurisian formals he's wearing."

Miga, still standing over the warden, said, "Jurisian. He's gotta be the one, then."

"Get up." Cromberg grabbed one of Kane's arms and hauled him to his feet. "Keep those hands where they are. Walk." The two masked men escorted him toward the door.

Without looking up from Ankledge, Miga said, "I'll take him. You two secure this room. Disarm those guards and get them out of here."

"What about him?" With his emitter barrel, Cromberg indicated Ankledge's unconscious form.

Miga hesitated. Her mouth twitched. "Leave him here, away from the others. When you're done with the guards, one of you take a post outside this door. And let the Hub know we've got him. Understood?"

Cromberg stood watch over Ankledge while the other intruder went to the guards.

Miga stood before Kane, sizing him up, holding her emitter pointed toward the ceiling. She had a scarred face and gray streaks in her thick hair. Musky body odor emanated from her—from all three of them, in fact.

"You come with me," Miga said.

She walked behind him down darkened corridors, keeping her emitter pointed at his back, occasionally giving directions. Kane kept his hands behind his head. Only the emergency lighting marked the way. Judging from the signs on the walls and the sketchy map Kane had in his memory, they appeared to be headed toward the Hub.

They left the guest wing and proceeded through office space lined with orderly workstations, all of them empty and silent. Some papers lay scattered on the floor, and a file cabinet had been overturned, but those were the only signs of violence. Kane saw no bodies, no blood.

"Where are the others?" Kane asked.

"Don't worry about it. Keep moving. Take a left up here. Through that door."

Beyond the door was another corridor, tiled instead of carpeted, leading to a stairway heading down.

"Listen, I'm just a visitor here," Kane said as they descended. He had to proceed with care; he couldn't use his hands to steady himself, and he still wasn't used to Petra's gravity. "I'm sure you've figured that out. But I know the warden. If you have demands, I could relay—"

"Shut the fuck up about the warden."

"I can be your liaison with him. I'm sure I can—"

"If you mention him one more time, I'll pulse you and drag your ass the rest of the way. Got it?"

Kane shut up.

He's gotta be the one, she'd said, meaning him. But that didn't make sense.

They wound their way in silence interrupted by occasional rumbles of thunder and sporadic thuds of heavy arms fire coming from somewhere outside. Bravo Squad, Kane figured—still wasting their ammunition.

They entered the Control Complex proper and proceeded straight to the Hub. She no longer needed to give him directions; Kane followed the signs on the wall.

They paused outside the steel doors to the Hub. She stepped forward and rapped on the door with her emitter. "Miga," she said, loud enough to be heard on the other side.

Within moments, the door opened. A man armed with a very large assault rifle stood there. He had spiky white hair and pale skin and wore tattered clothes like Miga's. He stepped aside to let them in.

The Hub appeared strangely normal. All the monitors continued to display satellite images and constant scrolls of data coming from all over Petra, just as they had during Kane's tour of the facility. The only real difference was that instead of workers in black-and-gold uniforms, armed men and women in threadbare, ragged clothing had taken positions throughout. They all looked over at him and Miga. Kane counted fifteen of them.

Miga led him around the perimeter of the Hub to a darkened, glassed-in area that overlooked the main floor with its rows of workstations. She held the door open and motioned him inside.

Kane hesitated, frowning, then stepped in. Miga let the door shut behind him and waited on the other side.

Kane waited, peering into the darkness. He glanced over his shoulder, looking through the glass. Miga stood with her back to him. The others were either watching the monitors or talking among themselves.

"Hello, Kane."

The voice, a man's, came from his right. Kane started.

"Sorry. I was just resting my eyes for a few minutes. Let me find the switch."

Kane heard fumbling sounds and a small *thunk*, as of something falling over.

And that voice…it sounded familiar, though he couldn't place it.

A muted click, and a small lamp lit, illuminating a modular desk, topped with some scattered files, a multi-panel computer monitor, and a paperweight lying on its side. This was a supervisor's office, most likely. Behind the desk sat the owner of the voice. He wore a long tan overcoat, stained and ragged like all the others' clothes, but his face was clean-shaven, his brown hair shoulder length but kempt. Like Miga, his features were weathered and drawn, aged beyond his years—but his were still somehow boyish, with a sharp nose and prominent brow. Slowly, the man stood.

Kane took an unsteady step backward. He was looking at a ghost.

"Hal?" That was impossible, but the name came to his lips before he could stop himself. "Halleck Ellum?"

It could not be. But even as he said it, Kane became certain that Hal Ellum indeed stood before him, Hal Ellum, who had been dead for—how long had it been?—fifteen years now. Kane went numb with shock.

A smile flickered across Hal's face. "Surprise."

CHAPTER FOUR

Dazed, Kane found a nearby office chair and fell into it. His legs would no longer support him.

"Hal Ellum is dead," he said. "He died on Juris, during the Cassean War. I attended his funeral."

"Really? They had a funeral for me? That was nice of them." The man with Hal's face shook his head. "Did they produce a body, too?"

No, of course they hadn't. Hal Ellum had been *declared* dead, years after an investigation had failed to turn up any evidence of his whereabouts. Kane's mind raced, attempting to make some sense from this senselessness. An identical twin, a son, a clone—something, *anything*. "No. No. No."

"It's me, Kane. The same guy who sat with you in a bar in Elva City and convinced you to testify against the war. Remember? You were drinking citta beer that night."

The memory came easily to mind. The lighting in the bar had been dim, like this office. He and Hal Ellum had sat in a corner, the place empty but for the two of them.

No one but Tayla knew about that meeting.

"It can't—" Kane stopped himself. "How in the hell can you possibly—"

"They had to get rid of me, Kane. And they figured they could get away with it if my body was never found. So they came for me in the middle of the night, put me on a classified Portship, and brought me here. Fifteen years ago."

"That's crazy. Juris isn't even part of the Petra Compact."

Hal slammed a hand on the desk. "God damn it, Kane, *look* at me! I'm here, right now, right in front of you! If that's crazy, then so are you."

Kane gripped the padded arms of the chair, breathing hard. He looked right and left, claustrophobic.

Hal came around the desk and sat on its front edge. In a lower voice, he said, "I'm sorry. I know this is a shock to you."

Shock didn't even begin to describe it. Kane had been shocked before. He knew that dreamlike sensation, that sense that what was happening wasn't quite real. This was another order of magnitude. Kane welcomed the unreality of it, clung to it, even as it seemed to crumble.

"Kane, they made a secret deal with Rolf Ankledge—and probably paid him handsomely for it. It's really that simple. They paid the price and *disappeared* me. They dumped me here on Petra, never to be heard from again—by anyone. I'm sure they expected I wouldn't last more than a few weeks. At the most." Another smile flickered across his features. "They miscalculated. And their day of reckoning has arrived at last."

"Who?" Kane's voice was hoarse. "Who could have done this?"

"Who else? Who had the resources? And the motive?"

"Grange?"

"You know how paranoid he was. Him and that entire pack of Virtue Party cronies, all those lying bastards who brought us into the Cassean War."

Kane had met Prime Minister Ronel Grange once—at a medal ceremony, just after Kane had returned from Cassea. After the ceremony, Kane had taken a very long shower, shaking despite the steam heat, despondent, feeling like a whore. No, worse—like a murderer.

He had sought out Hal Ellum, the most outspoken leader of the protest movement, only a few days later.

In a monotone, Kane said, "We voted them out of office in the next general election. The Silvers took power."

"Good for you. Good for Juris. A little late for me, as it turned out."

"Grange is dead. So are Bressis, Elamil, and Hamera. The rest of them never went into politics again."

"I know. Even here, I manage to occasionally get some news from home."

"And you…" Kane struggled to piece it together. "We thought…everyone assumed you'd been killed. But no one had any proof. You had a lot of enemies. Not just Grange. Even some in the anti-war movement hated you."

"I made them look bad. Ineffectual."

"And all this time, you were here."

Hal nodded. "Here. In this fucking hellhole." Venom crept into his voice. His lips peeled back from his teeth as he spoke. "My case isn't an isolated one, not by a long shot. Rolf Ankledge has set himself up like some crazed little pig-god. You have no idea what's been happening on this planet, Kane. No one knows. But that's about to change." He pointed. "And you're gonna help me change it."

"Me."

"You."

The door opened, and Miga came in. "We're ready."

"Good." Hal stood. "Come on. No one here's going to hurt you." He went out without looking back. After a moment, Kane got up and followed.

Hal stood with Miga and a group of his armed compatriots near a monitor that displayed a graphic representing the Hub. Kane hung back a few steps, looking over shoulders. Miga was giving Hal a status report: "…locked down. One of the teams out there has been trying to blast their way in, but it sounds like they've given up. Allcomm traffic indicates that the fire at the armory is now contained, so we can expect those units to join the main party soon."

Hal nodded. "Has there been any word on Roman and Berian?"

Miga glanced around at her colleagues before answering. "They're alive. A team of medics found them, along with those guards we ran into outside the Hub. They've been taken to the infirmary. I don't have anything on their condition."

"We can't do anything for them, then."

"No."

"Shit." Hal nibbled at his lower lip. "And the storm?"

Miga flicked a control, bringing up a radar image—a mass of green, yellow, and flashing red just beginning to swamp the island. "It's tracking west-southwest at twenty klicks an hour."

"Slow moving bastard."

"It won't be out of here until dawn. No way we can launch until then."

"We can hold out a lot longer than that if we have to."

"Launch?" Kane stepped forward. "You're going to launch?"

They all turned to him. Hal's smile reappeared. "That's right. We're getting out, Kane. Escaping. The jailbreak of the millennium."

"Damn right, brother," the pale, spiky-haired inmate said, and clapped Hal on the shoulder.

"Who's going to pilot the ship?"

The prisoners looked at each other and chuckled. And Kane finally understood what he was doing there.

His dawning horror must have registered on his face. Hal said, "Maybe you should go back to the office. There's a couch. You look like you need to lie down."

Kane found the couch along the wall opposite the desk. He collapsed on it, one arm slung over his eyes. The wear of repeated shocks had taken a toll on him. Exhaustion made every body part sag as if weighted. He would have slept if not for the endless loop playing through his memory, starting at the first explosion all the way to that moment of realization.

The rumbles of thunder became regular, jangling counterpoints to his thoughts. The storm had made landfall.

The office door opened again. Kane took his arm away from his face and opened his eyes. Hal looked down at him. Backlit by the lamp on the desk, his face was hidden in shadow. He went to the chair Kane had used and swiveled it so that it faced the couch. He sat and leaned forward, resting his elbows on his thighs. "Bet you didn't think you'd be doing this when you got up this morning, did you?"

"This is insane," Kane said.

"Yeah. Probably."

"You want me to help you escape."

"We need to get to that Portship you have in orbit."

"I..." Kane's mouth opened and closed as he tried to figure out what to say next. "How did you do this, Hal?"

He told Kane a story of luring down a skimmer on a surveillance flight and taking the crew with them on a transport they had stolen during a raid. They'd manufactured the story about a malfunctioning transponder, then had the skimmer crew give the clearance code as the transport approached the island.

"Forced them at gunpoint, you mean," Kane said.

"You know, I tried asking nicely, but they weren't disposed to listen."

"What about the explosion at the armory?"

"I was wondering when you'd think of that." Hal's smile returned, lingering.

Kane sat up. "Wait. You couldn't have set that off. You had just touched down. The armory's nowhere near the landing field."

"Got that right."

"You've had inside help."

"Not all the staff on this island are automatons. Some of them have consciences. They know what's going on here."

"How many?"

Hal shook his head. "Sorry, my friend. That's classified. Those people have to remain anonymous if they want to stay alive."

Kane fought through the shock, concentrating. It occurred to him how close the inside help had come to killing him earlier in the day. If Emma hadn't intervened, he might well have been at the armory when it—

Emma Goring. She had steered him away from the armory.

Was it possible they had managed such a high-level penetration? She'd been unusually forthcoming about the condition of the skimmer fleet. She'd known a lot about his background, too. If he was right about her, that would mean—

"My God. You…you knew I was coming."

"Of course I did. You didn't think it was coincidence, did you? This visit of yours has been planned for months. When I found out about it, I knew the time had come." His smile faded. "I was being a little facetious back there, Kane. This is about more than just an escape. Much more. You have to understand that." He sat back, running a hand through his hair. "Like I said, I'm not the only political prisoner on Petra. I wasn't even the first." He nodded toward the door. "Most of the others in that room can tell you similar stories. They come from all over Ported Space, from every world in the Compact—Land's End, New Xizang, even Cassea. Petra was supposed to be the last resort for the most violent offenders.

That's part of the charter. Murderers, rapists, other predators. The final solution, even better than the death penalty."

That much Kane already knew. It was one of Petra's selling points. True life imprisonment without the possibility of parole—an arrangement that satisfied both the far left and the far right. Capital punishment had been discarded by every member of the Compact.

His mind still reeled from the thought of Emma Goring feeding information to prisoners, of plotting the destruction of the armory. She and God knew how many others.

Hal went on: "But it didn't take long for certain powerful people to realize what they could get away with here—as long as they were willing to pay the price." Hal held up his hands. "Look around you, Kane. Look at the way Warden Ankledge lives. You'll see where all that money went."

Kane couldn't deny it.

"It has to stop," Hal said. "It's not enough that we escape. These people have to be exposed. Brought to justice."

At the bar in Elva City, Hal had said much the same thing about Cassea: *It's not enough to end the war. Grange and the Virtue Party lied to get us into it. We have to wake up the populace if we want to get justice.*

"Fifteen years you've been here," Kane said, "and you haven't changed a bit."

Hal shifted in his seat and adjusted his overcoat. "Oh, I've changed. Spending years fighting—and killing—for your survival…that'll change you. But they haven't managed to beat the dissident out of me yet." He leaned forward again. "Kane, I'm not a religious man, but when I learned you were coming to Petra, I felt like a prayer had been answered."

Kane put his hands up in front of him. "Stop. Just stop."

"Stop what?"

"The hard sell. You're working me, just like you worked me in Elva City."

"What?" Hal's weathered face was a mask of disbelief. "I never worked you. Let me refresh your memory, my friend. *You* came to *me* in Elva City. It was *your* idea to testify before Parliament. All I did was help stiffen your resolve a little."

"You wanted more than that. You wanted me to join the movement. You wanted to take to the streets with clubs and stones. Riots. Storming the Parliament House. Ronel Grange's head mounted on a pole. And me out in front, leading the way—the war hero turned rebel. And now, you're—"

"Now I'm *what*?" Hal stood, fuming. "Now what am I doing? *Look* at me, Kane! Look what they've done to me!"

Outside the office, Miga and some of the others turned to see what the shouting was about. Hal glanced at them and spoke in a lower voice, his lips skinning back from his teeth. "I did nothing to deserve this. I was a dissident, that's all. I spoke up when others were too apathetic or too frightened. For that they took my life away and dumped me on a planet full of psychopaths and sociopaths, most of them barely human anymore. And let me say it again, Kane: *I'm not the only one*. It's happening all over the Compact. But you sit there in your best Jurisian formal wear and tell me to stop giving you the *hard sell*." He looked Kane up and down. "You son of a bitch."

Silence fell, but for the thunder outside. Hal stood glaring at him. Kane rubbed his brow, avoiding his gaze. His head still ached from the sirens.

Hal squatted, interposing himself in Kane's line of sight. "I have to know, Kane. Will you help us?"

Kane chuckled humorlessly. "Do I have a choice?"

"You're not a hostage."

"That's not how it looks from where I'm sitting."

"I already told you—no one is going to hurt you. I won't allow it. I came here tonight to ask for your help. I was counting on you being the same man I met in Elva City."

"If I were to help you…" Kane became dizzy at the thought. "My God, can you imagine how huge it would be? It would be an interplanetary scandal. It…it's unprecedented. Ported Space has never seen anything like it."

In a monotone, Hal said, "I'm not feeling much concern for the well-being of Ported Space. It doesn't seem to give a shit about any of us here."

"There would be nowhere we could run. Nowhere." Kane licked his lips. "And I would *have* to run, wouldn't I? If I help you, I'm as much of a fugitive from justice as you are. I have a family back on Juris, Hal. A wife and child. I can't do that to them."

Hal bowed his head, settling on his haunches. "You're not going to help us."

Kane put a hand on Hal's shoulder. "Listen to me. You have

control of this facility. That puts you in a position to make demands. You should be able to make whatever arrangements you need to get off this planet. I might even be able to act as an intermediary between—"

Hal shoved Kane's hand away. "Spare me."

"It could work, Hal. And I'll tell you something else: when I get back to Juris, I could demand an investigation. I have some pull there now."

Hal got to his feet and headed toward the desk. "No doubt you do." He flopped into the chair. "Actually, you haven't changed, Kane. You're still trying to fix the system from within."

"Hal, that's been working. My testimony before Parliament—"

"Helped get the Silvers elected. Helped throw out one corrupt political party in exchange for another. That was as far as you were willing to go."

"Things have changed on Juris."

"Have they? Have they really? Then why are you here? Why does Juris want to join the Compact?"

"We're just considering—"

"Still have that draconian code on Juris? What's the matter, Kane, are all the prisons full?"

Some estimates put Jurisian incarceration numbers at two percent of the total population. Maybe more.

What have they turned you into, Kane?

Kane said, "Let me go back to the dining room. Let me talk to Warden Ankledge. I might be able to arrange something for you."

Hal flapped a hand at him. "Oh, do whatever you want. Just get the hell out of here."

Kane emerged from the office and found himself facing Miga. She brought her emitter, at rest on her shoulder, into her hands, just holding it, not pointing it…yet. "What are you doing?"

"I need to talk to the warden. Will you escort me back to the dining room?"

"Talk to the…" Miga looked through the glass door at Hal, still seated at the desk. He glanced in her direction and nodded.

She regarded Kane as she might a snake. "Why?"

"See if I can bring this to a peaceful resolution."

"Are you going to take us to your Portship or not?"

Kane didn't like the way she was holding her weapon, Hal's assurances of his safety notwithstanding. Hal could always change his mind. "No one's going anywhere until the storm passes. In the meantime, I want to talk to the warden. I can find my own way if I have to, but I'd prefer to have your help."

The others were watching them. He became acutely conscious of his formal wear, and of the fact that he was unarmed. All it would take at this point was one unstable person, one misstep in an already tense situation.

"Come on," Miga said. She led him toward the exit.

They made their way back from the Hub in silence. At least Kane no longer had to walk with his hands on his head. He stole glances at her as they navigated the winding halls, but she only stared straight ahead, her scarred jaw set. Outside, the thunder rumbled on and on.

Kane said, "Will you tell me what you did with the other workers, the other guards?"

"We ran them out of the Hub and out of this wing." Her words were clipped. "They're on the other side of the emergency doors."

"But…there were some fatalities, right?"

"You're a fucking genius. People die on Petra every day."

"What about the skimmer crew?"

"What about them? One died back on Mainland. He would have killed us if he'd had the chance. We left the other two in the hangar."

"Merciful of you."

"Hal's idea. He wants casualties kept to a minimum. He thinks it might make a difference when we testify in front of the interplanetary tribunals he keeps talking about—assuming there ever are any."

They came to the guest housing, with its carpeted floors and luxurious appointments. Kane knew the way from here, but he let Miga escort him, anyway. No need to make her more suspicious than she already was.

Just before they emerged into the reception area, she stopped him, standing in his way with her emitter still in her arms. "I saw the way you were talking to Hal back there. I couldn't make out what you were saying, but I guess I don't have to." She stepped closer to him, holding the emitter up so that its barrel was bare inches from Kane's face. "Listen up, Jurisian. We didn't come through all of this just to surrender to that fucking butcher you call the warden."

Kane focused on the barrel of the emitter. "I'm not asking you to—"

"We're getting off Petra. You understand me?" She tapped the barrel to his chin. Her sour breath washed over his face. Her voice dropped to an icy whisper. "I don't know what Hal promised you, and I don't care. We're getting off Petra, one way or the other. Think about *that* while you're chatting with the warden about a peaceful resolution."

She held his gaze for long moments. It unnerved Kane worse than anything that had happened since arriving on Petra. Murder burned in her eyes, rage the likes of which he hadn't seen since the war.

Back in the Hub, he'd feared one of the inmates might do something rash. He began to suspect that he'd walked out of there with the most unstable one in the bunch.

She shoved him toward the reception area. "Get moving."

Cromberg, he of the pelt, stood watch outside the dining room doors. No longer masked, he had craggy features, dark skin, a crooked nose that appeared to have been broken more than once, and eyebrows as bristly and bushy as his beard. He stood up straighter as Kane and Miga approached. "What's going on?"

Miga looked around. "Where's Raxel?"

The other inmate, Kane supposed.

"Hauling away those guards." Cromberg chuckled. "He got hold of a dining cart. What the hell—it beats dragging them."

"What will he do with them?"

"Tuck 'em away somewhere safe. It's not like we can just open a door and toss 'em out."

Miga looked past him to the double doors. "Any trouble from our friend?"

"Not a peep." Cromberg glanced at Kane. "What's he doing here?"

Miga shook her head. "Ask him."

Cromberg raised his bushy eyebrows. "Well?"

Kane sighed. "I just want to talk to the warden. That's all."

"Hal said you were gonna help us. Said he knew you, from before. Said you would understand."

"I am trying to help you."

"Shit," Miga said. She addressed Cromberg: "Go back to the Hub. I'll take over here."

"You sure?"

"Yeah."

With a shrug, Cromberg headed across the reception area, turned a corner, and was lost to sight.

Miga motioned toward the doors with her emitter. "Go on. Talk all you want. But just remember, when the storm passes, the time for talking's done."

CHAPTER FIVE

Rolf Ankledge sat in one of the upholstered chairs, staring into the darkened fireplace, when Kane entered. The warden was on his feet in a moment. "What happened?" His words were somewhat slurred; his jaw had swollen where he'd been struck.

"Are you hurt?" Kane said.

Ankledge rubbed his jaw. "I'll heal. What happened?"

"They…they took me to the Hub."

"They want your ship, don't they?"

Kane nodded. He had no inclination to fill Ankledge in on the details of his past. It was none of the man's business, anyway. And if even half of what Hal Ellum had told him was true…

Halleck Ellum. After all these years. No one had known about Kane's association with Hal; as far as the rest of Juris knew, Kane had testified before Parliament of his own volition, a decorated veteran who had seen enough of the war to question the rationale for it.

All I did was help stiffen your resolve a little. That was one way of putting it, Kane supposed. But it had been more than a pep talk in Elva City. Hal had shown Kane the evidence he had gathered, copies of classified intelligence briefings showing there had been serious doubts regarding the claims that the Cassean government had been behind a series of raids on Jurisian vessels in the shipping lanes. The briefings concluded that the most likely culprit had been one of the crime cartels that plagued Ported Space. Hal wouldn't tell him how he had come by the information, but at that point, it hadn't really mattered. The documents only confirmed what Kane had already figured out on his own during the Cassean campaign. In all the recon missions he had flown, he had never once found evidence of a direct connection between the raids and Cassea. And the bombing missions he had been sent on seemed more intent on crippling Cassea's manufacturing infrastructure than its military capacity.

Ankledge had said something Kane had missed. Kane swept his rambling thoughts aside. "Sorry, I was a little distracted."

"Was that their only demand? Just to escape?"

"Basically."

"How many are there?"

Kane thought back, counting. "At least nineteen. Plus two that are wounded."

"All inmates?"

"Yes. And all of them well armed."

"No."

"Beg pardon?"

Ankledge shook his head. "No, they can't all be prisoners. This attack was coordinated on at least two fronts. They managed to breach our security even before they landed. Some of my own people must be in on this."

Kane feigned hesitation. "I suppose that's possible."

"Are you sure you saw no one but prisoners?"

"I'm positive. As far as I can tell, you and I are the only hostages." The word came naturally to his lips, despite Hal's insistence that Kane was not a captive. "If anyone helped them, they're either in hiding or outside the Hub."

"Snakes. Traitors." Ankledge spat on the floor. "There's no pit deep enough for them."

Kane had to change the subject, lest an inadvertent slip betray him. "Warden, we should talk."

"What did they say? Threaten to execute you, I take it?"

"Let's sit. Please." Kane extended a hand toward the chairs. They sat.

Ankledge tapped his fingers on the arm of his chair—measured, rhythmic taps. His rage seemed to recede. Some of the air of confident command he'd shown when they first met resurfaced. "Go ahead, Pythen."

Kane took a moment to arrange what he wanted to say. "They've taken control of the Hub. All your people are outside, and they can't get in. We can't even communicate with them. Like it or not, Warden, these prisoners have the upper hand. You'll have to negotiate with them. You can—"

"Absolutely not."

"Warden, this isn't—"

"No." Ankledge raised a bony finger. The joints were swollen, making the digit look crooked. "Petra is *my* planet, Pythen. Nobody tells me what to do here. Nobody. I don't *have* to do anything."

Kane glanced toward the door. He thought of Miga on the other side of it, of the deadline she'd given him. "That attitude could very well get us killed. What do you propose to do, then? Just sit here?"

"Yes." Ankledge let his hand drop to the arm of his chair. The emergency lighting cast a shadow over his eyes. "That's exactly what I propose to do."

"Warden, they're dug in behind bombardment-resistant fortifications. They've cut off your communications. And they have access to your emergency stores—plenty of food, plenty of water. You're not going to starve them out."

"Let them have your lander."

"What?"

Ankledge stared into the fireplace. "Let them take it. You can even offer to preset their course for them, if that will make them happy."

Kane's breathing slowed. "Why would I do that?"

"That vessel will never make it to your Portship. It will never make it out of the atmosphere." For the first time since the base had been attacked, Ankledge smiled—a mirthless smile, made unnerving by the shadowy emergency lighting. "What do you know about Petra's security, Mr. Pythen?"

"Only what you've allowed to be known."

"That's right. And here's a thing you don't know about: our satellite system is capable of more than mere surveillance. There are also orbiting platforms armed with smart missiles up there. In an emergency, the system is automatically armed. If the satellites detect any unauthorized launch—from Control or anywhere else on the planet—those platforms will open fire."

Kane swallowed hard. "You're sure the system had time to arm before the prisoners took over the Hub?"

"The system was armed within moments of the explosion at the armory. I checked it myself, before the Hub got locked down." Ankledge's fingers kept tapping as he talked. The remaining traces of his anger faded. "It's our last line of defense, Mr. Pythen—the final guarantee that no one leaves Petra without my permission."

"What if the prisoners deactivate it?"

"Impossible without authorization. Only Chief Mehr and I have those codes." The warden turned a languid gaze to Kane. "When they come back for you, tell them they can have your lander." More thunder rumbled. Ankledge glanced toward the ceiling. "They'll have to wait for the storm to pass. That will take until morning, at least. So settle in, Mr. Pythen. Maybe try to sleep a little. We've had a fine meal, and now we can just pass the time relaxing in front of a comfortable fire. This will all be over soon."

Hal Ellum emerged from the office. The others turned toward him. He straightened, pushing his shoulders back. Ever since his days on Juris, an eternity ago, he had understood the importance of bearing, of carrying oneself with confidence, no matter the situation.

Cromberg entered the Hub from the direction of the guest quarters. He stopped when he saw Hal and brushed some hair away from his craggy face. "What's going on?"

"I was about to ask you that," Hal said.

"Miga took over for me at the dining room. Raxel is securing the two guards we took out."

"Good. Thanks." Hal turned his attention to one of the weather monitors. The storm was lashing the island with eighty kilometer per hour winds. According to the security readouts, the surveillance skimmers that hadn't made it back to Control before it hit had given up on circling. They were heading for emergency landing fields elsewhere on Petra to hole up for the night. Some outlying stations on Control were reporting downed trees, and the emergency crews working at the armory had fled for shelter. But the structures here had been built to handle much worse. From inside the Hub, only the frequency of the thunder gave any real hint of the conditions outside.

Cromberg cleared his throat. It did nothing to smooth the rough edges of his voice. "You could try answering *my* question now."

"What do you want me to say? Nothing's going to happen until the storm passes. Be patient."

"Why did your boy walk out of here? What does he want with the warden?"

The others were watching and listening. Damn Cromberg for doing this, challenging him publicly.

Hal supposed he should have expected no less. It was Cromberg, after all.

"He's not a hostage. I told you that. He can come and go as he pleases."

Cromberg crossed his arms. "And supposing he asks to be let out of here. What would you do then? Open a door for him?"

"If he asked, and if I could do so without endangering us, yes, I suppose I would. But he hasn't asked to be let out, has he?"

Cromberg grumbled. "I'll tell you something: he sure didn't seem very happy to see us."

"Your face doesn't exactly make *my* heart flutter, either, Cromberg."

That drew a laugh from the rest of the team. Cromberg remained impassive. "We need this guy, Ellum. You'd best make sure he knows what team he's on." He leaned close and spoke in a lower voice so that the others couldn't hear: "If you don't, I will."

Hal knew better than to react. "Cromberg, everything's fine. Try not to worry so much."

Cromberg stared hard at him for a moment longer, then relaxed his posture. "What about Roman and Berian?"

"They're in the infirmary. That's all we know at this point."

"So we're just going to leave them here?"

"If you have any bright ideas, I'd love to hear them."

Cromberg uncrossed his arms. "Just don't seem right."

"We can't do anything for them in here, outside of basic first aid. They knew the risks."

"Yeah. Guess we all did." Cromberg looked out over the rest of the Hub and raised his voice. "Where's the damned food? I'm starved."

He went off in search of provisions. Hal watched him walk away.

Hotheaded though Cromberg could be, he had a good grasp of the situation. If Kane *did* ask to be released, Hal could not be sure he'd be able to keep his word to him. It was easy, perhaps too easy, for Hal to rationalize it by telling himself that extreme situations demanded extreme actions. Foolish, at this point, for him to worry about salvaging the shreds of his honor. Even more foolish for him to have placed so much faith in Kane Pythen, for trusting this entire escape plan to the ethics of a man he'd known briefly fifteen years ago.

Not that he'd had much choice. If Kane Pythen hadn't been sent to Petra, Hal would never have attempted this in the first place.

There had to be a way. Maybe if he could convince Kane to set the lander on autopilot…but no. That would only get them into orbit. The captain of the Portship would still have to let them aboard. And even if they somehow got through the Portal, where would they go from there? Someone—a world not part of the Petra Compact—would have to shelter them, at least for a little while.

Without Kane, the task became exponentially harder. Maybe even impossible. The bastard.

Still mindful of his bearing, Hal stood straight, working to remain outwardly calm, but inwardly wondering how much longer he would be able to hold this together.

Rolf Ankledge sat in his chair with head back and eyes closed. Kane watched him, disbelieving. "I don't understand this," he said.

Ankledge spoke without bothering to open his eyes. "What's not to understand?"

"Why don't you talk to them? Why don't you tell them what you've told me? If you make them see their position is futile, you could end this standoff right now."

"In the first place, I doubt they would believe me. And even if they did, that's no guarantee they'll surrender. They might decide they won't be taken alive, maybe take us with them."

"I doubt that." Kane spoke with more confidence than he felt. It all depended on how much control Hal had over his people. He thought again of Miga, waiting outside the door.

"No, this way is better," Ankledge said. "Easier."

"They'll all be killed."

Ankledge opened his eyes and raised his head. "Do you know how many of my people *they've* killed?"

"I thought you might prefer to avoid unnecessary bloodshed."

Ankledge's narrow eyes seemed black in the firelight. "Are you sure you're Jurisian?"

Kane hesitated before replying. "Warden…is it possible these prisoners might have legitimate grievances?"

Ankledge's fingers stilled their rhythmic tapping. "What did you say?"

"I think you heard me."

"What kind of *grievances*?"

"Wrongful imprisonment, perhaps."

"I didn't convict them, Mr. Pythen. Their guilt was established beyond doubt back on their respective worlds. They all had opportunities for final appeals before they were sentenced to Petra. That's part of the Compact."

A question rose to Kane's lips: *What's Halleck Ellum doing on Petra, then? Where are* his *appeal records?* Instead, he said, "What about the conditions on Petra? Maybe they're protesting their treatment."

Ankledge's fingers began tapping again, hitting the upholstered arm of the chair with more force than before. "Exactly what did they tell you when they took you to the Hub?"

"Vague hints, that's all." It had the virtue of being the truth. "But this is something that's been on my mind since before I even got here: how do these prisoners live? Do you have any idea what happens to them once you drop them off in the wilderness with nothing but a few days' worth of provisions?"

Ankledge shifted his jaw and winced. "It's a prison, Mr. Pythen. I shouldn't have to tell you that it can get ugly."

"How ugly?"

"We don't walk among them."

"And you don't care, do you?"

"Oh, for God's sake." Ankledge sneered. He stood and walked away from the fireplace. "Look around you, Pythen. Look what they've done here. Do you need any more evidence of how dangerous they are? You can't expect me to have sympathy for these vermin."

A planet full of psychopaths and sociopaths, most of them barely human anymore, Hal had said.

Kane spoke to Ankledge's back: "They're not complete savages, not all of them. We're still alive."

"And damned lucky to be."

Kane stood. "You're not telling me everything, Warden."

Ankledge glanced at him over his shoulder. "Neither are you." He turned to face Kane. "What do you know, Pythen? What do you *think* you know?"

"I think you should talk to these prisoners."

"You're forgetting yourself again. Whose side are you on, anyway?"

A good question. And Kane didn't have an answer, not yet.

Though dawn was still many hours off, he already felt time slipping past. And he was getting nowhere here. "I'll tell you this much, Warden: I'm having a hard time seeing a difference between you and them. Everyone on this planet seems hellbent on destruction. It's ridiculous." Kane headed toward the doors, passing the warden without even looking at him.

"Where do you think you're going? *Hey*! Where are you—"

Kane pushed through the door and into the reception area. Miga, startled, leveled her weapon at him. Kane stopped.

"Kane! You get back in here! You don't—" The door swung shut, cutting off Ankledge's shouts. With the injury to his jaw, raising his voice like that must hurt like hell. The thought brought Kane grim satisfaction.

"Where are you going?" Miga said.

On instinct, Kane started to raise his hands, then let them fall to his sides. "Hal says I'm not a hostage here. Is that true or not?"

"What?"

"Answer me."

Her features twitched at his tone. It wasn't quite a flinch, more like a nervous tic. For the briefest of moments, Kane wondered if he had just goaded her into opening fire.

Then the fleeting expression, whatever it had been, vanished. The emitter's barrel wavered. "It's true," she said. "For the moment."

"Then stand aside. And point that damned thing elsewhere."

"Where are you going?"

"What does it matter? I'm unarmed, I'm locked in, and my allcomm's dead. I just want to take a walk. The guy you need to guard is in there." Kane cocked a thumb over his shoulder.

Slowly, she raised her emitter and settled it against her shoulder. "I don't like this."

"That makes two of us." Kane walked past her, headed for the corridors. He half expected her to shoot him in the back, but she didn't.

Kane found the flight of stairs he had taken when coming down for dinner. He traced his steps back to his guest quarters.

The room, like the rest of the wing, was dark but for emergency lighting that cast strange shadows. He had neglected to draw the curtains before he'd left. Steel blast shields had gone up over the windows, part of the lockdown, denying him any view of the storm. Beyond, thunder growled, and the shriek of the wind reverberated in the floor. Kane pulled the heavy curtains shut and rested his forehead on the wall.

Whose side are you on?

He didn't know whom he trusted less—Halleck Ellum or Rolf Ankledge.

His case sat on the edge of the bed, still open. The formals he wore felt stiff, binding. Slowly, he pulled off the white jacket and unbuttoned the shirt. Every movement wearied him. He took his time changing back into the clothes he'd been wearing when he landed.

As he rummaged through his case, he came across a storage cell tucked into one corner. He didn't know how it had gotten there; he had no memory of packing it. Curious, he unclipped his allcomm from his belt, thumbed it on, and inserted the cell into its slot.

The allcomm screen lit. The info scroll from the storage cell informed him that it was a message from his wife. From Tayla. She must have slipped it into his things prior to his departure.

A moment later, her face appeared on the screen—her dark hair tied back, her normally bright eyes marked by bags.

At that moment, he felt every inch of the light years that separated him from his wife and daughter. A dead certainty seized him that he would never see them again.

"Kane," she said, "I don't know when you'll see this—probably not until you get to Petra. But I just wanted to say…" She took a breath and glanced away for a moment. "I guess I'm not sure what to say. I hate that we had that argument just before you left. But I won't apologize for what I said. Maybe it came out wrong; I don't know. It's something that's been on my mind for some time now."

She cleared her throat. Kane settled onto the bed.

"I keep waiting, Kane. I know somewhere inside you is the man who testified before Parliament against the war, the man who got into Enforcement to reform the system, not to become part of it. But I think you've lost sight of that. They've been using you as a kind of badge of honor, a shield to defend their policies. You know that, right? And now they've sent you across Ported Space to Petra. You know full well what answer they want from you. They expect your rubber stamp. Are you going to give it to them? The man I knew ten years ago, the man who testified against the war, he wouldn't have hesitated to say no. Now…I'm not so sure."

Kane bowed his head.

She continued: "I haven't lost faith in you, Kane. I know you have your doubts about Petra. And I know you feel trapped. I wish there were some easier way out of this, but there isn't.

"Maybe it would help you to know that I don't care about the money. Shamlyn and you and I will be fine without it. We'll figure something else out, some other way to leave Juris. This decision you need to make now, this decision about Petra—it's really the same question you've been ducking for years. This prison world is an abomination, and you know it."

Tayla objected to Petra on general principles. She didn't know the half of it.

"You need to tell them so," she said. "They will listen to you if you say it. They won't have any choice.

"I keep waiting, Kane. I can wait a bit longer, but don't make me wait forever. I love you. Shamlyn loves you. Come home as soon as you can."

She stopped. Kane looked at the screen, just in time to see her image fade to black as the message ended.

He set the allcomm aside and lay back on the bed. He had never felt so alone in all his life—not even in those dark days before he'd first met Hal Ellum, when it had seemed that the world had gone insane. He silently cursed Rolf Ankledge, Hal Ellum, the Republics of Juris and Cassea, and the Petra Compact.

Whose side are you on?

His own, and his family's.

We'll figure something out, she'd said. But Portal passage to another world, especially for emigration purposes, didn't come cheap. The bonus he'd been promised, along with their savings, would be barely enough to get them through and set them up elsewhere, even on some backwater world like Aeolus.

Someone knocked on his door. Kane started and sat up.

The door creaked open. Hal Ellum stood there. "I've been looking for you."

"Congratulations. You found me."

Hal stepped inside and let the door shut behind him. "Miga allcommed me after you left the dining room."

"I needed to be alone. To think."

"Do you want me to go, then?"

"No. Stay, if you want. It doesn't matter."

Hal lingered at the door. Kane tried to imagine how he'd feel if Hal died while trying to escape from Petra. Curiously, he felt nothing. But then, Hal had been dead in his mind for fifteen years.

Hal's unexplained disappearance had been cause for deep concern at first. It had happened shortly before Kane's scheduled testimony before Parliament. He did not doubt that Grange and the Virtues had been behind it in some way; Hal was the most public—and most incendiary—spokesman for the anti-war movement. Kane had wondered at the time if the Virtues had learned of his recent liaison with Hal Ellum. If so, they would have come after him next.

But by then, Kane was too angry to be dissuaded. The evidence Hal had shown him had convinced him to testify. The Silvers were ecstatic at the prospect and had promised he would be taken care of. He hadn't been interested in their promises. What he needed was protection from possible retaliation.

He had thought that some hint of Hal's whereabouts might shake loose after the hearings, after Kane's testimony. But there was nothing—no body, no arrest records, no tearful confessions, not even the vaguest whiff of a lead. Even as he became aware that no reprisals against him were forthcoming, Kane became more and more certain that Hal was dead. So did Hal's compatriots in the anti-war movement. The riots he had been so keen to incite broke out in earnest.

The election cycle swept the Virtues from power, putting the Silvers in charge. The riots eased; cease-fire talks between Juris and Cassea began. The Silvers offered Kane the post of his choosing. He decided on Enforcement, to see what he could do about curbing the excesses of the infamous Jurisian penal code. And his anger began to fade.

In Kane's introspective moments, he had to admit the presence of another emotion—relief. Hal's disappearance had absolved Kane of the need to choose. He could be a concerned citizen and nothing more.

And now the choice he'd been able to avoid fifteen years ago stared him in the face.

"I'm sorry for losing my temper back there," Hal said.

"Don't worry about it."

"I have to worry about it." Hal stood with his hands behind his back, leaning against the closed door. "You offered to be a mediator between us and the warden. If that's the best I can get from you, I'll take it."

Kane drew in a shuddery breath and ran a hand over his face. "I'm thirsty. Does the plumbing still work, or did you shut that down, too?"

"Be my guest."

A pair of drinking glasses sat atop a table in the corner, next to a coffeepot. Kane got up, grabbed one, and filled it with water from the bathroom faucet. He emptied it in one long drink. His head cleared a little. He ran the faucet again, splashed cold water on his face, then dried it off with a thick, fluffy hand towel.

It would be easiest to let Hal and his band of inmates go. To let them die. To return to Tayla. But if he did that, he didn't know if he would deserve her.

"I need to tell you something," he said. "But no one can know I told you."

Hal's brow creased. "Pardon me?"

"You forced it out of me at gunpoint. You threatened to kill me if I didn't help you. I had no choice at all. Understood?"

Hal's laugh sounded like a bark. "You're worried about your reputation?"

"I'm worried about my family. You and I both know this doesn't end once you Port away from here, assuming you even make it that far. I have to protect my wife and daughter from what's going to come down afterward."

Hal was silent, his brow still furrowed.

"You're right about Juris, Hal. It's as bad as it's ever been. I spent years fighting to reform the Ministry of Enforcement, but I couldn't do it alone, and no one else was interested. The war and the riots provided enough instability for most people's lifetimes." He took a breath. "I have no love or loyalty for my homeworld anymore. But I'm not interested in joining the revolution, either. I just want to get out of here, gather up my family, and take them as far from Juris as I can. I might be able to help you get off Petra, but after that, you're on your own." Kane tossed the towel onto the bed. "That's it. That's the deal. Take it or leave it."

Hal's mouth formed a resigned half-smile. "I guess I'll take it. I've made worse deals."

They shook hands. Hal's was rough and hard with calluses, the grip stronger than Kane remembered.

"You can't launch," he said. And he told Hal about Ankledge's automated defense system.

Hal's face went solemn as Kane spoke. When he finished, Hal said, "Yes, we know."

"You *know*?"

Hal nodded. "Pretty typical of Ankledge, really. At this point, I'm sure he *wants* it to happen. Probably thinks it will teach everyone on Petra a lesson."

Kane thought with amazement of Emma Goring again. "Yes, probably. Why haven't you done anything about it yet?"

"If you weren't going to help us, there wasn't any point." Hal dug an allcomm from his stained overcoat. "This one's authorized to allow communications," he said by way of explanation. "Get your things together. We're heading back to the Hub. I think it's time I met the warden."

Kane stuffed his formals into his case and shut it. As he slung it over one shoulder, Hal put a hand on his arm.

"Kane. What you just did...it means a lot to me. I know it couldn't have been easy. Thank you."

"I haven't done anything. You forced me at gunpoint."

"Right. Sorry." He activated the allcomm.

Miga Bronn acknowledged the order and returned her allcomm to its place on her belt. She still had no idea what was going on, or where that chickenshit bastard Kane Pythen had run off to, but Hal had promised to explain once she got back to the Hub.

Before opening the doors to the dining room, she checked her hands. No shaking. Good. Well…maybe just the faintest hint of a tremor. Nothing she couldn't handle.

She steeled herself to open the door. When she felt calm enough, she went in, emitter held at the ready.

Warden Ankledge, seated by the fireplace, rose when he saw her, waiting.

"Alone at last," Miga said, and wondered why she had. She glanced at her hands again. The tremors had not worsened. She doubted that anyone but her would notice them.

Being in the presence of this pig-god warden caused a strange tension in her. Of course, she hated the man, as did everyone on Petra. But this was something different, a blind instinct to broil him where he stood. And that wouldn't do.

Her mind did that to her sometimes, taking her down dark alleys before she could stop herself. There were gaps in her memory, she knew—sealed places from before she'd come to know Hal Ellum and the rest of them. But those were bad things to be thinking about right now. She had a job to do.

She motioned with the emitter barrel. "We're ready for you now. Let's go."

CHAPTER SIX

Rolf Ankledge walked in front, hands up, with the wild woman trailing, her emitter pointed at his back. He was grateful for the opportunity to stretch his legs. His joints, growing more arthritic daily, ached from sitting so long. The change in the weather hadn't helped, either.

He had managed to doze a little while sitting in front of the fireplace, thanks to the wine he'd had at dinner, before all this madness had started.

They had taken his base. Destroyed his armory. Murdered his men. Anger stirred in him again, but he took deep breaths to quell it. As he had told Pythen, this would all be over soon. These savages had surprised him, had probably managed to scuttle the deal with Juris, but come daybreak, he would be back in control. Then he could turn his attention to repairing whatever damage they'd inflicted. Assuming he could get Pythen to play ball, there was even still a chance the Jurisians would come on board. They still needed Petra.

Ankledge and the woman passed into the darkened administrative and record-keeping area. God, the *smell* of her. She reeked of sweat and dirt. His stomach churned.

He had to wonder where she was from. She was dressed like a Mainlander. She seemed articulate, as did her cohorts. Northern Mainland, then, no doubt from those outposts past the Fracture. That stood to reason. Surveillance flights and satellite data had shown too many signs of organization—bigger farms, hints of advanced structures. And that was even after the bombing campaigns. If there was ever going to be serious trouble on Petra, Ankledge had always suspected it would come from there.

But those momentary lapses of hers concerned him. Ankledge had seen such blank expressions before, in the faces of flight crew members that had gone down in Bone Tribe territory and been rescued. The Bone Tribes stayed in South Mainland.

He held his silence, kept his moves slow and easy—nothing that could be construed as provocative.

They came at last to the Hub. The woman rapped on the steel door. "It's me," she said.

The door opened. Ankledge stepped through.

The savages were *everywhere*, standing over consoles as if they belonged there, poring over monitor data as if they understood it. It chilled him to think of all the information they had access to.

It would all be over soon. He had to keep reminding himself.

They all went silent and stared as Ankledge entered. North Mainlanders, all of them. A beardless man in a tan overcoat, standing near one of the weather displays, stepped forward. Next to him stood Kane Pythen, also with his hands raised. He must have gone back to his quarters after fleeing the dining room; he'd changed out of his formals. A wild man with a bushy beard held an emitter on him.

Ankledge stared down the man in the overcoat.

The man stared back. The moment stretched.

"Warden Ankledge," the man said. "You can put your hands down now, I think."

Ankledge let his hands fall to his sides.

"I thought it was time for us to meet. I'm Halleck Ellum."

The name rang faint bells, but Ankledge couldn't say from where, nor could he place the accent.

It didn't matter at this point. He supposed he should say something warden-like, something they would expect to hear from him. "Release us now, and you'll be taken back to Mainland."

Chuckles sounded throughout the Hub. "My, how reasonable of you," Ellum said. "Thanks, Warden. But what if we don't *want* to go back to Mainland? Or even Southland? Or Farside?"

"Whatever you have planned, it can't work. You have to know that. You won't escape from Petra."

"We've come this far. Before today, a lot of people might have considered that impossible. Maybe we can pull off another miracle yet. Especially after you deactivate your automated defense system."

Ankledge took a moment to comprehend Ellum's meaning. He glared at Pythen. "You *told* them?"

Pythen, his features drawn and sagging, opened his mouth to speak, but Ellum beat him to it. "No, we knew about the system before we landed. We know a lot of things, Warden."

Ankledge held his jaw shut to keep from gaping. "Impossible."

"Like prisoners taking control of the Hub?"

Snakes. Traitors. And in alarmingly high places. That he could have been so betrayed—he would have raged had the situation been different. But it would have to wait. He had to think fast. "The system is automatic. It can't be deactivated until the base lockdown is lifted."

"Nice try," Ellum said. "You can override it."

"No, I can't." Ankledge projected quiet confidence. He could show neither weakness nor anger now.

"Really." A faint smile played at the corners of Ellum's mouth.

"Ellum, tell your people to stand down. This isn't going to work. Surrender now, before anyone else dies."

The wild woman jabbed Ankledge in the back with her emitter. "You shut your mouth. Or *you'll* die next."

Ellum held up a hand. "Easy, easy." To the warden, he said, "So how good is that defense system?"

"It's state of the art."

"That's too bad. For you, I mean." Ellum's smile spread. "I guess we'll have to put *you* aboard that lander and launch it. Then we'll see for ourselves just how good it is."

Ankledge considered possible responses. No use pointing out that destroying the lander would do them no good; they knew as well as he did that Control had other landers. And though he had been lying about his inability to disable the orbiting missile system without lifting the lockdown, he had been telling the truth about its capabilities. It was indeed state of the art. Multiple tests using drones had confirmed its accuracy.

These prisoners knew a lot, much more than they should. When all this was over, every single person on Control, from the officers down to the kitchen staff, would be subjected to a very thorough investigation. And any who had helped these prisoners would soon learn first-hand just how hard Petra could be.

But no matter how much inside help they had, there was still plenty they couldn't know. Farside, for instance, wouldn't show on any of the surveillance monitors in the Hub. The continent had been programmatically blocked. That had been part of the arrangement. And he and Tomas Mehr were the only two on Control who knew about Farside.

Ankledge cleared his throat. "All right, then. I'll deactivate the missile system on one condition: you let me talk to my people. You've done a lot of damage out there, and I need to know how bad it is."

Ellum glanced over Ankledge's shoulder at the wild woman, then at the bushy-bearded man holding a gun on Pythen, and lastly at Pythen himself. The Jurisian shrugged. Ankledge didn't like that interaction. It didn't fit with that of a man being held hostage. And why had the prisoners allowed him to wander the halls freely?

"You can use my allcomm," Ellum said. "But if you attempt to feed them any information that might help them—how many of us there are, what kinds of weapons we have, anything—I'll cut you off."

"Fine. Give it to me." Ankledge held out a hand.

"First, you'll deactivate the missile system."

Ankledge swallowed a sharp response. He didn't like being ordered around. When he felt in control again, he said, "I'll need a workstation."

"Over here." Ellum led them to a desk on the perimeter of the Hub, outside of Chief Mehr's office.

Halleck Ellum. Ankledge had heard that name before, a long time ago. But he'd heard a lot of prisoners' names in his time here, many of them quite famous—or infamous. All the celebrity serial killers came to Petra sooner or later. They numbered in the thousands.

And that accent of his—North Mainland for certain, but underlaid with one Ankledge did not know. He was usually pretty good with accents.

Ankledge sat at the workstation. Ellum leaned close, looking over the warden's left shoulder. On his right stood the wild woman, her emitter pointed at his temple.

The monitor displayed any number of emergency messages—the armory, the landing field, the Hub, even a wind advisory for the storm. Ankledge ignored them and input his login.

The graphics disappeared, replaced by a menu of executive functions. Ellum leaned even closer, watching every keystroke. From here, Ankledge could lift the lockdown himself, but he wouldn't survive the attempt.

No matter. Let Ellum have his suspicions. Ankledge had other plans.

He accessed the satellite network and the defense system. All indicators showed that the missiles were armed and ready for launch. Ankledge input the security code from memory—a twenty-digit string of characters that only he and Mehr knew. The system accepted the code and displayed a message confirming that the escape alert had been cancelled on the warden's orders.

Ankledge backed his chair away from the workstation so that Ellum would have a better look. "Satisfied?"

Ellum stared at the display, going over it several times before straightening. "Good enough. Step away from the workstation, Warden."

Ankledge stood and complied. "I've done my part," he said. "Give me the allcomm."

Ellum handed it over. "Remember what I said."

"I will. But you remember what *I* said: this will never work, Ellum."

"We'll see about that."

Ankledge input Chief Mehr's access code. Mehr's voice came on the line: "Chief."

"Tomas, it's me."

Several seconds of silence followed. "Warden? How did you—"

"Chief, I'm being held at gunpoint here. They're allowing me to speak to you, but they're listening to every word we say. Understood?"

"Understood, sir."

"Give me a situation report."

"All our people are under shelter, waiting out the storm. Most of them are in their quarters. I had Bravo Squad quit their idiotic shelling, too. We've taken up positions at every exit from the Hub. I can't communicate with the skimmers who were caught in the air when the assault began. I assume they've gone to their designated emergency landing strips."

"What about the wounded?"

"All in the infirmary. Five aren't expected to survive."

"Son of a bitch," Ankledge said under his breath.

"We, ah, also have two of the enemy assailants there."

The rest of the prisoners visibly tensed. They crowded closer to Ankledge. Ellum said, "What's their condition?"

"Say again, Warden?" Mehr asked.

"The leader of these..." The word *vermin* rose to his lips. Ankledge thought better of it. "The leader of this uprising wants to know how they are."

"One's been shot in the leg. Shattered femur. The other took a hit in the chest. He's lost a lot of blood. The medics have stabilized him for the moment, but he'll probably die without surgery."

The bushy-bearded one mumbled something unintelligible. "Quiet, Cromberg," Ellum said.

"Warden, what's *your* condition? Are you injured?"

"No. But they're holding me and Kane Pythen hostage."

"You let those prisoners know that if anything happens to you, I can't guarantee the safety of their people in the infirmary."

Cromberg lunged. "Son of a—"

Ellum stopped him with a hand to the chest. "No. Not now."

Cromberg turned away, muttering again.

Ankledge said, "I think they understand the situation, Chief."

"What the hell do these prisoners want?"

Ankledge glanced at Ellum. The man shrugged. "Go ahead and tell them. They have to find out sooner or later."

"They want to escape. They plan to take a lander up to the Jurisian Portship in orbit."

Mehr laughed. "And how do they expect to get back to the landing field?"

"We'll discuss that later," Ellum said, his voice tight.

Ankledge said, "Chief, I need to tell you something."

"I'm listening, Warden."

"They know about the satellite system and the missile platforms. They've had me log in to the network and disarm the missiles."

The allcomm went silent for a moment. Mehr said, "I understand. What are my orders?"

He had to choose his words with care here. They were watching and listening. "No heroics, not from you or anybody else. No foolish rescue attempts. These prisoners have control of the Hub, which means they can monitor your every move in the complex. You know as well as I do that outside of Farside, they have eyes everywhere on Petra. And with the lockdown in place, no unauthorized communications can leave the island."

He paused.

"Understood, Warden."

Ankledge suppressed a smile. Tomas had always been quick.

The warden raised his voice so that everyone in the Hub could hear him. "I also expect the medics to do everything in their power to help the two prisoners who were wounded. Acknowledge, Chief."

"Acknowledged."

Ellum held out a hand. "Give it to me."

"The leader of the uprising wants to speak to you." Ankledge handed over the allcomm, pleased to note that his hands were steady as he did so.

Ellum cleared his throat. "Chief Mehr, is it? This is Halleck Ellum speaking."

Another moment of silence on the line. "Mr. Ellum, what are the chances that I can talk you into vacating the Hub?"

"We'll vacate it when we're ready, Chief. Here's what's going to happen: I need you to send a maintenance crew to Hangar…" He glanced over his shoulder at Pythen.

"Five," Pythen said, still watching the security monitors. "It's in Hangar Five."

"Hangar Five," Ellum said into the allcomm. "That's where the Jurisian lander is parked. Your crew will refuel and prep the lander for launch. The lander will be ready by the time the storm blows over. That gives you until early morning, according to the weather satellites. We can monitor the lander's status via allcomm, and we will be watching the maintenance crew from here. Any malfunction in the security cameras in the hangar will be considered an attempt at sabotage and will necessitate reprisals. *Any* malfunction, no matter how minor. Is that understood, Chief Mehr?"

The more Ellum spoke, the louder that faint bell of recognition rang. The juxtaposition of Ellum's voice and Pythen's struck a chord with Ankledge.

"I just want to be clear," Mehr said. "Are you threatening to hurt the hostages, Mr. Ellum?"

"Not necessarily. I can trigger a riot alert from here. Your crew in the hangar bay would be gassed. And there are other defense systems I can activate from the Hub, too. I trust you know that."

He knew, probably better than Ankledge did himself. Mehr had had occasion to trigger riot alerts.

"Yes, I know," the chief said. "Your demands are understood, Mr. Ellum."

"Just a minute; I'm not finished."

"Go on, Mr. Ellum."

"You're going to withdraw all your people from outside the Hub. You will also make certain there are no guards anywhere between the Hub and the landing field. In fact, I want all your guards to move to the Holding Area, where we can keep an eye on them."

Halleck Ellum. Ankledge had heard that name before. He knew it. And that accent…it was elusive and familiar at the same time. He had a hard time placing it, but the more he heard, the more certain he became that Ellum sounded a bit like…

Well, like Kane Pythen.

Had he been alone, Ankledge would have smacked himself in the forehead. Of course—Halleck Ellum was Jurisian, just like Pythen.

But Juris wasn't part of the Compact yet. And that meant—

"Ahhh," Ankledge whispered, quietly enough that no one noticed. Mehr was talking, acknowledging Ellum's orders.

It couldn't be. That had been—how long?—at least ten years ago. Maybe longer. But the evidence of Ankledge's senses couldn't be denied. It was unlikely, but not impossible. The entire situation began making more sense.

"Begin withdrawing your guards now, Chief," Ellum said. "And get that maintenance crew to the hangar."

"Mr. Ellum, that could take a while." Mehr sounded apologetic. "I'm not sure it would be safe to put a crew on a tram in this weather."

Ellum sighed. "No stalling, please, Chief. It's only a Category Two. Tell them to put on rain gear and get moving."

"I'm afraid it's not as simple as—"

"Chief, just do it. No excuses."

Mehr paused. When he spoke again, his voice was subdued. "All right."

"Good. That's all for now. We'll contact you if we need anything else. And remember—we're watching you."

"I'll remember. Mehr out."

The line went blank as the chief disconnected.

So. Halleck Ellum, the Jurisian troublemaker from the war. During the entire clandestine transaction, those anonymous suits from Juris had never mentioned the name of the prisoner they wanted extradited to Petra, and Ankledge had never asked. But he had remained well informed, even in this remote corner of Ported Space. The deduction had been easy enough to make.

Despite being held at gunpoint, he felt oddly upbeat, now that he had a better handle on events. But it only took one nervous finger on an emitter trigger to turn this into a disaster.

Ellum looked over his assembled people. "The ball's rolling now. You each know your jobs. First shift is up for the next four hours. Everyone who isn't first shift needs to get some sleep. We need fresh eyes watching these monitors at all times." He tapped Cromberg, still standing with his back to the rest of them, on a shoulder. "I want you tracking the weather. We launch as soon as the storm clears the island."

Cromberg grumbled and nodded.

"If you see anything suspicious, however insignificant, let me know immediately so we can decide on an appropriate response. No independent acts. Enough people have died. Come tomorrow, we leave this place behind forever."

Silence greeted this. Ankledge tried to get a read on the inmates' collective mood. Their hard stares bespoke grim determination.

"Not Roman and Berian," Cromberg said, his gravelly voice sounding more like a growl than human speech. Others around the room nodded.

Ellum stared him down. "No, not Roman and Berian, Cromberg. Even if we could get them out of the infirmary, you heard what Mehr said: both of them are hurt bad. We can't do anything for them."

"Right." Cromberg stormed away, headed for the Hub's meteorology center.

Ellum took a deep breath. "Anyone else have a comment?"

Some of the inmates exchanged glances; others looked away. No one spoke.

"Then let's get to work. These next few hours are critical."

Truer words were never spoken.

CHAPTER SEVEN

Someone had brought up a container of emergency provisions from storage and left it in the center of the Hub's main floor. Several food packets had already been opened; the silver wrappers lay scattered around the container. Kane was still full from dinner, but he helped himself to a bottle of water and swigged it while he watched the others go about their business.

They spoke in low voices, scanning their respective security monitors, pointing out movement they observed—guards retreating from the posts, other Petra personnel heading for the Holding Area, a maintenance crew boarding a tram headed for the landing field, all as Hal had ordered. Muted thunder provided a backbeat.

Ankledge had asked to be taken back to the dining room, but Hal had declined. "Better not to have ourselves spread out at this point," he'd said. He'd directed Miga to put the warden in the supply closet where they'd found the emergency provisions, just off the perimeter of the Hub. As a fellow hostage, at least as far as Ankledge was concerned, Kane knew he should have gone with the warden. He'd made an excuse about needing to use the washroom, even asking Hal's permission to go.

Ankledge seemed to buy the charade, at least for the moment. But Kane didn't like the way the man studied everyone with his squinty gaze, as if he were constantly weighing, judging, calculating.

A hand fell on Kane's shoulder. Startled, Kane whirled.

"Hey, relax," Hal said. "It's all coming together."

"Will you stop acting like we're best friends? Jesus!"

"Sure. Sorry." Hal stepped back a pace.

Kane glanced toward the supply closet where Ankledge was being held. The door was shut, and Miga stood watch next to it, her feet apart, emitter in both hands. No way the warden could have seen anything, but still.

Kane's gaze lingered on Miga. "You really think this will work, Hal?"

"It either works or we die. We all knew that going in."

"You say that so easily."

"You haven't lived through what we've lived through."

Kane pulled his gaze away from Miga. "How *have* you survived? How do you live in a place like this?"

Hal laughed, but his lined face remained emotionless. "That's a long story, Kane. Don't have time for it right now. But you'll hear it all once we Port away from here. Soon, *everyone* will hear it." He straightened his overcoat's tattered lapels. "We even have access to records from the Petra prisoner archives. All kinds of dirt in there, for someone who knows where and how to look. Let them try to bury the story. Just let them try."

Even here on Petra, after doing fifteen years of the hardest time imaginable, Halleck Ellum seemed to have all the answers. He had been much the same on Juris.

Kane nodded toward Miga. "What about her? What's her story? A political prisoner, like you?"

"No one knows. She doesn't remember."

"Doesn't—beg pardon?"

"Trauma. Miga has more scars than on her face. She escaped from the Bone Tribes." At Kane's quizzical look, Hal said, "That's just what they're called. They've overrun the southern half of Mainland. Psychopaths. They don't know how to farm. They're not even very skilled hunters. So they go after the easiest prey on Petra—new inmates."

"God."

Hal nodded. "Do you know what the guards around here call a prisoner drop in southern Mainland? Feeding time."

"So how did she survive?"

"The Bone Tribes have been known to keep…harems, I guess you'd call them, although maybe *pens* would be a better word. The conditions aren't as glamorous as they sound."

Kane closed his eyes. He felt sick.

Hal said, "She has no memory of anything prior to her escape. She doesn't know where she's from, how she got to Petra, or why."

"And you trust her with a weapon?"

"She's saved my life three times. I think she's more than earned the right to a little flaky behavior." Hal leaned against a console and studied Kane's face. "You look exhausted. Why don't you get some sleep? It's going to be pretty quiet here for the next few hours."

Kane had to admit it sounded good. With every passing moment, his limbs felt heavier. If he didn't sleep soon, he would simply drop where he stood. But… "One more thing first," he said. "Let me talk to my Portship. They need to know what's going on."

Hal handed over his allcomm.

Kane took a few moments to pull the correct code from the recesses of his weary brain. He input it and waited for the connection, wondering what he was going to say.

The Portship had a crew of six, all of whom had opted to stay aboard rather than join Kane on Petra. Lucky for them. The captain was a woman named Sason Hemly, a career pilot with grizzled features and a voice almost as gruff as Cromberg's. "Kane? Is that you?"

"Yes, it's me."

"What the hell's going on down there? We've been trying to reach you for *hours*. We received a strange message from the base about an emergency lockdown. Since then, nothing."

Kane rubbed his forehead. "There have been some…developments down here."

"Because of the storm? Are you hurt?"

"Listen very carefully, Sason. Do exactly as I tell you, and everything should be fine."

"All right. Go ahead."

"You'll, ah, need to prepare the ship for some visitors."

She took the news as well as could be expected. Kane balked at telling her the truth; he hated lying to her, but she would never let the lander back aboard otherwise. So instead, he used the excuse she had unwittingly provided for him, that the storm had caused some damage at the base, necessitating the lockdown. He also explained that he would be bringing some "Petran emissaries" with him. Yes, he knew that hadn't been planned; he and the warden had discussed it over dinner. He told her to expect the lander to launch from Petra after the storm cleared out. Yes, he realized that was well ahead of schedule, but the itinerary had changed. He would explain it all when he got back aboard.

She was less than pleased, but at least she didn't seem suspicious. Kane finished the call and dragged himself to the supply closet.

Miga stood aside just enough to let him enter. Kane eyed her hold on the emitter, expecting her to point it at him at the slightest provocation. She gave no sign that she noticed, staring straight ahead.

By normal standards, the closet was a large space, a box three meters square. Shelves lined the walls, full of storage cells, backup batteries, and more boxes of provisions. Ankledge sat in a corner, on a cushion upholstered in the same material that covered the furniture in the offices. A matching cushion lay at Kane's feet.

"Provided by our friends," Ankledge said, indicating the cushions.

Exhausted, Kane wasted no time lying down. The pad—from a couch, he guessed—was just large enough to fit his curled body.

"Here," Ankledge said. A moment later, a folded blanket landed on Kane.

He sat up and unfolded it—thin and black, with the Petran insignia sewn in one corner. Ankledge pulled a twin from an open box on the bottom shelf nearest him.

"Thanks," Kane said.

"What's your game, Pythen?"

Kane closed his eyes. "I don't have a game. I just want to get back to Juris alive."

"What did you mean back in the dining room? What *legitimate grievances*"—he sneered as he said it—"were you talking about? Were you trying to make some kind of political statement?"

"You sound like you're worried about something, Warden."

"I might be worried about disinformation being fed to you by this Halleck Ellum. I might be concerned you would try to circulate it. That you might be sympathetic to him."

Kane opened his eyes and faced the warden. "Got some secrets that need protecting, do you?"

Ankledge fixed his squinty gaze on Kane. "None at all."

Kane thought he preferred seeing the man seething with rage. The scandal that Hal Ellum threatened to break—if indeed as far-reaching as he claimed—might well shatter the Petra Compact. Rolf

Ankledge would be finished. Ported Space would call for his head. He should be scared, if nothing else. Kane found his demeanor unnerving.

"In that case," he said, "you have nothing to worry about. Now if you don't mind, I need to sleep." He lay back down and closed his eyes again.

"Jurisians," Ankledge said under his breath, and then was silent. Kane gave thanks for it.

Through the closet door, Miga heard the men talking, but could not make out the words. She wasn't sure if she should care. She hadn't been as impressed with Kane Pythen as Hal seemed to be. The man seemed far too rich, too pampered, to care about Petra.

Eventually, they quieted. Probably asleep. Good. She passed the time scanning the Hub from one end to the next and back again, repeating the drill methodically. It kept her thoughts from drifting.

In particular, watching Hal amused her. He flitted from one part of the Hub to another, never staying in one place very long, chatting with the others, giving them reassuring pats on the back. Rallying the troops, as he always did. It worked well when hiding in caves or shelters from raiding parties and Warden Ankledge's bombers. For some reason, the routine didn't play in the Hub. He looked and sounded as genuine as ever, but the words and gestures felt artificial to her, and she wondered why that should be.

It might be her, she realized. She hadn't been herself since all this had begun. Those blind spots in her memory, the places she thought of as dead in her, seemed to press and clamor for attention. Dark things stirred there.

She found herself longing to be outside, away from these walls of steel and concrete. The raging storm concerned her not at all. It was just rain and wind. She'd survived years on Mainland at the mercy of the weather—subfreezing blizzards, biting dust storms, sweltering summers, sometimes with only a hastily built shelter for protection. She hadn't experienced such climate-controlled comfort since…

Since…

Since before.

Random images and sensations flashed through her mind: huddling dry and warm under covers while rain beat on the roof, the smell of simmering soup, drunken laughter among friends and family. Then they were gone, leaving a residue of regret.

She would much rather have been caught outside in the storm.

Hal retired to the office he'd commandeered, no doubt to catch some sleep himself.

Cromberg approached her from the meteorology center. He walked slowly, stiffly.

She favored him with a small smile. "Your back bothering you?"

He grumbled. "Always."

"How's the storm?"

"Spinning in place. But all the forecasting models say it will clear out by dawn. Damned bunch of computerized horseshit, if you ask me." He stretched and yawned. "My shift's over. I'm going to find some floor. You should, too. Where's your relief?"

"In the infirmary. Roman was my backup."

"Miga, you need to stand down for a few hours." He cocked a thumb at the closet behind her. "You're not going to have any trouble from those two."

"I'm fine."

He peered at her. His dark eyes were piercing. "You sure about that?"

"You heard Hal. In a matter of hours, we'll be gone. I can hold on for a few more hours. You and I have both made it through worse."

Cromberg gave a short hiss. "Hal talks a lot. Too much, sometimes, I think. This guy Pythen isn't everything Hal said he was."

"No."

Faraway thunder rumbled.

"Listen to that," Cromberg said. "Almost makes me wish I was out there instead of in here."

Miga smiled. "Get some sleep."

"You sure you're OK? I can—"

Something outside exploded. The blast was unmistakable, and somewhere *close*. The force of it shook the Hub. Monitors in every section flashed red emergency messages.

Cromberg turned to Miga, eyes wide.

"Miga!" Fallon, the Petran-born blond boy, the one who had knifed the Petran skimmer crewman back on Mainland to get this ball rolling, stood at a security station, urgently motioning to her and

Cromberg. The two of them ran to him, the other prisoners on their heels.

"What happened?" Miga said.

Flustered, Fallon fumbled gestured at the console. "I-I don't know. The board just went red."

She slung her emitter to her shoulder and shoved Fallon aside. "Let me see." Miga bent over the console, scanning the monitors. She spotted the problem. "One of the comm towers is out. Tower 10."

Cromberg leaned in next to her. "How? Lightning strike?"

Miga tapped some keys, looking for more information. The readouts were too vague. "I don't know. Maybe." She sat at the station and attempted to run a diagnostic check, guessing what she could of the system's operation from the onscreen prompts. It was difficult. She hadn't done any computer work since…

Since…

She shook free of those thoughts and managed to bring up an overview of the comm system. The towers and dishes that kept Control in contact with itself and the satellite system clustered atop the mountainous spine of the island. The overview told her what she already knew: Tower 10 was out and needed immediate repair.

She was about to give up on gleaning any more information when another message caught her eye:

ATTENTION: Jamming system failure. Security lockdown is compromised. Acknowledge?

"Jamming system," she said in a murmur.

"What was that?" Cromberg said.

Miga backed the chair away from the station, thinking. Suspicions stirred. She whirled in the chair. "Which of you has been on the surveillance monitors?"

Two men near the back of the assembled crowd raised their hands. She recognized Orem, with his spiky white hair, but couldn't remember the other one's name. Not that it mattered. "Where are they now? Are they in the Holding Area like they're supposed to be?"

The two men exchanged glances. Orem said, "A lot of them are already there. Some are still heading that way."

"Does that account for all of them? Even the security forces?"

"How should we know? It's not like we took roll. They all wear black uniforms, anyway. I couldn't tell security forces from secretaries."

Miga was on her feet in a flash. She elbowed her way through the others until she stood face-to-face with Orem. "Security forces are the ones carrying the weapons, dummy. Where are they?"

Though he towered over her, he backed away. "I-I saw a lot of guns in there. But we didn't take roll, or anything. How…" Orem looked around in vain for support. His cohort turned away, mumbling.

"Worthless piece of shit." Miga brought her emitter around to the ready position and headed toward the supply closet.

The others trailed her. Cromberg kept pace. "Miga, what the hell's going on?"

"Fucking bastards." Her rage boiled. Orem had a point, of course, but she was past caring. Ah, but she had to keep control, not do anything rash. The anger threatened to blot out conscious thought. It had happened before; she knew the warning signs very well.

She reached the closet, tore open the door, and slammed the light panel. The overheads flickered to life. Ankledge, lying near the rear, came awake instantly. Pythen stirred and held up a hand against the light.

The others hung back at the door. Miga stepped over Kane, leaned in, and jammed the emitter barrel under the warden's chin. Her face was bare inches from his. "What are they up to?"

Ankledge's eyes widened slightly. "All right, just calm down. No need for—"

"*Goddamn it, what are they up to*?" Her finger rested on the discharge. Just a little more pressure would cook the warden alive. She even knew how it would smell.

"I don't know what you're talking—"

"Tower 10 just blew up, you son of a bitch. That's the one that jams all the unauthorized allcomm signals. We can't monitor the outside communication now. Why did they do it?"

Ankledge kept very still as he spoke, very calm. "How could I know anything about that? I'm in here with you."

"You know those people. What are they planning? Tell me, or I swear to God I'll kill you here and now." Her rage had reached critical mass. The rest of the room was fading, as were Cromberg and the others. In their place, gibbering, half-seen faces danced.

Distant screams echoed out of the dark places inside her. Hal, the plan to escape, the dreams of exposing Petra—all dissipated like smoke.

Someone barreled into her from behind, knocking her off her feet. The emitter discharged with an electric *crack*; the burnt smell of ozone filled the room. Miga crashed into wall shelving; equipment fell to the floor.

She thrashed and spun. Kane Pythen grabbed her in a bear hug, pinning the emitter between them. He yelled in her face; the words were only noise to her.

A hulking shape loomed behind Pythen, seized him by the shoulders, and pulled him off her, throwing him back. She lunged, ready to tear the man's throat out if she had to.

The hulking shape resolved itself into Cromberg. He stopped her with a hand to the chest. She lunged again, and he grabbed her by the arms.

The closet was in an uproar. Everyone was yelling. Fallon and some of the others had Pythen against the shelves on the opposite wall. He struggled in vain to free himself. Cromberg screamed Miga's name over and over as he held her back. She was tiring. The red fog of rage that had clouded her vision began to break up; memories of gibbering faces and screams receded.

"Miga," Cromberg said, calmer now. "Stop. Just stop."

Pythen was still bellowing. "Idiots! If she kills him, the rest of us are dead!"

Someone else—it may have been Orem—said, "Fuck it, we're all dead, anyway. You heard what she said. They're coming for us. Cook them both!"

Some of the others yelled their assent.

"No." The single syllable, spoken with firm command, silenced everyone.

The crowd just outside the closet parted. Hal stood there, hands on hips. "What the hell is going on here?"

Ankledge spoke from his place on the floor. "You'd better keep these animals on leashes, Ellum."

Cromberg released Miga and clouted Ankledge, knocking him backward. "Watch your fuckin' mouth, there, Warden."

"Enough!" Hal elbowed people aside and stepped into the closet. "Goddamn it, we have *four hours* left until dawn. Four hours until we can escape. And you want to blow it now? Did I just hear someone say *cook them both*? What in the *hell* are you thinking?"

Miga, still breathing hard, recovered enough of her faculties to speak. "They've taken out the tower that jams the allcomm signals. They're getting ready to move against us."

"We don't know that." Hal rubbed at his eyes. "Miga, we're in the middle of a goddamned tropical storm. That tower could have been downed by lightning, or even wind."

"Just that tower? That one, and no others?"

"That *is* awfully convenient," Cromberg said.

Hal pressed his lips together, forming a thin line. "Fine. And suppose you're right? Suppose they are planning something? They still can't get to us in here."

"We have to go out sooner or later," Miga said.

"And we'll do it just like we planned. The way will be clear from here to the landing field. All of the security people will be on the other side of the base, too far away to take any action. We've been over this a thousand times, Miga." Hal extended a hand. "Let me have the emitter for a while."

Miga cradled it against herself. "You don't trust me anymore, is that it?"

Hal sniffed the air. "Smells like someone fired a weapon. Who was that? Was it you, Miga?"

"It was an accident."

"Doesn't look that way to me." Hal looked toward Fallon and the others holding Pythen. "You. Let him go. Now."

They complied, looking sullen. Pythen stepped away from them, his lip curled—whether with disgust or anger, Miga couldn't say.

Hal took another step toward Miga. "Let me have the weapon. Just for a while. Until you calm down."

"You're going to throw me out, aren't you?" Her voice cracked as she said it. "Throw me to *them*. Abandon me here."

"You know me better than that, Miga." He extended a hand to her again. "Hand it over, please."

She looked around the room for support. Cromberg stood nearest to her. His gaze wavered, alternating between her and Hal. Fallon and the others who had seized Pythen stood with eyes downcast. Her cheeks burned. Her anger had vanished, leaving her exhausted and uncertain.

Maybe Hal was right.

With shaking hands, she thumbed the safety and gave the emitter to Hal. She wanted to collapse, right then and there, but she would not allow herself. Instead, she raised her chin and faced Hal. "You can't just throw me away. Not after everything I've done for you."

"No one's throwing anyone away. I want you to get some rest. That's an order. Cromberg, you stand watch over these two." Hal indicated Pythen and Ankledge. "And confiscate their allcomms."

Cromberg nodded.

"Everybody clear out of this room. From now on, no one goes in or out of here without my permission. Understood?"

The others mumbled acknowledgment.

Hal raised his voice: "Understood?"

"Understood," they said in unison.

"Good." He turned and exited the closet.

The others followed suit, emerging single file. No one spoke. Miga left last, casting a glance over her shoulder as she did so. Pythen remained on his feet, shaking his head. Ankledge, still seated on the floor, met her gaze. One cheek was red and swollen from Cromberg's blow. Even so, she could swear she detected the faintest trace of a smirk playing at the corners of his mouth. Or she might have been imagining it.

CHAPTER EIGHT

When he was certain that Miga had gone to get some sleep as he'd ordered, Hal turned his attention to the security system. He went to the station Miga had been working at and pored over the data. Fallon stood behind him.

There was no way to tell what had damaged the tower. Surveillance video playback would be useless, given the storm and the lateness of the hour. The thought of Chief Mehr and his security forces being able to talk over channels Hal could not monitor made him extremely uncomfortable. He had no idea how Mehr could hurt them while they were holed up in the Hub and he and his men were stuck outside, and therein lay the problem. There was too much he didn't know. At least he'd had the sense to confiscate Ankledge's allcomm.

He was so very tired. He had managed to cop maybe an hour of sleep before this latest fiasco. It became clear that he would have to remain awake and alert the rest of the night. If he could just hold this together for the next four hours or so...but then, planning the breakout of the millennium had no easy parts, nothing that could be taken for granted.

He got out his allcomm and retrieved Chief Mehr's access code from its memory. Mehr answered within moments: "Chief."

"This is Halleck Ellum."

"We've pulled all our people from around the Hub, Mr. Ellum. You should be able to see that from where you are. The maintenance crew tells me they should have the lander refueled and prepped for launch in another hour."

Hal worked to keep his voice calm, even. "Are all your people in the Holding Area like I ordered, Chief?"

"Most of them. We have about thirty in some bunkers near the armory, pinned down by the storm. And there are a number of off-duty personnel who never made it out of their quarters when the alarms first went off. I don't know how many."

No, of course not. Hal had expected that. Control's noncom housing was too far away to be a factor. "And that's all of them? You're sure?"

"I'm sure."

"None of them are skulking around outside?"

"In this weather?"

"Good. Then you won't mind if I do a thermal scan of the area."

"Be my guest." Mehr may have paused before responding. Maybe.

It would probably do very little good. The storm would play hell with heat signatures, and Mehr would know that. Hal would run the scan anyway. The monitor prompts would guide him through it.

"Is there anything else?" Mehr said.

"No. That's it for now."

"How is the warden? May I speak with him?"

Hal glanced toward the closet. "He's asleep. So's Kane Pythen."

"I see."

"I'm running that scan now, Chief. If any of your people aren't where they're supposed to be, we're going to have a problem."

"I understand."

"Good. Out." Hal snapped off the allcomm.

Navigating the menus to initiate the thermal scan took longer than he would have liked. He had been fed some information on the Hub's systems prior to their departure from Mainland; they had all pored over it. But Mainland was now two thousand kilometers distant, and a lot had happened since then, and he was running on perhaps three hours of sleep out of the last thirty. Fallon, who had spent his entire young life on Petra and knew next to nothing about computer systems, became bored and wandered away. If Mehr did have people in the jungle or up in the hills, he would have plenty of time to get them back, and Hal would be none the wiser.

Thirty minutes later, he found the controls to activate the scan. All the security monitors showing the exterior of the Control complex switched to thermal displays. The view was worse than infrared—all dark grays and blacks, no definition, no movement.

Standing at the meteorology station, Fallon looked over at him. Hal pointed to the monitors. "Don't watch me. Watch *them*. Yell if you see anything larger than a treerat."

Fallon turned his attention back to the screens.

Hal stretched and rubbed the back of his neck. That damned tower. It could have been lightning. Probably it *had* been lightning. That only made sense. But he couldn't put Miga's suspicions out of his mind. The people who had put him on Petra—him and God only knew how many others—Hal would put nothing past them.

He peered at the dark screens before him, alert for any hint, any sign of untoward activity. The shadows seemed to dance, mocking him.

"Damn them all," he whispered. They were in the Holding Area—most of them, anyway. It would be a simple matter to initiate an alert and release riot gas in there. He could even control the concentration from here. A low dose would knock them all unconscious in under a minute. Higher doses…

Oh, it was tempting. But the word would get out sooner or later. And if it did, no one in Ported Space would listen to him. They would dismiss him out of hand. The deaths of a few hundred prison guards and personnel was paltry repayment for the millions that had died here on Petra, but no one Out There would give a damn.

The allcomm chirped. Mehr, he assumed.

But it wasn't. The display showed a different access code, one he recognized. He connected.

"Are you sure it's safe?" he said.

Emma Goring spoke in a low voice, rushing her words: "For the moment. I'm in a bathroom, alone. If anyone comes in, I'm disconnecting."

She wouldn't be calling unless it was important. Hal got up and headed for the office he'd been using. Best for the two of them to talk in private; he didn't want the others crowding him. "All right. Go ahead."

"Have you been communicating with Chief Mehr?"

"Yes. You knew that. We had to make our demands to *someone*." He reached the office and closed the door behind him. "The missile platforms are disarmed. I watched Ankledge do it. Now we just—"

"Hal, you have to launch as soon as you can."

"That's the plan. If it weren't for the goddamned storm, we could launch within the hour."

"Jesus."

Hal frowned at the allcomm. "Emma, what's going on?"

"I don't know. Something. After you spoke with Mehr, there was a great deal of activity down here. The chief spoke to several security details. Sent them on errands."

Hal went cold. "What kind of errands?"

"He's not telling me anything, and I can't ask without him getting suspicious."

Hal hesitated to ask, then pushed ahead with it: "Could they have destroyed one of the communication towers? One of them is down."

"Which one?"

"Tower 10. The one that blocks unauthorized transmissions."

Silence on the line. Hal checked the display to make sure he hadn't lost her. According to the allcomm, the connection was still open.

"Hal, get your people out of there."

"What are they doing, Emma?"

"Communicating without your knowledge. Making plans. Taking up sniper positions, maybe. I don't know. But that was no accident. We've had worse storms than this hit the island. You have to get out of the Hub."

"And go *where*? Right now, we're in the safest place on Petra. Safer than you, even."

"Hal, you're in danger."

"We've been in danger ever since we forced down that skimmer. Damn it, Emma, you have to give me something concrete here."

"I don't *know*. But you have to do something."

"We're watching them. That's about all we can do."

"You're blind in the storm."

"Not as blind as that. Emma, you—"

"I hear someone coming. I have to go."

"Get me something concrete. Find out what they're—"

The line went dead.

Hal stared at the allcomm, heart racing. Thank God he'd had the sense to take the call in private. If the others had heard it, he'd have a full-scale revolt on his hands.

He looked out the glass front to the main floor beyond. All his people remained focused on their tasks. No one seemed to be watching. Exuding as much outward calm as possible, he put the allcomm back in his overcoat pocket.

What he owed Emma, he could never repay. Though not the only friendly on Control, she was far and away the most important. Without her feeding them information and supplies, none of this would have been possible. And she had done it all at great personal risk, solely because she believed in it. She had refused his offer to take her off Petra in the escape. "My term is up in six months," she had told him. "After that, I go home. I can hold out that long."

If she said trouble was coming—

But he could not command the weather. And she had no idea what Mehr was planning, if anything.

Communicating without your knowledge…taking up sniper positions, maybe…

Snipers made no sense. The tram would take them into the hangar. They would be shielded the entire way. And the destruction of the armory limited Mehr's firepower. What's more, the chief wouldn't want to chance killing Ankledge. It had to be something else.

With the allcomm signals unblocked, could Mehr have reactivated the missile platforms? Hal tensed at the thought. But no, if that had happened, it would have shown up on the Hub's security status screens.

It was maddening. Emma and Miga had him jumping at shadows.

He couldn't tell the others. The fracas in the supply closet made that much very clear. He would lose what little control he had over the situation. No choice, then, but to wait out the storm, maintain a sharp lookout, and hope that Emma could find out Mehr's plans before he put them into action.

Hal sagged against the glass door and let out a shaky breath, wondering if dawn would ever come.

CHAPTER NINE

Kane slept unevenly the rest of the night. His exhaustion warred with the disturbing memory of the madness he's seen in Miga's eyes when he'd tackled her. He shifted positions on the floor, unable to get comfortable, certain he would never get to sleep…only to awaken with a start an unknown time later, staring into the darkness of the supply closet, realizing he'd been dreaming of Tayla and Shamlyn—and the cycle would start again.

Ankledge snored through the night.

On the umpteenth iteration, Kane snapped awake to find the overhead lights were back on. The warden stood near the door, stretching.

Ankledge noticed him and paused in mid-stretch. "If my internal clock's still accurate, it's nearly dawn."

Eyes scratchy and muscles aching, Kane roused himself.

Ankledge said, "They'll be coming for us soon, I imagine."

Kane shrugged. "You know as much as I do."

"Before that happens, I need to say something to you."

Kane got to his feet, waiting.

Ankledge took a deep breath, raising his chin. He bore a black eye from Cromberg's blow. "You might have saved my life last night."

"I overreacted. She probably wouldn't have done it."

Ankledge crossed his arms. "She had every intention of doing it. That woman is coming apart. It's only a matter of time before she kills someone."

Kane couldn't deny it.

"I don't know what to make of you, Pythen. I'm not sure where your loyalties lie."

That makes two of us, Kane thought.

"Even so," Ankledge said, "I suppose I owe you something. You saved my life; maybe I can save yours."

"What are you talking about?"

Ankledge cocked a thumb over his shoulder, indicating the door. "Are you going with them to your Portship?"

"I have to. They want me to pilot the lander."

"The launch can be automated, can't it?"

"It would have to be programmed."

"You could do that with an allcomm, couldn't you? The signals are no longer jammed."

"What are you getting at, Warden?"

"Don't get on that lander."

"I don't—I thought the missile platforms had been deactivated."

"They have been."

Kane stared into the warden's narrow eyes. "What have you done?"

"Don't get on the lander. That's all I'm telling you. If you do, I'm not responsible for what happens." He uncrossed his arms. "It's best if you don't know any more than that. Then they can't force it out of you." His mouth twisted in a grotesque imitation of a smile. "That's all. The debt's paid now. The rest is up to you."

Disinformation, Ankledge had said. It sounded plausible on the surface...but Hal Ellum's very presence here was proof to the contrary.

"You know, if there's something you'd like to talk about, it's not too late for you to come clean, Warden."

Ankledge shook his head. "Pythen, you're way out of your depth. This isn't some damned game. There's much more at stake than you realize."

"Enlighten me, then."

Before Ankledge could reply, the door opened. Cromberg leaned in, looking at Kane. "You. Out here." To Ankledge, he said, "You stay put."

Kane kept his gaze locked on the warden. He studied the man's face, looking for any sign of—what? Guilt? Remorse? Fear? But Rolf Ankledge was a study in authority and confidence. One could not tell by looking at him that he was being held hostage. His upright bearing and unflinching gaze lent an air of strange dignity to his black eye. Everything about him bespoke total control.

Kane broke the stare and went with Cromberg.

They weren't going anywhere.

Hal stood at the meterology center, staring at the radar image, silently cursing what he saw. A mass of green, blue, and red still covered the island. It seemed not to have budged in the night. Hal touched a control that ran a loop of the last several hours, if only to get some reassurance that the storm was indeed moving. The night that he had at one point considered eternal had ended too soon.

And Emma hadn't called back. He didn't dare call her.

"I thought it was supposed to be out of here by dawn," Kane said.

Hal had been too wrapped up in the weather and his own thoughts to hear Kane approach. He turned away from the screen and rubbed tired eyes. "It's a slow moving son of a bitch. Another hour, maybe."

"Cromberg said you wanted to see me."

"Yeah. Is there any way you can launch in this?"

"*This?*" Kane started to laugh, but stopped when he caught the look on Hal's face. "Is it still a Category Two?"

"Yes."

"No way."

"Are you sure?"

"I'm sure there's no way *I'm* going to attempt to launch in these conditions. You're welcome to give it a try on your own if you like."

Hal slumped into a nearby chair. "I figured. I had to ask." He lowered his voice. "You're the only one I can say this to, Kane: Miga was right. Mehr and his men are planning something."

"I know."

All tiredness fell from Hal. "How do you know that?"

Kane leaned in closer. "Ankledge was just telling me not to get on the lander."

"Did he say why?"

"No. Let me have my allcomm."

Hal had it—and the warden's—clipped to his belt. He was garnering quite a collection of them. He handed Kane's to him.

Kane switched it on, tapping keys. "I'm going to initiate a scan of the lander. If they've planted a bomb or messed with any of the onboard systems, I should be able to pick it up."

Hal thought Mehr would have known better than to try something so obvious. But it couldn't hurt to check. "Kane, how would Ankledge know what Mehr is doing?"

Kane shook his head, intent on his allcomm display. "Some sort of contingency plan they had worked out in advance?"

Hal's weary mind worked slowly. "No, the missile platforms were the contingency plan. That was their last resort. Unless...Ankledge has been communicating with Mehr."

"Impossible," Kane said. "We were locked in that closet all night. Trust me, he slept through. The only time he talked with Mehr was out here."

"And we were right there with him the whole time. We heard everything they said."

Kane looked up from his display. "A coded message, maybe?"

"Could he have sent a text message while he was talking? Without us noticing?" Hal unclipped the allcomm he had appropriated and brought up its log. He scrolled through the latest entries. The conversation with Emma was the most recent. Prior to that was the talk with Mehr. Before that was Kane's transmission to his Portship, preceded by the first call to Mehr, the one Ankledge had placed. Nothing in the log that shouldn't have been there.

Hal closed his eyes for a moment, remembering. "What did he say to Mehr?"

Kane paused before replying. "He told Mehr about the defense system being disarmed. And Mehr asked what his orders were."

Hal had listened closely at that point, intent on ensuring that the warden wouldn't try to feed Mehr any helpful information. "Yeah. He told the chief not to try any rescue attempts. He even mentioned that communications were cut off."

"A hint to destroy the jamming tower?"

"Maybe. But why? Who would he..." Something shadowy and elusive stirred in Hal's thoughts. "Hang on. There was another thing he said. Something about how we could watch them everywhere, except..."

It came to him. Hal opened his eyes.

Kane finished the sentence for him: "Farside."

No surveillance flights ran there. And there was no satellite coverage, either. It didn't show up on any of the monitors in the Hub—the Petran equivalent of the Lost Continent.

"Motherfucker," Hal said.

"But that doesn't make any sense. There's nothing on Farside. It's empty. Never settled."

"You sure about that? Willing to bet your life on it?" He slammed a hand on the console beside him. "Mother*fucker*!" He jumped up and ran for the security station. Kane followed.

Fallon saw them coming and stepped aside.

Every available monitor was giving him video, infrared, and thermal scan data. Hal pounded at the keys.

Miga spoke from behind him: "What are you looking for?"

Hal whirled. She had emerged from wherever she'd been sleeping. She regarded him with bleary eyes, outwardly calm, evincing none of the rage she'd shown earlier. Nonetheless, in his peripheral vision, Hal caught sight of Kane retreating a few steps.

Miga ignored Kane. "Well?"

Hal took a breath to settle himself. If Miga could be calm, so could he. "I need the long-range tracking satellites. And hurry."

She elbowed past him and leaned over the workstation. Deftly, she wound through the menus. "Tracking satellites won't give you weather data."

"I know."

She reached the satellite control screen and stopped. "Got a particular region you're interested in?"

Hal and Kane spoke in unison: "Farside."

She looked from one to the other.

The rest of them gathered around the workstation, except for Cromberg, still guarding the warden. Uncomfortable warmth suffused Hal. "Something in the vicinity of Farside, anyway."

He expected Miga to question him, but she only bent back to the console. She had been the best of them at picking up the technical information Emma had smuggled out. She remained stoic as she tapped the keys.

The security monitors changed, displaying the tracking data—high-level satellite views of Petra, upon which were superimposed graphics showing any air traffic. With all skimmer surveillance grounded, the monitors should have shown nothing but the outlines of Mainland, Southland, and the ocean between them.

One of the monitors, showing an equatorial ocean view, picked up a set of unidentified blips.

Solid lines indicated the blips' track so far. The lines ran off the map to the west, in the direction of Farside. Dashed lines showed the projected flight plan—straight toward Control.

Miga said, "What the fuck is this?"

Hal bit his lip. "Reinforcements, apparently."

"From where? *Farside*? You mean to tell me that Ankledge has a base there?"

"That's what it looks like."

Moans and cries of dismay went up from the rest of them. "Quiet!" Hal said. "Focus, all of you. Miga, give me an ETA."

He watched her for signs of another outburst. Her hands seemed steady as she worked, in control.

At her bidding, the monitors shifted views again, this time zooming in on the errant blips. Text and numerical data scrolled alongside them.

"They're supersonic," Miga said. "About two thousand kilometers west-southwest of here. At their current speed, they should arrive"—she looked from the monitors to Hal—"in about an hour."

"Jesus Christ," someone behind Hal said.

The storm. The goddamned storm was going to get all of them killed. "Any idea what kind of craft they are?"

Miga shook her head. "No transponder data. We can't identify them."

Kane, still gazing at the graphic, moved up to stand beside Hal, Miga's presence notwithstanding. "They're military."

"How do you know?"

"Anything in that much of a hurry to get here is armed, I assure you. No point in calling in a fleet of freighters."

"Calling in?" Miga raised her eyebrows and looked to Hal. "Mehr called them, didn't he? That's why he took out the tower."

"Yes." Hal said it evenly. "You were right. It wasn't an accident."

"Fuck that."

Cromberg's voice took Hal by surprise. Cromberg had stepped away from his post for a better look at the monitors; he stood behind the rest of them, on the walkway around the perimeter of the Hub. His brow had formed a solid ridge over his eyes. "Fuck who was right or wrong," he said. "What are you gonna do about that?" He pointed to the blips.

They all looked to Hal. The mantle of leadership fell on him, its weight familiar. It was hardly the first time that lives depended on him. But it felt different. To be so damned *close*—

Hal turned to Kane. "How was the scan?"

Kane's gaze shifted from Hal to Miga to Cromberg to the tracking data. In the few minutes since Miga had put up the graphic, the blips had already edged closer to Control.

Kane glanced at the allcomm in his hand and sighed. "It looks clean. But Hal, we might not even be able to get off the ground."

"If you're right about those ships, we either launch now or not at all. They'll turn the landing field to slag. We're not gonna be stopped after coming this far. We'll never get this opportunity again. Program the lander from here, if nothing else. You don't even have to fly it."

"The computer won't let you lift off in these conditions. You'll need someone at the controls." Kane passed a hand over his face, his expression pained. "The storm's definitely moving out?"

Hal nodded. "In about an hour."

"And how long will it take for us to get from here to the hangar? Fifteen, twenty minutes?"

Hal thought about it. There were still some last-minute steps to be taken. "Yeah. Something like that."

Kane drew in a shaky breath. "It's got to weaken sometime." He rolled his eyes. "All right. Let's go."

Hal clapped him on the shoulder. "Knew I could count on you."

"I thought we were in a hurry."

"Right." Hal raised his voice. "We're launching. You all know the drill from here on out. Cromberg, bring the warden here."

They moved.

CHAPTER TEN

The wild man with the heelocat pelt and the raspy voice, the one who had clocked him twice, ordered Ankledge out of the supply closet, keeping the emitter trained on him. The warden's jaw still ached, and his bruised eye had swollen. The wild man—Cromberg was his name, if Ankledge's memory served—still needed to answer for those injuries. That time was coming soon, very soon.

And they all knew it. Ankledge spotted the tracking data on the monitors as soon as he stepped out of the closet. He suppressed a smile at the sight of those unidentified blips closing in on Control. If they'd figured it out, his life might very well be forfeit. But there were still angles to be played.

At least the air out here was a little less stale than in the closet—although of course the omnipresent stink of the inmates still permeated the Hub. Not that Ankledge smelled much better at this point, he was sure. He needed to piss, too.

Halleck Ellum stood in the center of an eddy of activity, as his lackeys hustled to finish packing. He was speaking loudly into his allcomm: "...time to argue with you, Mehr. Everyone into the cells. Now." He snapped off the unit before Mehr could reply.

He caught sight of Ankledge and motioned him over. "Morning, Warden. You've been a clever boy, haven't you?"

"Don't know what you're talking about."

Ellum cocked a thumb at the monitors. "I don't suppose you'd care to tell us who your friends from Farside are, would you?"

Ankledge was conscious of Cromberg's emitter pointed at his back. He could be blasted with it any minute. "No, I don't. But I'll make you a deal. I'll call them off if you surrender."

Ellum gave a tight-lipped smile. "I'll make you a counterproposal. Call them off, or I'll kill you where you stand."

Ankledge chose not to reply. He'd said everything that needed saying. If Ellum decided to do it, so let it be. He would not bargain with this man.

Ellum stepped closer to Ankledge and lowered his voice: "Don't think I wouldn't do it, Warden. I have no further use for you. I'd be doing all of Ported Space a favor."

"Then do it."

The two studied each other. The silence lengthened.

Ellum's gaze drifted toward Kane Pythen, who observed the exchange from the security station. Ellum stepped back. "You know, I think you might actually prefer it. Then you could be a martyr. But I'd rather you stay alive to face what's coming to you. Goodbye, Warden. The next time you see me, it will be in front of a multi-world tribunal, along with all the signatories to the Petra Compact. You're finished."

Ankledge would have laughed if it weren't for Cromberg. This Jurisian was as self-righteous as Pythen. "You expect to be welcomed as a hero when you get back to Ported Space? Some kind of great liberator? You're kidding yourself. They'll see you as the most dangerous terrorist humanity has ever known."

"Perhaps. And they'll see you as history's worst mass murderer. Maybe they'll execute us together." Ellum looked past Ankledge's shoulder. "I've heard enough. Cromberg, if you please."

Something slammed into Ankledge from behind. He had just enough time to identify it as a pulse from the emitter before he tumbled into unconsciousness.

They rode the tram in silence.

The sky had grayed with the dawn. Wind and rain lashed the tramcar. Tropical trees bobbed and swayed. Branches littered the track ahead, but the tram handled them without difficulty. The incessant thunder had died down, at least.

Kane observed their progress from a window seat, next to the young inmate, Fallon. The rest either sat or stood, holding handrails placed throughout the cabin. All eyes were on the weather. But Kane's thoughts were on those last moments in the Hub.

He had been shocked when Cromberg had shot the warden, but Hal had assured him it was just enough of a jolt to render the man unconscious.

Kane had knelt at the warden's crumpled figure, felt at his neck for a pulse. The electric smell the discharge hung in the air. The pulse was there, weak but steady. He had stood and said, "Fine. Do we go now?"

"Not just yet," Miga said. "One last thing." And she opened fire on the security station in front of her.

She sent pulse after pulse into the console. Sparks and flames shot up; wiring and circuitry flew. Smoke filled the air. Fire alarms blared. Still, she kept firing until the console before her was so much slag. Half the monitors around the Hub went dark.

When she finished, she brushed a lock of hair from her face and regarded Kane and Hal. "They have backups. But they'll take a while to get operational. Should keep them from reactivating that damned missile system anytime soon."

Kane coughed, waving away smoke.

And then the rest of them opened fire.

They blasted every computer, console, and monitor in the Hub, working from station to station. Kane shielded his eyes from flying debris. Fires broke out; water showered from automated suppression systems in the ceiling. Cold water drenched Kane as he retreated toward an exit. The smoke stung his eyes and burned his lungs. He crouched against a door along the perimeter and watched the chaos with equal parts horror and fascination.

It was more than a scorched earth strategy to slow down Ankledge, and it was more than mere vandalism. Kane could see their faces—teeth gritted, eyes blazing. Some of them were even crying, though he doubted they were aware of it. In that moment, he felt the release of years, even decades, of their collective pent-up rage.

More significant, though, was the unmistakable sense of its depth—this outburst had done little more than scratch the surface. Kane recalled the murder in Miga's eyes and realized that all of them had been similarly scarred, to varying degrees. That well of rage might just be bottomless.

And in that moment, he wondered how wise it would be to let these people escape Petra. Unjustly imprisoned or not, they had been so bent by their ordeal that they might be incapable of functioning in civilization.

Of course, civilization had done this to them in the first place.

Finally, it had ended, leaving the Hub a smoking, sodden ruin.

The tram rounded a bend, bringing the hangar into view. The gray curtain of rain turned it into an indistinct monolith. They would be there in a matter of minutes.

The outburst in the Hub had slowed them down. He turned his gaze skyward, searching in vain for any break in the clouds or for any hint of those approaching ships, whatever they were.

The tramcar took them into the hangar, to whatever fate awaited them.

CHAPTER ELEVEN

Icy water roused Ankledge from unconsciousness with a start. He shivered and opened his eyes to madness.

Blasted, blackened electronic wreckage and bits of broken glass surrounded him; cold water drenched him. The shattered remains of monitors hung on the walls. The air was hazy and smelled burnt. For long moments, Ankledge could do nothing but lay there, muscles twitching at random, not even sure where he was.

Gradually, he regained control of his limbs. Every fiber of his body ached, as if they had been clenched for hours on end. He dragged himself into a sitting position, glancing around, aghast.

This was his Hub, he realized. It looked like it had been bombed.

Full memory returned. *They* had done this. First they'd hit him with an emitter, and then they'd done this.

It occurred to him to wonder how long he'd been out. The destruction of the Hub was so total that he could see no indication of the time of day. It could have been minutes, or hours. Or days.

That he wasn't dead told him the emitter pulse had been low amperage. And water from the fire suppression system still poured from the ceilings, though no flames were evident. It couldn't have been very long, then.

Ankledge grabbed the remains of a nearby workstation and pulled himself to his feet. He had no allcomm, and with the Hub in ruins, no way of communicating.

The southeast exit hung ajar. That must have been the way Ellum and his band of savages had departed for the hangar. They might still be on the ground. If he hurried…

He lurched across the Hub, staggering from ruined console to ruined console, glass and circuitry grinding under his feet. His muscles remained reluctant to obey him, but he bore down, refusing to fall. He reached the exit and pulled himself through.

A darkened corridor stretched before him, ending in a T-junction ten meters ahead. Halfway there, an emergency comm unit hung on the wall, undamaged. Ankledge half-ran, half-staggered to it.

He detached the receiver and tried to punch in Mehr's access code. His muscles betrayed him again, causing him to fat-finger it twice before he got it right.

The comm's transmit tone sounded once, twice, three times. "Come on, Chief," Ankledge whispered. "Come on, answer."

On the fourth tone, Mehr connected. "Chief."

"They're making their move. They shot up the Hub, and they're heading for the hangar. They knocked me out with an emitter. I'm not sure how long they've been gone—ten minutes, maybe."

Mehr was silent for a moment. "Warden, where are you calling from? I don't recognize the origin code. Are you all right?"

"To hell with the origin code! I'm telling you, the Hub's been destroyed, and the prisoners aren't waiting for the storm to pass. They know a message has been sent to Farside. Our friends need to hurry if this is going to work. Tell them…" The effort it took to frame his words exhausted him; he sagged against the wall. Without it, he would have dropped to the floor.

"Warden?"

Ankledge summoned his strength again. "Tell them that nothing gets off the ground. Nothing. And tell them to watch out for the base defenses! Even with the Hub destroyed, they're still active. I can't take us off full-alert status from here." He sagged again. The base's cold site was three levels down; he wasn't sure his legs could carry him that far. "It…it'll be a while before we can lift the lockdown. Too long. This…this will be over before then."

"Understood."

"Nothing gets off the ground, Chief. Nothing."

* * *

Though he had already scanned the lander from the Hub, Kane couldn't help running another systems check before launch. The remote scan might have missed something; no sense in braving the storm only to have the lander detonate in midair.

Hal hovered near the forward controls with him, but asked no questions. The others busied themselves with stowing their weapons and supplies and strapping in.

Cromberg and Fallon had pulled open the hangar doors while the others boarded. The landing field stretched beyond, its tarmac black and glistening from the incessant downpour. Like the tramcar track, blown down branches and fronds littered the way, but nothing big enough to be an obstacle. The winds blew around bits of detritus. Skimmers, transports, and other craft stood parked in the open, dark and lifeless.

The systems check proclaimed the lander clean and ready to launch. Kane held his breath as he queried the shipboard computers for a weather report. He didn't exhale until he read it through.

Hal sat in the copilot's chair. "How's it look?"

"The storm's let up a bit. It's down to a Category One."

"Thank God."

"It's still far from ideal. The computer recommends scrubbing the launch. I'll have to override it." He input the command passcode that put the lander entirely under his control, then hit the switch on the primaries. The engines responded; a vibration thrummed through the deck.

Kane glanced behind him into the cabin. "Are Cromberg and Fallon on board?"

"Right here." Cromberg, dripping wet, crouched in front of a storage compartment, stuffing it with a bag of supplies. Fallon was already strapped into a seat near him.

Kane glimpsed Miga Bronn, seated in the front row, her eyes faraway, before turning back to the controls. "All right. We're going." He stabbed a stud that sealed the lander with a hiss.

"None too fucking soon." Cromberg slammed the compartment shut and stood. "They'll be on us any minute."

Kane jerked on the yoke harder than necessary; the lander lurched forward. A thump from the rear of the cabin, followed by growling curses, told him he had knocked Cromberg on his ass.

The lander emerged from the hangar. Rain pelted it; a gust of wind rocked it on its wheels. Kane waited until the vessel cleared the hangar doors before accelerating.

He urged the lander along as fast as he dared, aware that Cromberg was probably right. At best, they had bare minutes. Next to him, Hal peered through the forward viewport, searching the sky. Kane resisted the temptation to do the same, focusing on following the runway diagram on his heads-up display.

It was all too reminiscent of the flying he had done during the war. The instincts, long dormant, were still there, guiding his hands. He found himself wishing he were in a military craft; this civilian tub had no weaponry of any kind.

The lander rolled along, emerging from the close confines of the hangar, taxiing toward the runways. Kane risked a little more speed. The tarmac was smooth, but the wind made the ride as rough as on a gravel road. Visibility was down to three kilometers. The sky seemed to be lightening, hinting that sunlight was waiting to break through. Kane feared it wouldn't be enough. The computer was right; this launch should be scrubbed.

He thumbed on the comm and sent a signal to the Portship. Sason Hemly answered.

"Sason, this is Kane. We're lifting off. Get ready for us."

"You're doing *what*? Unless I'm mistaken, you're still socked in from that storm."

"It's clearing off." He hoped. "We'll be fine. I just wanted to let you know we're on our way."

"Kane, what the hell is going on? You have no business launching in that weather."

"I'll contact you again after we lift off. Out."

"Kane, you—"

He cut her off.

Warning indicators flashed all over his display, telling him what he already knew about the conditions outside and that he had not received clearance to launch from Control. Hal noticed them and cast a nervous glance toward Kane. "Can you do it?"

"I don't know. It's gonna be rough."

They reached the end of the runway. Kane throttled up; the primaries went from a low rumble to a scream. The lander accelerated. Pelting rain blasted the viewports, reducing visibility even further.

Something flashed in Kane's peripheral vision, to his left. Moments later, a rumble sounded.

"Christ," Hal said.

Kane recognized both the flash and the rumble. Not thunder and lightning, but heavy artillery fire.

Another flash. And another. And another. All coming from his left—from the direction of the Hub. The base defenses were firing.

To Hal, he said, "We're too late."

Hal never heard. He was pointing out the viewport, his face ashen.

Through the slashing rain, Kane glimpsed black shapes in the sky. Artillery fire from the base erupted in a barrage. As he watched, pinpricks of light flashed from the incoming ships.

He slammed the throttle back, braked hard, and yanked the controls to the right.

The wheels locked; the lander skidded sideways down the runway. If the tarmac hadn't been rain-soaked, the lander might have rolled. Curses and moans of protest sounded in the cabin.

Sections of runway exploded, maybe twenty meters ahead. Kane straightened the controls, bringing the lander around two craters that hadn't been there moments before.

Gouts of flame erupted around the craft. Shells rained on the landing field, striking hangars, other runways, even some of the parked skimmers and transports. He brought the lander around in a circle, gazing skyward as he did so. The attacking ships roared overhead, trailing sonic booms felt more than heard in the din. At that speed and in these conditions, he couldn't make out any detail. He guessed there were at least five of them.

Whoever they were, they had missed on their first run, but they would be back. He had to get the lander off the ground. Airborne had become the safest place to be.

He steered the lander down an adjacent runway and throttled up again. Though the driving rain again hid the invaders, Kane knew they had overshot the base and were banking hard for another pass.

Control's defense systems released another barrage. A fireball burst in the air, two o'clock from the lander's position, brilliant even in this weather. Something fell from the sky, trailing flame and black smoke. The base artillery had scored a hit.

The lander hurtled down the runway, the primaries screaming once more. Kane knew he had to be heading straight for the attackers. The position of that explosion told him they were maybe twenty kilometers distant. At their speed, they couldn't be very maneuverable; they would have to make wide loops to double back.

Halfway down the runway, gaining speed. Liftoff velocity would take another ten seconds. He wasn't sure he had that much time.

He spoke through clenched teeth: "Come on, come on, come *on*..." Hal had braced himself against the low ceiling of the cockpit, agape and wide-eyed.

Five seconds. Four. The yoke trembled in his hands. Rain plastered the viewports despite the high-pressure air jets intended to keep them clear.

Three seconds. Two. Artillery fire burst overhead.

Liftoff velocity. Kane pulled back on the yoke; the lander left the ground. Wind gusts tugged at it as it ascended.

The attacking ships barreled into view over a ridge just ahead, much lower to the ground than before—no doubt to avoid the base defenses. Kane got a better look at them this time, just before they unleashed artillery fire of their own.

Something slammed into the lander. It bucked and slewed in the air. Damage indicators glowed red on the heads-up. Then the attackers were past them again.

Kane wrestled to maintain control of the lander, but the afterimage of those ships seemed burned on his retinas. He literally could not believe what he had just seen: angular, wedge-shaped aircraft with blunt noses and flared exhaust ports. They were so familiar that he had to wonder if he'd hallucinated them.

Of course they were familiar. God knew he had seen his share of them. They were Cassean bombers.

The lander pitched forward. Kane forgot about the attackers for the moment and fought for altitude. The lander responded sluggishly, as if its starboard side had just tripled in weight. And ahead loomed the ridge those Cassean ships—could they actually have been Cassean?—had just cleared.

He wrapped both arms around the yoke and threw all his weight backward, willing the lander up. Beside him, Hal murmured; he might have been praying.

They got close enough to the ridge to resolve individual fronds on the trees...then they were up and over, still gaining altitude, but far too slowly.

Kane allowed himself a glance at the damage indicators. Starboard avionics and attitude jets were out, and the ship's autorepair couldn't fix them.

"Shit."

"What is it?" Hal said, his wide-eyed expression frozen in place.

"I don't have any starboard controls."

"Can't you compensate?"

Kane leaned hard to port just to keep the lander level. "Yeah. I can keep us in the air. But I can't fire the launch engines."

"Why not?"

"I won't be able to control the ship, not with that kind of thrust." He hit the port attitude jets. They kicked in enough to allow him to focus again on gaining altitude. The lander approached the cloud layer. "Just trust me, Hal. If I fire the launch engines, we all die."

"What do we do?"

"We get the hell away from here as fast as we can."

"And our pursuers?" Hal jerked a thumb over his shoulder.

"We lose them in the storm."

"We do *what*?"

"You heard me."

They hit the cloud layer—a charcoal gray wall that obliterated their visibility. Turbulence buffeted the lander. Kane and Hal juddered in their chairs.

Hal had to shout over the din. "This is insane. You mean the storm that had us pinned down for hours?"

"Kind of funny, when you think about it."

Hal said nothing, only stared at him.

Kane jostled and jockeyed with the lander. "I don't really have time for a discussion here, Hal. They'll never follow us into this damned thing. I can fly through it long enough to discourage them from trying. Then we can get above the weather and find somewhere to land."

"But we can't launch."

The lander hit an air pocket and dropped ten meters. Kane's stomach seemed to jump into his mouth. Someone behind him screamed. He swore again and fought to regain his tenuous control over the flight. He spared Hal a glower—all he had to give at the moment.

"God," Hal said. "I don't believe this."

Kane flew the lander, too preoccupied to even feel shock. His gaze flitted from one part of his heads-up to another in an attempt to take in all the data at once. The winds were bad up here, no doubt, but he'd flown through worse. Of course, those were battle conditions, and in military aircraft. Whether the lander could take this kind of punishment remained to be seen.

A headwind lifted them. Kane rode it as long as he could, then fired compensating thrust and gripped the yoke before the wind shift could twist it out of his hands. He operated by pure feel. The lander continued to climb and fall, climb and fall, but the trend was up.

Miga, close enough to hear their conversation, spoke from behind them: "So where do we go, then?"

"It's your planet," Kane said. "I'm just visiting. You tell me."

"Where are we?" Hal asked.

Kane risked a glance at the navigation instruments. "We've left Control behind. We're over the ocean now. Bearing due east. Roughly."

Hal twisted in his seat to face the rest of them and raised his voice. "All right. We can't launch, and we can't go back to Control."

Cromberg, who had managed to strap in before liftoff, craned his neck to be seen. "Where, then? Back to Mainland?"

Kane spoke while maneuvering through a burst of wind shear: "Too far northwest. If we head in that direction, we lose the cover of the storm."

Miga said, "There's nothing between here and Southland but ocean."

Hal turned to Kane. "How much fuel do you have?"

"The tanks were filled before we left."

"Can you get to Southland?"

"Hal, no!" Miga said. "That's over four thousand clicks!"

Kane worked the attitude jets while trying to recall the lander's tank capacity. "Yeah, I can make it."

Miga's voice became shrill. "That'll take *hours*! They'll spot us on satellite!"

"No, they won't," Kane said. "Not after what you did to the Hub."

"He's right," Hal said. "It will take them hours to get the recovery site operational. And they'll have huge messes to clean up, all over the base. It may be days before they can even think about us."

"Maybe, but...Southland? You've heard the rumors about that place. Control won't even make prisoner drops there anymore."

"Why not?" Kane said.

"Not sure," Hal said. "The word I've gotten is that pilots are scared to fly there lately."

Rumors and frightened pilots. Kane had heard enough. The storm, the damage to his lander, those Cassean ships back there—and *that* would bear more serious scrutiny, assuming he survived the next few hours—and now this. "To hell with it. We're going to Southland."

The rest of them were silent for a moment.

Miga said, "And after that?"

"You'll have a few hours before we get there. Figure it out. Now shut up and let me fly."

They shut up and let him fly. The wounded lander limped eastward, buffeted but not stopped by the storm. Kane tried not to think of Tayla and Shamlyn. It was difficult.

PART TWO

SMALL GODS

CHAPTER TWELVE

It was their third attempt at bringing up the cold site. Ankledge stood in the center of the room, arms crossed, and waited for another disaster.

The cold site was a third of the size of the Hub, little more than an unfinished basement level with unpainted block walls. It smelled of old dust and disuse. The place would have felt like a dungeon had it not been for the assortment of freestanding workstations and desks and the cables snaking across the stone floor. And it was literally *cold* down here, well below the Petran surface—though that would change once the hardware got up and running.

If they got it running.

The first two attempts at powering up had resulted in electrical overloads. The Casseans had been far from precise in their bombing run. In addition to reducing the landing field and hangars to smoking ruins, their stray rounds had hit—among other things—the power plant and some of the generators. The complete damage report was still being assembled. With the Hub out of commission, the cleanup teams had nothing but allcomms to coordinate their efforts. But the initial indications were that the Casseans had done a number on Control.

Idiots. No wonder the Jurisians had beaten them.

Chief Mehr, looking exhausted but otherwise none the worse for wear following his incarceration in the Holding Area cells, stood conferring with a knot of techs. His uniform bore tears and stains from a long night of battling the armory fire and, later, dealing with the takeover and the storm. But he wouldn't go to bed, even if Ankledge ordered it. Not until they regained some measure of control. Mehr understood the stakes here without being told.

He detached himself from the techs and crossed the room to Ankledge. "They're ready to try again, Warden."

"Fine. Go."

The chief nodded to the techs. They dispersed to begin the power-up process again.

One by one, the workstations flickered and whirred into life. Ankledge realized he was holding his breath and chided himself for his foolishness.

As he watched the techs scurry about the level, he said, "Do you ever find yourself missing home?"

"Land's End?" Mehr said. "Daily."

They shared a chuckle.

The makeshift meteorology center came on line. Then the security station. So far, so good. They were the two biggest power drains. Communications came next, followed by the tracking systems—not that there were any surveillance flights to monitor at the moment.

As instructed, the techs stopped what they were doing to run checks on the power grid. These were the bare essential systems. If they could keep at least this much running, some progress could be made.

And none too soon. It had been—Ankledge checked his replacement allcomm—seven and a half hours since the storm had blown its last.

The techs nodded among themselves and smiled. One of them gave a thumbs-up to Mehr.

"Looks like we're up," the chief said.

"Hold here for another ten minutes. Make sure. If it's still running after that, instruct them to bring up each of the auxiliary systems in half-hour intervals." He raised a bony finger. "Make damned sure they're ready to pull those systems offline at the first *hint* of a spike."

"Yes, sir."

"And start bringing those stranded skimmers back from the emergency landing fields."

"Right away."

Ankledge ran a hand over his smooth scalp. "I'm getting a shower. Then I'll be ready to talk to the Casseans. Half an hour."

"I'll tell them."

Ankledge left the cold site and made his way to his quarters. On the way, he encountered various guards and staff, who passed him in the halls with subdued greetings and downcast eyes. He set a brisk pace, walking with shoulders back and head up, projecting confidence and authority.

Morale was at an all-time low. Understandable. Control had never seen an incident like this. Nothing even came close. There had been incidents of attacks on surveillance skimmers and transports, their pilots taken hostage. Control never negotiated with inmates; many of those hostages had died, often in grisly fashion. There had been attempts at infiltrating the island, stowing away on transports and the like. Those that hadn't been discovered in flight had never made it off the landing field. On one memorable occasion, a small army of inmates had assembled a fleet of makeshift boats and rafts and tried an outright invasion, sailing from Mainland, following the island chain to Control, armed only with clubs and spears. Surveillance had spotted them from the outset, but Ankledge had ordered no action to be taken, figuring the open ocean would kill them soon enough. But the fleet had gotten incredibly lucky with the weather, catching a week of doldrums. The would-be invaders had rowed and rowed, inexhaustible. At last, when they had gotten within sight of Control, he had ordered a bombing run to take them out. God only knew what they had been planning to do once they made landfall.

No, nothing like this, not in forty years.

And it wasn't just the attack and the standoff. It was the knowledge that they had traitors in their midst. That thought, more than any other, rankled Rolf Ankledge to his core. Those traitors would be among the first orders of business. He would find them, however many there were. Find them and make examples of them. Thanks to Mehr, he already had an excellent idea where to start.

She made a point of keeping Pythen away from the armory, the chief had told him—one of the first things he'd said upon being released from the Holding Area.

The shower calmed Ankledge. He allowed himself some extra time, breathing in lungfuls of the steamy air, washing away the last of Halleck Ellum's stink, purging himself of the attack. The Casseans would be waiting for him in his private office, but to hell with them. They had been waiting two hours; a few minutes more wouldn't do any harm.

He emerged from his quarters clean and relaxed. No allcomm messages from Mehr had come in during his shower, meaning there had been no further electrical problems at the cold site. Very good. He wanted no distractions while dealing with the Casseans.

His private offices were on the top floor of the main Control complex, higher even than the guest suites. The double doors, Petran blackwood adorned with a gold-plated rock-and-eagle insignia, parted silently as he approached. The blackwood motif continued inside, comprising the bookcases, conference table, and the massive desk. Oil paintings of Land's End seascapes, done in a variety of styles, hung on the walls. The northern exposure was all tinted glass, affording the best view on the island short of the mountains, hidden for the moment by heavy curtains. Plush carpet cushioned and quieted Ankledge's footsteps.

The three Casseans, all dressed in distinctive orange-red military uniforms, stood as Ankledge entered. Two of them—majors, by their stripes—at the conference table, the other, a colonel Ankledge had met once before, at one of the chairs near the desk.

Mardell, the man's name was. Pudgy, balding, bespectacled, with eyes that seemed to bulge from their sockets.

Ankledge could not help being amused, and he didn't bother hiding his smile at Mardell's little entourage.

"I apologize for keeping you gentlemen waiting," Ankledge said, stowing the smile. He crossed the room and shook Mardell's hand.

"Warden," Mardell said. His hands were smooth and dry, his grip just a bit soft. He smelled of a musky cologne so strong it had to be fresh. He'd also spruced up a bit before this meeting.

Ankledge took his place behind the desk. "Please sit."

Mardell remained on his feet, as did his functionaries. "We've been here for hours."

"It's been a very trying day. For all of us."

"I realize you're a busy man, Warden, but so am I."

Ankledge steepled his hands in front of him. "Colonel, in the past thirty hours, this base has been attacked—not once, but twice. The first attack inflicted forty casualties, blew up my armory, and destroyed the Hub. The second attack—by your trigger-happy flyboys"—the two majors stiffened at this—"damaged not only my landing field and a substantial portion of my aircraft, but also the power plant, the docks, and even some of the comm array. Thank God my people were hidden in the Holding Area at that time; I'd hate to think how many more would have died. I, personally, have been assaulted, held captive, and shot with a pulse emitter." He paused. "I think it's safe to say, Colonel, that I've been considerably more than *busy*."

Mardell reddened and pointed a shaking finger at Ankledge. "Perhaps I need to refresh your memory on a couple of items, Warden. *You* called *us*, asking for help. Those *flyboys* came under fire as soon as they were in range—by *your* weapons system. They had to defend themselves just to stay alive…to say nothing of completing the mission you begged us to take on."

"You knew the base had been attacked. Chief Mehr warned you that the defense systems had been activated. I'm sorry if some of your ships got scratched, Colonel, but—"

"*Scratched*? You blew one of them out of the sky, killing both crewmen aboard. You don't—"

"And if you want to talk about the *mission*, Colonel, why don't you brief me on the outcome? How is it that a single unarmed lander managed to evade *five* Cassean bombers? Perhaps your pilots are in need of some target practice." Ankledge let his hands rest on the arms of his chair and took a breath to calm himself. It was fine for Mardell to lose his temper, but Ankledge would maintain control.

Mardell glared. His mouth opened and closed, as if he were working to come up with some crushing rejoinder.

Ankledge gestured to Mardell's empty chair. "Colonel, please sit. We won't get anywhere by kicking sand at each other."

Mardell glanced over his shoulder at the two majors and settled himself into the chair. The functionaries followed suit.

"That's better," Ankledge said. "Now then—"

"It didn't evade our bombers. Our in-flight vids clearly show a hit. The lander was listing to starboard and trailing smoke when it vanished from sight. Then it went straight into the storm. That aircraft is in pieces and at the bottom of the ocean by now."

So Ankledge had been told. And it was probably true. "I hope you're right. We have to be sure. As soon as we get the harbor cleared, we'll send out ships to scout for debris."

"Of course." His pudgy face remained stuck in a scowl.

"And we'll want to review those in-flight vids. It will help us pinpoint the lander's position." And confirm the truth of this Cassean's words.

Mardell drummed his fat fingers on the arm of his chair. "We'll transmit dupes to you as soon as they're ready."

"Fine. Although I'd advise you not to have too many copies lying around."

"I'll keep as many as I need."

Ankledge didn't like the sound of that. "Do you mean to show those vids to your superiors?"

"I have to."

"Why is that?"

"Unlike you, Warden, I'm accountable to a chain of command."

"I'm accountable to the Petra Compact. Why are you taking this offworld?"

Mardell rolled his eyes. "Don't play stupid with me. I've reviewed those vids; I saw the markings on that lander. It was a Jurisian craft."

Ankledge kept his gaze steady. They had come to the crux of it now. He had to proceed with careful confidence. "Yes, it was."

"And would you mind telling me what the hell a Jurisian ship is doing on Petra?"

"Would you mind telling *me* what the hell Cassean ships are doing on Petra?"

Mardell's glare returned.

"I didn't think so," Ankledge said. "We have an agreement, Colonel. I don't ask what you're doing in Farside. You paid for the use of the land, and for privacy. You don't want anyone asking questions, and I frankly don't want to know—although I'll bet I can guess." He shrugged it off. "But never mind. My point is that, by the same token, I don't need your permission to entertain visitors."

Mardell considered this in silence. His two functionaries watched him. Their faces—young, clean-shaven—were blank, expressionless. They didn't comprehend everything that was happening here.

Mardell cleared his throat. "Is Juris joining the Petra Compact?"

"They're considering it."

Mardell's face cracked in a smirk. "Not anymore, I imagine. How are you planning to explain to them the loss of their lander?"

The man's smile irked Ankledge. "Shall I tell them that it was shot down by Casseans?"

The smirk vanished. "That's a poor joke, Warden."

"Not a joke. Merely trying to point out that we both stand to lose in this situation."

"Where are the Jurisians? What have you told them?"

"The Jurisian dignitary was on board the lander when you shot it down."

Mardell absorbed this with more aplomb then Ankledge was expecting. He must have been expecting it. "How did that happen? You mean to tell me the Jurisian was aiding these prisoners?"

"He was a hostage, like I was. They needed him to fly the lander."

Mardell shifted in his chair. "That lander didn't get here on its own. Where's the Portship that carried it?"

"Still in orbit. They're understandably anxious about the situation down here." That was an understatement. The insufferable captain of the Portship had been demanding hourly updates via allcomm. "All they know at the moment is that the lander was lost in the storm."

"Get it out of here."

Ankledge's chest tightened at the imperative. "I would like nothing more, believe me. But I doubt they'll leave without hard evidence that the lander is indeed destroyed. And we can't exactly show them the video, can we?"

Mardell shook his head, his lips pursed as if pulled taut by a drawstring. "That Portship is an unexploded bomb, Warden."

"You think I don't know this?"

"How are you going to explain the lander taking off in the middle of a Category Two storm?"

"I'll tell them the truth…as much of it as I can, anyway. They already know the island was locked down. It won't be too hard for them to piece together some version of what happened. I'll tell them the prisoners forced a launch attempt in those conditions, but the storm proved too much for the lander." Ankledge worked a control on the arm of his chair; the curtains on the north wall opened halfway. He stood and looked out. Late afternoon sun colored the jungle and the base structures red-orange. Beyond, the ocean glittered. The western horizon was still dark with the tail end of the slow-moving storm. Ankledge extended a hand to the ocean. "It will help us immeasurably to find some wreckage, even if it shows burn marks. We can always claim a lightning strike. It's worked before."

Mardell rose. "So there's no way to prevent word of this from getting out. There's going to be a full-scale investigation."

"Of course there's going to be an investigation. Did you honestly think otherwise?" Ankledge hadn't expected this level of naïveté from the man. Then again, he was a soldier, not a politician. Ankledge looked out the window again. "All regularly scheduled flights to Petra have already been suspended. That alone will be enough to attract attention. But by the time any investigation occurs, we'll be ready. Any damage the investigators see will be attributable to either the assault or the storm. All our records will be in order. And if there happen to be gaps—well, we can attribute that to the uprising, too. We'll get through this, Colonel. The Compact will get through this."

"And what about your own people? Can you keep them from talking out of turn when they return to their homeworlds on leave? Or when they retire from Petran service?"

The mention of his staff set Ankledge's teeth on edge. It reminded him of the traitors that had destroyed the armory and allowed the inmates to penetrate the Hub. Good thing he was facing away from the Casseans. "You let me worry about my people, Colonel. Most of them were secured underground when your ships flew over. They'll only find out what I let them know." And the harsh example he planned to set with the conspirators would dissuade others from asking too many questions.

"No," Mardell said.

Ankledge turned away from the view. "I beg your pardon?"

Mardell drew himself to his full height, such as it was. "I'm afraid that's not good enough, Warden."

"*What's* not good enough?"

"None of it. There are too many witnesses. Too many holes in the story. It won't hold up to scrutiny."

Ankledge held his temper in check, but it was getting difficult. "Don't underestimate me. No one thought an idea like Petra could work until I showed it could be done."

"To be sure." Mardell motioned to his functionaries. They stood. One of them brought the colonel his coat. "But I'm a conservative man by nature. I have a very low tolerance for risk. And we have a lot to protect here." He held out his arms as his aide helped him into his coat. "For that matter, so does every member of the Compact. You might want to consider notifying the other signatories."

"I'll take that under advisement."

"Don't think about it too long, or others may make the decision for you." Mardell buttoned his coat. "Not me, you understand, but I have a report to send. You'll issue the necessary clearance for the Portal, yes?"

Mardell had his own Portship in orbit. As far as the Jurisians knew, it belonged to Ankledge. Mardell used it as a courier between Petra and Cassea. "Of course," Ankledge said.

"Thank you, Warden." Mardell and his aides headed for the doors.

"Colonel."

Mardell looked back.

"It *will* hold up to scrutiny…if we all stick to the story."

"Hang together, or hang separately, is that it?"

"Those are the choices."

"Not my decision to make, thank God. Good night, Warden."

The double doors slid open. Mardell and his aides left.

Ankledge remained standing for long minutes after the doors had shut again. He considered withholding Mardell's access to the Portal—but that would accomplish nothing, except antagonize the Cassean and delay the inevitable. Sooner or later, his higher-ups would send another Portship through to find out why Mardell hadn't reported in so long.

He took several deep breaths, attempting to regain the serenity he'd felt when he'd walked into his office.

Hang together, or hang separately.

The lander wreckage. That had to come first. The sooner Ankledge could confirm the unfortunate death of Kane Pythen, the sooner this would end. He sat and started making the necessary calls to coordinate the search effort.

CHAPTER THIRTEEN

The storm had been bad. The aftermath promised to be no picnic, either.

Kane flew the wounded lander over the vast blue of the ocean, but had no time to admire the view as he had upon his arrival. He had managed to stabilize their flight with the attitude jets, but the extra thrust had cost them. He kept a nervous eye on his instruments. The fuel level neared redline.

It had taken too long to escape the storm. The lander had lost necessary maneuverability. Kane had to steer north and get out of the storm entirely. He'd managed it, but not before the pounding had taken an additional toll—not the least of which was the loss of the comm system.

The winds had damaged the hardware. And the missile hit they had taken hadn't helped. With Control and its radio towers well over the horizon, Kane's only hope to contact Sason was the lander's antenna. His allcomm's signal was far too weak to reach the Portship unaided. And there were no towers left standing anywhere else on Petra.

The last Sason knew, Kane had been attempting an emergency launch during a tropical storm. Now he couldn't reach her at all.

The lander flew eastward, toward Southland. Midafternoon sun slanted from aft. Fair-weather cumuli dotted a dark blue sky.

The cabin was silent. The lander had been airborne for ten hours; the passengers had spent much of that time napping. Kane had remained at the controls. Exhaustion gnawed at the edges of his awareness. He kept it at bay by snacking on dried fruits taken from Control's emergency provisions. If things got really bad, he could scare up some amphetamines from the lander's medkit.

Hal, still yawning from a nap of his own, took the seat next to Kane. "How are we doing?"

Kane glanced at his instruments again. "We should make it. Barely. But we won't be going anywhere else. Not unless there's a fuel depot nearby."

Miga and Hal had chosen their destination—a place called Ferrum, a deserted Bellerophonian coastal settlement—using the Petran geographical data on Kane's allcomm. As Bellerophon's only Petran settlement, it had to have a landing field.

The name had been wishful thinking, apparently. Ferrum would be in ruins by now, but as long as Kane could set the ship down, he didn't care. They had to get on the ground before Control managed to resume satellite surveillance. Once they landed, they could see to repairing the comm hardware and call down one of the Portship's other two landers. And hope that Southland's fearsome reputation among Control's pilots was exaggerated.

Hal said, "Anything I can do to help?"

"Not unless you know how to fly." Kane squinted out the forward viewport. He thought he spotted some kind of shadow on the horizon. He pointed. "What does that look like to you?"

Hal leaned forward. "Highlands, I think."

Kane looked over the navigation readouts. "That jibes. We should be down in less than an hour." He throttled back a little to begin their descent.

Hal strapped himself in. "Kane, I've been thinking."

"Yeah?"

"Those ships back there, the ones that hit us—"

"Weren't Petran. You noticed."

"You recognized them?"

Kane nodded. "They were Cassean."

Hal looked over his shoulder as if afraid of being overheard. "Are you sure?"

"I only got a quick look at them, and that was in the middle of a goddamned tropical storm." Kane rubbed tired eyes. "But I suppose I've seen enough of them in my day. Yeah, I'm sure."

"What the hell are they doing on Petra?"

The lander wobbled as their speed decreased. Adjusting the thrust of the attitude jets proved problematic. "Those were military aircraft, too. Bombers."

"So…what? The Casseans are conducting some sort of military operation on Farside?"

Kane managed to smooth out their flight again. But things would just get bumpier the closer they got to landing.

Hal continued: "Like what? Combat drills?"

"Mighty long way to come just to train," Kane said. "It's got to be something they don't want anyone to see. Anyone. Not even Ankledge. There are no surveillance flights over Farside. No satellite coverage."

"Secret weapons testing?"

"Maybe." The idea had some merit. But Kane had had too long to think it over while everyone else had been napping. It had led him to some dark conclusions he wasn't sure he believed. "Cassea's been under martial law since the war ended. Did you know that?"

Hal shook his head.

"Juris annihilated the infrastructure. The government couldn't operate." It shamed him to consider his part in that.

"Doesn't surprise me. But I'm not following."

"Fifteen years under martial law. That's a long time. It makes for a lot of dissidents. Underground movements. Guerilla campaigns." He spared Hal a glance. "You know. Like the one you wanted to start."

Hal looked at him sidelong. "Are we gonna have this argument again?"

"No. But I'll tell you, I'm beginning to understand something about Petra: it's the perfect dumping ground for incriminating evidence. The perfect hideaway for any unsavory business a government might have."

Hal leaned back in his seat. "Yeah. That's Petra, all right."

"The Virtue Party paid Ankledge to drop you here. That was *their* unsavory business. I was thinking that Cassea's unsavory business might involve dissidents, too."

Hal held a finger to his lips, tapping. "But that wouldn't explain why they'd need to maintain a presence here. They could just dump their dissidents the way the Virtues did." He gave a short, humorless laugh. "Hell, the way a lot of Petra signatories do."

Kane had thought of that. "Maybe they don't want to dump their dissidents."

Hal turned to him, frowning.

"Everything is off the map here. That makes Petra—and especially Farside— an ideal black site."

"God," Hal said. "Just when I think this place couldn't get any worse."

"I could be wrong."

"Yeah, but it fits. And they pay off Ankledge, so he asks no questions."

"If we can figure it out," Kane said, "so can he."

"Doesn't matter. He still has plausible deniability."

There was one more thing. Kane hesitated to mention it. He'd really had too much time to think on this flight. "Hal, there's a helluva lot of bad things going on here. I get the feeling we're just scratching the surface. I don't think even you have considered the magnitude of the scandal if word gets out."

A slow smile spread across Hal's face. "There you're wrong."

A bitter taste flooded Kane's mouth. "You'll get your revolution after all, won't you? Not just on Juris, but all over Ported Space."

"Tear the whole fucking mess apart. Burn it all down. Yeah, I've thought about it, Kane. Dreamed about it, even."

Kane glanced toward the cabin. "And do *they* share your dream?"

Hal's smile faded, but his eyes were bright. "All of them wound up on Petra thanks to a system that doesn't work anymore. Or maybe it never worked at all. In any case, it's long past time to throw that system away."

The words *you're insane* rose to Kane's lips, but he saw no need to repeat himself. He really didn't want to have that argument again. "Hal, the Casseans already know what's happened on Control. If the other Petra signatories find out, they'll stop at nothing to keep their secrets safe. Nothing."

"Then we need to get this lander repaired and get off Petra before they do." Hal's gaze was steady, his face solemn and still as stone.

Kane looked away, out the viewport. The shadow on the horizon had resolved itself into the coast of Southland. "Ferrum will be over there." He pointed to the southeast. "I'll make a pass. Look for anything that resembles a landing field." He raised his voice and called over his shoulder: "Everyone strap in back there. This landing could be a little rough."

Not much was left of Ferrum.

The latticework of roads was still visible, but the structures had collapsed to rubble. Not even the shells of buildings remained, as far as Kane could tell. If there was any kind of housing or shelter, it was too small to be seen from the air. To the south, a meandering river emptied into the ocean. Nothing moved below.

The landing field was identifiable as a flat, empty expanse on the northern side of the settlement. A few outlines remained that hinted at a runway.

Kane killed as much of the lander's speed as he dared and tried to bring it down at a gentle angle. The attitude jets fought him every step of the way. As he came around on final approach, he was dismayed to see the remains of the runway pitted, cracked, and overgrown with weeds.

At last he killed the thrusters and forced the lander to the ground. It hit hard enough to jolt him in his seat. The straps bit into his waist and shoulders. If not for the restraints, he would have slammed into his instrument panel. He prayed the landing gear would hold up.

The lander shuddered and bounced and slewed. Kane throttled all the way down and braked hard. He could barely see from being tossed around in his seat. The ruins of the landing field hurtled past the viewports. Hal yelled something, but Kane couldn't hear over the roar of the lander's passage.

The ship hit some unseen obstacle that yanked the yoke from his hands. He groped for it, bending back a fingernail in the process. The lander veered off into a stand of scrub brush and rock. He regained the yoke and steered hard to starboard, trying to will the aircraft back to a clear patch. The landing gear locked on him, sending the ship into a skid. Given its mass, and at this speed, it had to be pulverizing whatever lay under its wheels, and everyone aboard was paying the price.

He let off the brake and leaned to port. The lander fishtailed, squealing. Kane feared that at any moment the craft would start to come apart.

At last, the lander began to slow, though it continued to take a pounding. Kane couldn't get it back to the narrow track that had once marked the runway. The nose dropped into a dip he couldn't avoid, again jerking the yoke from his hands. He flailed to retrieve it. His teeth clamped down on the inside of his cheek, setting the left side of his face afire.

The lander slid into a ditch and slammed to a stop.

It lay canted, enveloped in the cloud of dust kicked up by the landing. The viewports became obscured. Kane's hands hurt from the grip he'd had on the yoke. He tasted blood where he'd bitten his cheek.

Hal had gone pale and haggard. A sheen of sweat shone on his face. Someone in the cabin was moaning.

Kane looked over his instruments. Myriad indicators flashed red and yellow, but at least the fire alarm wasn't going off. He throttled up a little to see if he could get out of the ditch. Wheels spun, but the lander remained stuck. He tried reversing, with the same result.

"Shit." He powered down the lander and unstrapped himself. He got out of his chair and walked gingerly along the canted deck. Everyone was still strapped in. One of the storage compartments had popped open; packets of provisions lay scattered in front of it. He scanned the cabin, checking the hull for cracks or broken glass. The lander seemed intact. "Is anybody hurt?"

Miga rubbed her scalp. Her hand came away bloody. "I hit my head," she said.

"I'll get the medkit. Anybody else?"

There were contusions and bruises aplenty, but no broken bones. Kane located the medkit. Cromberg yanked it out of his hands and went to help Miga. Kane left him to it.

He opened the hatch, letting in sunlight and a hot, dry breeze. The debarkation ramp deployed as well as it could. With the lander sitting at an angle, the ramp didn't quite reach the ground, but it got close enough. Kane worked his way down. He spit over the handrail to clear his mouth of blood.

His feet crunched on the stony soil. The surrounding scrub brush had small blue and purple flowers that gave off a pungent scent. Once he got some distance between himself and the lander, he walked in a circle around it, surveying the damage.

They would have to dig to free up the landing gear enough to get out of the ditch. The artillery hit on the starboard side had stove in the hull and left it blackened. Part of the wing had been shorn. The comm hardware was badly bent, jamming the mechanism that aligned the array. Steam vented from the engines. Fluids leaked from a dozen different places, stinking of burned lubricant.

The others made their way off the lander, expressing varying tones of dismay and disbelief as they took in the situation. Hal emerged, first looking west, shielding his eyes against the sunlight, then south, toward the ruins of Ferrum.

Kane walked over to him. "How's Miga?"

"Scalp wound. Cromberg patched her up and gave her a painkiller. He did a quick scan. No sign of concussion."

"Good."

They looked around. What had once been Ferrum was still, seemingly barren, without so much as scurrying rodents or even insects. The rhythmic rush of the ocean, less than a kilometer away, was the only sound. In the near distance, spindly trees began mingling with the brush, becoming more numerous and dense as the land rose to the east. Beyond stood forested hills. The hazy outlines of the highlands marked the horizon.

Hal looked back toward the lander, where the others milled. Cromberg and Miga had debarked. Miga had a white bandage tied around her head, but looked otherwise fine.

"What do you think?" Hal said.

Kane inhaled deeply. The breeze came from the south, bringing with it only a hint of the ocean. He would have welcomed a swim at the moment. "I have some tools. We should be able to get the comm aligned again. That'll be enough. I just need to get in touch with the Portship. Sason can send one of the other two landers down on automatic, or even remote pilot it, if she has to."

Hal straightened. "Thank God. I didn't want to get my hopes up."

"Well, it's still going to take a while."

"Then you'd better get started on that comm array. It'll be dark in a few hours. I'll see to posting lookouts."

Kane glanced toward the ruins. "You expecting company? This place is deserted."

"You're not from around here." Hal walked toward the others.

CHAPTER FOURTEEN

As dusk fell, Kane and Fallon sat atop the lander, sweating over the comm array. Fallon had removed his shirt in the heat. Numerous scars and burns marred his muscled arms, back, and chest. He silently obeyed Kane's instructions, loosening bolts here, applying a prybar to a bent housing there, communicating in monosyllables when he had to.

Hal had set up lookouts to the north, south, and east, forming a triangular perimeter, a hundred meters from the lander at each point. They had concealed themselves in brush or behind rock outcroppings. Kane couldn't see any of them from where he sat. The others busied themselves near the lander, handing tools up to Fallon and him as needed, patching up leaks where they could, or removing some of the larger stones and chunks of broken concrete from around the landing gear. Hal seemed to think it a good idea for the ship to at least be mobile.

Kane finally resorted to a cutting torch to free up the dish. It had been too long since he'd last used one; he was out of practice, and he fumbled with adjusting the flame and cutting straight. He was hesitant to trust Fallon with it—care would be needed to prevent damaging the transmission hardware—but the young man only nodded when Kane asked him if he knew how to use the tool. Kane handed it over and showed him what to cut, and what not to cut. Fallon went to work, slicing through hull plating with precision Kane could not have hoped to achieve.

The comm array would never be flight-worthy after this, but the lander's flying days were done. All he needed to do was get in touch with his Portship—assuming Ankledge hadn't blasted it from orbit. Not even he would be so bold. But Kane remembered what he had said to Hal, about the lengths to which the Petra signatories would go, and he wondered.

Fallon finished cutting and shut off the torch. Kane wiped sweat from his forehead, reached into a provision packet nestled between the hull and the comm housing, and pulled out an unopened water bottle. He offered it to Fallon, who declined with a shake of his head.

"You sure?" Kane said. The westering sun, bloated and orange, had just set, but the day's residual heat lingered, radiating off the lander's hull, and the southerly breeze had dropped off.

"I'm fine," Fallon said.

With a shrug, Kane popped the top and took a long pull. The water was still cool. Condensation formed on the sides of the bottle. Before he could stop himself, he gulped down half of it. Shamefaced, he replaced the cap and put the bottle away. Fallon was too intent on freeing the trapped dish to notice. He wedged a prybar into the cut he had just made and leaned on it. Kane grabbed a prybar of his own and did the same.

Metal screeched and gave. At last, the dish came free.

They eased up on the prybars. Kane got on his knees and bent low, bringing his face to the level of the hull, looking for any sign that wiring had been exposed or damaged. The hardware appeared intact. The dish pointed down at a comical angle, but that could be easily adjusted. Kane straightened, satisfied. "That should do it."

"Really?" Fallon cast a doubtful scowl on the array.

"I still need to align it, which is going to be a chore. It'll have to be done from here, by hand. It's going to be pretty hit-and-miss, but I should be able to get it right."

"By tonight?"

"With any luck." Kane extended a hand. "Thanks for your help."

Fallon regarded the hand as a foreign object for a few moments before shaking it. "Welcome."

Kane dug into the provision packet. "You hungry? I'm starved."

"Hey, listen..." Fallon gazed westward, squinting into the sun. Some of his fair hair had fallen into his face, making it hard to read. "I, uh...sorry about what happened back in the Hub."

Kane flashed on the memory of his altercation with Miga, of being restrained by Fallon and some of the others. It had only been yesterday, but it seemed like an eternity ago. "It's fine."

"I didn't know what was going on. I just saw you going after Miga."

"Forget about it."

"I would have killed you right then and there if Hal hadn't stopped me."

Kane didn't know how to respond to that. He supposed he couldn't blame the kid.

"But you've done a lot for us," Fallon said. "I thought we were dead when those bombers hit us. You kept us alive, got us here. So thanks."

"We still have a ways to go yet." Kane glanced skyward.

"Yeah." Fallon brushed the hair out of his face, revealing a half-smile. "Never thought I'd be doing this."

Kane opened a small bag of dried fruit from the provision pack. He couldn't identify the slices of shriveled yellow flesh, sweet to the taste but with an acid bite, but ate them by the handful all the same. "You were born on Petra," he said.

Fallon nodded, sitting with one leg extended, the other bent, one arm resting on his knee.

"And your parents?"

"Dead. When I was a baby."

Kane had feared as much. "I'm sorry."

"The swells."

"Beg pardon?"

"That's how they died. They got the swells. You know."

Kane wasn't familiar with the term.

Fallon must have read it on his face. "Plague. Disease. You know disease?"

Kane nodded.

"You break out in running sores, and your body swells up all over, you suffocate." He rubbed the back of his neck. "Anyway, my folks gave me to Hal's people before I got sick, too. Then they went away to die. I never knew them."

"So you never knew what they—" Kane stopped himself, unsure if he should proceed.

"What they did to get sent to Petra?" Fallon shook his head. "No.

Never knew." He paused. "Hope it was something worthwhile, though. Hope they pissed off the right people."

"Yeah." Kane allowed himself a small smile. "I'm sure." He finished the fruit and stuffed the empty bag in a pocket. "If we're going to align this dish, I need to get my allcomm. And we'll need a light, too. It's getting dark." He slid off the hull to the wing.

Something whistled through the air behind him. He turned in time to see an arrow, a meter long, plunge into Fallon's neck and punch out the other side. Fallon gave a gurgling cry and reached for his throat. Blood spurted and gouted. He tried to stand, slipped, and fell off the lander. He hit the ground and lay prone, twitching and spouting blood.

More whistling cut through the air. A rain of arrows clattered on the hull. Emitters crackled in response; assault rifle fire boomed.

CHAPTER FIFTEEN

Hal heard the incoming arrows moments before they hit. He dropped the chunk of concrete he'd been carrying and ducked into the ditch. Lee and Ash, who had been helping with digging out, were caught in the open as the first wave of arrows landed. Some bounced off the lander, others stuck in the ground. Lee took an arrow in the leg and fell into the ditch beside Hal, bellowing. Two hit Ash, in the back and shoulder. She dropped with a groan and lay still.

Hal was caught without a weapon. Next to him, Lee thrashed and screamed, clutching his leg. He had a palm-sized emitter in a belt holster.

The sound of return fire filtered down to Hal. Good. The lookouts hadn't been hit. Flat on the dusty ground, he detected a rumble, felt more than heard, as of a stampede.

Hal grabbed Lee and clapped a hand over his mouth. "*Quiet!*" he whispered. "Do you want to lead them right to us?"

Lee clenched his teeth, eyes wild, making guttural noises. But at least he stopped screaming.

"Let me have your gun," Hal said. He reached Lee's holster, popped the strap, and removed the weapon. Lee, meanwhile, threw his head back, still grabbing his leg. The arrow protruded from his thigh. Blood soaked his clothes.

"Tend to that wound. I'll cover you." Hal scrambled up the embankment on his belly. More arrows fell around him; the rumbling swelled.

He reached the top of the ditch and peered toward the east. The attackers were emerging from the hills, riding bullos—gray and hairless, thick-legged and thick-skinned, but deceptively fast for all of that. The mounts had been smeared with streaks of colorful dyes, as had their riders. They wore little more than loincloths, but their faces and bodies were covered in reds, blues, and blacks. They bellowed war cries as they came on. Hal estimated there were twenty of them at most.

Like the Bone Tribes—but no. Bone Tribesmen tended to favor late-night guerilla action over full-on assault. These attackers seemed better organized, better equipped—and there were more of them.

An assault rifle cracked, and one of the bullos went down, bleating. Its rider went flying. Two trailing bullos charged headlong into the mess and also collapsed. One of them crushed its rider beneath its bulk as it fell.

Hal held his emitter at the ready and waited. This was a short-range weapon; firing now would only give away his position. He took the opportunity to scrabble closer to the lander's nose.

The others had taken up positions around the lander and were returning fire. The air became electric with the pulse of emitters. The attackers, still a hundred meters out, launched another volley of arrows, but found few targets. Everyone who hadn't been wounded in the initial outburst had gotten under cover.

Hal was calm. His people had handled much worse than this. Given their superior firepower and their defensive positions, they had the upper hand. The painted attackers, to their sorrow, had marked the lander as easy prey. They and their mounts took hit after hit. Their front rank collapsed, slowing their onslaught and creating havoc.

Even so, Hal had to wonder how many he had already lost.

The attackers closed to fifty meters, well inside the perimeter, but the mass of writhing and wounded bullos became a serious impediment. They began dismounting, some forgoing bows and arrows for crude spears. Cromberg had taken the easternmost lookout post; he riddled them with emitter fire from behind.

A spear slammed into the ground a scant meter in front of Hal. Still, he held his fire. It may have just been a lucky throw. Or these painted Southlanders were better than he had first thought.

He risked a glance at the floor of the ditch. Lee had broken off a length of the arrow shaft that had wounded him and had clamped it between his teeth to keep from screaming. He was tying a tourniquet, torn from his clothes, around his leg. He'd lost a great deal of blood.

Hal turned his attention back to the attack.

Twenty-five meters. Twenty. They came on, still bellowing, some of them brandishing their spears above their heads. With the threat of arrows eliminated, a couple of Hal's people had emerged from their firing places and clambered onto the lander to get better firing positions. Some of the Southlanders responded by pelting them with stones launched from slingshots.

Stupid of them to have left cover. Too cocky. They'd be lucky not to get brained.

Hal took aim at the nearest slingshotter and fired. The pulse dropped him. The stone he'd been readying flew straight up and then fell on top of him.

Something whistled through the air just over Hal's head, *thunked* into the lander, and clattered to the ground next to him—another spear, this one deliberate, not lucky. Hal looked to his right, where the shot had come from. A muscular man, bald, his head and chest painted a glistening black, charged him. Hal took aim, but a stone slammed into his hand, knocking away the emitter. It slid down the embankment, out of reach.

With a cry, the black-painted man launched himself at Hal, who rolled away. The Southlander missed, but managed to snag an ankle and pull Hal toward him. With his free foot, Hal kicked him in the face. The savage grunted but kept his grip. Hal kicked again and heard the crunch of bone.

The man released his foot. Hal scrabbled away, only to have that iron grip clamp on his ankle again. Hal lost his purchase on the embankment and slid to his stomach.

The spear that had just missed him lay within arm's reach to his left. He grabbed for it just as the Southlander yanked, pulling Hal into the ditch.

Spear in hand, Hal rolled over. The Southlander, a momentary silhouette against the setting sun, loomed in Hal's vision. Hal thrust the spear at the man's midsection. The savage, cat-quick, dodged, but he wasn't fast enough. The tip of the spear pierced his hip instead of his intestines, knocking him backward.

Hal yanked the spear out and scrambled to his feet. The

Southlander was on his hands and knees. Blood poured from the wound, but the man was uncowed. With a feral snarl, he lunged.

Lee tackled him from behind. Enraged, the Southlander threw him off. God, the man was strong, and seemed to feel no pain. Hal backed well out of his reach, keeping the spear ready.

The weapons fire had subsided, as had the war cries of the attackers. In his peripheral vision, he caught sight of figures running toward him.

The Southlander, panting, his nose ruined by Hal's kick, crouched, holding his ground. But his eyes had a faraway, detached look Hal recognized from his years on Petra. The man was high on tropograss, or some variant thereof. So it grew here in Southland, too. That explained the savages' recklessness and this one's imperviousness to pain.

Lee had landed on his back and was struggling to his feet. Blood covered his wounded leg.

"Stay put, Lee," Hal said. "I've got him."

Lee obeyed, sinking to the ground again.

Miga and Cromberg joined Hal, weapons raised. Cromberg sighted down his barrel, but Hal said, "No. Don't shoot."

"Careful, Hal," Miga said. "He's high."

"I know." Hal took a step forward. The painted man's eyes widened, but he kept still.

"Can you understand what I'm saying?"

The Southlander said nothing, but Hal caught a flicker of recognition in his face. "Are you the leader of this gang?"

He gave the faintest of nods, still panting.

"How many more of you are there?"

Again, the Southlander remained silent. Cromberg said, "There were seventeen of them in all. The others are dead. Turkey shoot."

Hal kept his gaze on the painted man as he replied to Cromberg: "No, they're too well equipped. There are more of them. Count on it." He waggled the spear. "How many?"

A line of drool ran from the Southlander's mouth and dribbled unheeded from his chin.

Hal edged closer to him. "Listen to me. You saw what we did to your people. You see what we're capable of. We have plenty of charge cartridges and shells for our weapons, enough to take on a hundred more of you if need be." That was a lie; they were running low on ammunition, but this man wouldn't know any different. "We don't want any more trouble with you. We'll be gone by dawn. I'm sparing your life so that you can tell the rest of your gang. Understand?"

The Southlander remained silent.

Miga fired a pulse into the ground in front of the man. A white flare burst, searing the earth black. A burnt smell filled the air. The Southlander grunted and retreated a few steps, casting a baleful gaze on her. "We're talking to you," she said. "Understand?"

"Miga," Hal said in a warning tone.

The Southlander continued backing away, circling toward the east. Blood ran in streaks from his wounded hip. Hal, Miga, and Cromberg advanced, keeping their weapons trained on him.

His mouth quivered, forming words Hal had a hard time understanding. He said something like *dur*, and something like *kofny*. Then he said it again: "Dur…kofny…" He straightened, and said very clearly: "He'll make you beg. He'll kill you all."

Hal couldn't tell if the Southlander was speaking of himself in the third person or of someone else. He guessed the latter. *Dur Kofny.* Hal didn't recognize the name.

The Southlander bolted, running past the bodies of the other attackers and the bullo carcasses, heading for the cover of the trees. He ran upright and without limping, unhindered by the hip wound.

Cromberg sighted again. "You sure I shouldn't just take him out?"

Hal put a hand on the barrel of Cromberg's emitter and eased it down. "No need."

Cromberg settled the weapon on his shoulder. "If he's a gang leader, he has to come back at us. Otherwise, he loses face."

Hal watched until the painted man was lost to sight. "Sure he'll be back. And if we had killed him, his followers would have charged us that much sooner. But now they have something to think about. That should give us the time we need." He turned to Lee, who lay in a heap, eyes closed. "See to him."

Miga picked her way over to Lee, squatted, and felt at his throat. She bowed her head and sighed. "He's gone. Fuckers got him in his femoral artery."

Hal had seen too much death for too many years to feel more than a twinge of sadness. But at least he still felt something. "They got Ash, too."

The others began to gather, some limping. Many bore fresh wounds. Kane stepped out from behind the lander, pale but unbloodied. Relief swept through Hal.

"Fallon's dead," Kane said.

"Sixteen of theirs, three of ours," Cromberg said. "That's five for one. Not bad."

Kane sagged against the hull. "I didn't have a weapon. I couldn't fight back."

"Good," Hal said. "If you get yourself killed, we all die here."

Kane closed his eyes.

Hal surveyed the scene, trying to get his mind working again. "All right. Man the lookouts again. All fresh eyes out there, understand? If you've already stood a post, you're done for the night. The rest of you stay near the lander. I'll want some help burying our dead."

"What are we going to dig with?" Cromberg said. "Our hands?"

"We'll raise cairns, if nothing else."

Cromberg nodded wearily and wandered in the direction of Ash's body.

"Kane," Hal said. "Where are you with the comm?"

Kane opened his eyes, gazing past Hal, looking toward the ocean. "We managed to free up the hardware. I need to align it, though."

"How long?"

"If I could scan automatically, it would take a matter of minutes. As it is—" He shrugged. "Could be an hour, could be a day. Depends on how lucky we get."

"We don't have a day."

"You think I don't know that?" Kane looked at Hal. "I could use some help, if you have anyone to spare."

"I'll join you once we get things cleaned up here."

"Fine."

"We really don't have a day."

"Yeah. Doing what I can." Kane walked away.

Hal watched him go, uncomfortably conscious of the corpses of Lee and Ash behind him. And Fallon was gone, too. He felt that twinge of pain again at the thought, and was glad for it.

CHAPTER SIXTEEN

Night fell. The day's heat ebbed. The breeze shifted to the west, bringing with it the salt smell of the ocean. Kane had a hard time concentrating on his work. His gaze kept wandering toward the darkness to the east. The forested hills had become black, monolithic. Detecting motion was impossible. The pounding of the surf would mask the whistle of arrows and the approach of those charging beasts—bullos, they were called.

He chided himself. The blue-white light of the flashbar Hal held for him would of course destroy his night vision. And the painted gang wouldn't be stupid enough to come at them from the forest again. More than likely they would attack from the south, using the cover of the ruined city. They wouldn't be riding noisy bullos this time; they would approach by stealth. Arrows would be less effective in the dark; knives were more plausible. He wouldn't see or hear them until they were upon the lander.

Better to just focus on the job at hand, to ignore the fact of his vulnerability up here. The sooner he got in touch with the Portship, the sooner he could retreat to relative safety inside the lander.

God, it had been too long since Cassea. And as a pilot, he had never been involved in hand-to-hand combat, anyway. It rattled him in a way dogfighting and dodging missiles never had. Sheer luck had saved him from Fallon's fate. At least in an aircraft, he had some measure of control over the situation.

Working the scan manually was tedious under the best of

circumstances, requiring time and patience. Kane had neither at the moment. He had mentally broken down the inky sky into a grid. He would point the dish at a sector, starting with the most likely prospects, and send a test signal with his allcomm. If he got no response after a minute, he'd reposition the dish and try again.

It was not a job to be rushed, and it required concentration, lest he miss a sector or overlook a faint signal. Determining the best part of the sky to search was a matter of educated guesswork. He started in the west, beginning about twenty degrees above the horizon and working up, moving south to north.

Hal held the flashbar and helped with the positioning of the dish, saying little. He seemed lost in his own thoughts. Kane had heard him saying eulogies over the graves of his compatriots. They had simply laid the bodies at the bottom of the ditch, then covered them with loose stones and broken concrete—the best they could do without tools.

Kane would have liked to stand there with the rest of them, paying respects to the fallen, but as Hal had said, they didn't have the time. So he had worked and listened.

"So Petra has killed three more of us," Hal had said, his voice strong in the twilight, his cadence measured. "We all knew, going into this, that some wouldn't make it. No, that doesn't make it any easier. But maybe we can take a measure of comfort in knowing that their deaths will be among the last. That Ash, Lee, and Fallon"—he had paused, the briefest hesitation—"that they gave their lives for something bigger than all of us. That thanks to their sacrifice, one of the ugliest chapters in human history is about to end."

Kane had stopped what he was doing. The fervor in Hal's voice had been undeniable.

"When I was first sentenced to Petra, I thought a lot about things like guilt and innocence. Those concepts don't have much meaning here. Those are words for rich people, powerful people. *Civilized* people."

Murmurs of assent had greeted this.

"Down here, the hard truth is that none of us are innocent. Maybe some of us didn't deserve Petra, and maybe some of us did, but we can't be called innocent anymore. Not one of us.

"Except Fallon.

"Petra made him everything he was. You all remember that he

almost didn't come on this mission. He wanted to stay behind, to protect the others. I was the one who talked him into coming. I told him that out of all of us, he was the one most deserving of freedom. I wanted him to be the first one of us to step onto the soil of some other world, far from here—the first one of us to breathe free air.

"That's not going to happen now. But we all know there are plenty more like him. We're going to finish this thing. We're going to escape this shithole. If we can't do it for Fallon, let's at least remember all the other Petra-borns—all those other innocents."

Another pause, and then: "Ash. Lee. Fallon. You were our friends, and you will not be forgotten. I swear to you that, someday soon, the rest of Ported Space will know your names.

"Goodbye."

Silence had followed. After a time, the others filed away from the gravesite, some alone, some in smaller groups, all of them quiet.

Afterward, Hal had clambered atop the lander to assist. Occasionally, Kane caught him glancing around, as if scanning for more attacks—only to snap his attention back to the comm when he saw Kane looking at him. He said nothing more about the importance of hurrying, thank God—not that there was any need. As darkness descended, the backwash of the flashbar made Hal appear spectral. A day's growth of beard, patchy with gray, marked his previously clean-shaven face. It aged him ten years.

It occurred to Kane that he was seeing the night sky over Petra for the first time—a moonless expanse of black, and a scattering of stars unfamiliar to him, somewhat more sparse than the view from Juris. The arm of the galaxy was not visible from here.

The dish was ready for another try. He sent the test signal again, eyes intent on the display. Hal leaned in for a look over his shoulder. The signal strength indicator remained at zero, without so much as a flicker. Kane forced himself to wait a full minute before giving up.

"Nothing?" Hal said.

"Nothing." He clipped the allcomm back to his belt, making certain it was fastened before letting it go. If it dropped to the ground and shattered, they would all spend the rest of their lives on Petra—however short a time that might be.

Hal settled back on his haunches and looked up, again seeming to retreat into his own thoughts.

Kane felt he should say something. "I'm sorry about Fallon. And the others."

"Thanks." Hal kept his gaze focused on the sky. "I talked him into this, you know."

"I heard. You said he wanted to protect the others." For a moment, Kane forgot about painted marauders and arrows.

"Yeah."

"What others?"

"About three hundred of us, at the moment. It fluctuates." Hal pulled his gaze away from the stars. "Safety in numbers, Kane. Loners don't survive on Petra. We have a…a community, I guess you'd call it. Back on Mainland. We build—as best we can, out of satellite and skimmer view—we farm, we defend ourselves, we hide from Ankledge's goddamned bombing runs. We survive."

"He bombs you?"

"God, yes. Whenever his skimmers or his satellites pick up something he doesn't like."

"Such as?"

"Signs of organization. Farming. Industry. Any structures more sophisticated than log cabins or sod houses. Or sometimes he wants to punish us for bringing down one of his ships. We have empty sites—decoys—we leave in the open just for that purpose, while we shelter in the caves. We rebuild the decoys after he bombs them."

"And your group—all political prisoners, all of you?"

"Some. Others, like Fallon, were born here. But it's not like we do background checks, Kane. If you can show yourself to be a productive member of a society, if you're not a danger to others, then we'll take you in."

Kane thought of Cromberg, wondering what his crime had been. But now wasn't the time. He leaned over to realign the dish.

Hal looked back to the sky and chuckled.

"What's funny?" Kane asked.

"I just figured something out." He pointed straight overhead. "See that bright one there? Know what it is?"

Kane followed Hal's finger and spotted a dazzling point of yellow-white light, just a few degrees north of zenith. He tried to recall what he knew of the Petra system. "One of the other planets?" Even as he said it, he doubted the guess. Petra's nearest celestial neighbor was its sun; the other bodies in the system were more than twice as far away.

Hal lowered his arm. "It's the Portal. I'm not used to seeing it so high. From Mainland, it's pretty low in the southern sky."

"*That's* the Portal? You're sure?"

"Positive."

"Damn. Serious miscalculation." If it was a typical Portal, it would be in a stationary orbit. And his Portship wouldn't be far from it. He had expected it to be more directly above Control, so he'd concentrated on the western sky. But then, the Portal had been built before Control had even been named. Kane wrestled with the dish. "Give me a hand with this, would you? I want to point it at the Portal."

Hal grappled with the other side of the dish. With a metallic groan, the hardware shifted.

"That's good." Kane pulled his allcomm from his belt and tried the signal again.

Hal released his hold on the dish, still looking up. "You know, when I first got here, I used to drive myself crazy staring. Every night it's up there, like some kind of taunt. Like an open door you can see but never reach." He looked away. "Had to give it up, though. I was getting obsessive about it. If I hadn't quit, I think I would have killed myself." He paused, shaking his head. "I gave up the night sky. Started working on my life here. I haven't stargazed in over a decade."

The allcomm signal indicator remained flat, but Kane was nonetheless encouraged. "Seems like as good a night as any to start again, don't you think?"

A half-smile formed on Hal's face.

Kane redrew the mental grid, centering it on the Portal this time. He'd circle outward from there. "OK, let's reposition it again. Just west of the Portal."

"Right." They got back to work.

They spent the next half hour at it, moving from sector to sector with a greater sense of direction and purpose. Kane made smaller adjustments to the dish, certain that they were close.

And then, with the hardware aimed about ten degrees west-southwest of that brilliant pinpoint of light, the signal strength indicator jumped from zero to twenty.

Hal, again looking over Kane's shoulder, said, "Is that it?"

"I think so." He still needed a better signal, though. "Move it a fraction further west."

Hal handed him the flashbar and nudged the dish. The signal strength dropped away to nothing.

"No, wrong way. Bring it back."

Hal obeyed, and the allcomm signal returned to its previous level.

"All right, now a little bit north. *Slowly.*"

Hal worked the dish while Kane watched the indicator. It jumped again, from twenty to the mid-fifties. "OK, that's the right direction. A little more, Hal."

The indicator rose into the green. Kane stilled the excited trembling in his hands. "That's it. Leave it there. Find something to wedge under the dish. I want to hold it in that position."

Hal looked right and left and spotted the toolkit Kane and Fallon had used to free the hardware. With a free hand, he picked it up and placed it under the dish, then eased himself away from it.

The signal remained strong. "Good," Kane said. "Good." He transmitted a text that read simply *Kane.*

The signal could be picked up by Control, but only if they were listening for it. Ankledge might think they were dead. Even if he didn't, would he think of looking here in Southland, so far from where they'd last been spotted? Kane thought not—hoped not.

It was academic, anyway. They had no choice at this point.

The allcomm chirped—an incoming transmission.

"Oh, thank God," Hal said.

Kane connected. Sason Hemly's voice came on the line, strong, insistent: "Kane? *Kane*? Is that you?"

Kane had never been so glad to hear another voice in his life. "Yeah, it's me, Captain."

"Sweet Jesus! They said you were dead. They said you went down in the storm."

"Right. Listen, Sason—"

"And why the hell were you attempting a launch in those conditions? Did you lose your mind?"

"I'll tell you everything as soon as I get back on board the Portship. But right now I need you to listen."

"Go ahead, Kane."

Hal seemed to be peering into the darkness. He edged aft.

"First thing," Kane said. "As far as Warden Ankledge is concerned, I *am* dead. You haven't heard from me, you have no idea where I am. Control can't know about any of this. Understand?"

Sason was quiet for a moment. "What kind of trouble are you in?"

"Not now. I need you to—"

A cry of alarm cut him off. It came from aft, where Hal had focused his attention. It was Orem, the white-haired one with the pale skin, the one who'd said, *Cook them both.* Hal had assigned him to the northern lookout post.

"Cut that light! Cut it! They're coming!"

Hal scowled at him. "Why aren't you at your damned post?"

"Fuck the lookouts! Get everyone back in the lander! Now!" He pointed north, the way he had come.

Hal and Kane looked in that direction, but saw only darkness. A faint rumbling cut through the whistling of the wind—not the tromp of stampeding bullos this time, but a mechanical sound…an engine.

Hal slid off the lander and motioned for Kane to follow.

Sason's voice nagged at Kane's attention. "…didn't catch that. Say again? Kane, talk to me. Repeat—"

Orem's eyes bulged in his pale face. "Kill that fucking light!"

Kane extinguished the flashbar. He followed Hal off the lander, first climbing down to the wing, then to the ground.

Orem ran for the debarkation ramp, yelling at the top of his lungs for everyone to get back to the ship, no doubt for the benefit of the other lookouts. Everyone else was already inside, either sleeping, eating, or tending wounds.

Kane and Hal stood their ground, looking northward. Hal raised his emitter.

Something large lumbered toward them—a blacker shadow among shadows.

Over the allcomm, Sason's voice became strident. "Kane? Kane, I've lost you. The signal is—"

Bright light blazed forth from the shadowy hulk. Kane and Hal shielded their faces with their hands and backed away. People were emerging from the lander, despite Orem's insistence that they get the hell back inside, that they were all screwed.

Kane couldn't make out the shape of the vehicle closing in on them, but he recognized the sound of the engine. "It's a transport, I think," he said.

Hal lowered his emitter. "They didn't—"

A report sounded, coming from the direction of the approaching vehicle. Kane crouched, but the shellburst detonated in the air, well above the lander.

"Warning shot," Hal said. He yelled over his shoulder at the others assembling behind him: "Hold your fire! Do what Orem says. Get back inside!"

The vehicle neared the lander, its wheels crunching over gravel, and stopped. Despite the light shining in his face, Kane discerned the outlines of a retracted-wing craft, somewhat larger than his lander—a transport, for certain. Ankledge must have somehow found them.

Figures approached, more shadows, holding what appeared to be assault rifles. Hal holstered his emitter and raised his hands. "Shut off that allcomm," he said out of the corner of his mouth.

Kane obeyed, cutting off Sason in mid-plea. Something inside him twisted at the act.

The figures neared, coming into the light, and Kane knew at once that they weren't from Control.

All of them had shorn pates, but bore no body paint. Instead, their foreheads were tattooed with large black Xs. Strips of dark cloth crisscrossed their chests, mimicking the marks on their heads. They were all armed with large assault rifles. Kane counted ten, with more moving in the shadows.

That warning shot had been something larger than a rifle. It had been genuine artillery fire from the transport's weaponry. It would be well armored, too. Kane saw the sense in what Hal was doing. They were outmanned and outgunned. He raised his hands.

"They want to talk," Hal said. "Otherwise, they would have just opened fire."

Kane nodded and glanced over his shoulder. The others had followed Hal's lead, discarding their weapons and putting up their hands.

The tattooed people—all of them with grim, hard faces and well-muscled arms—moved in, quickly disarming everyone. One of them, a woman with a horrid burn on her neck and jaw, pushed him against the lander, rested the barrel of her rifle under Kane's chin, and patting him down with a free hand. The burn was old and poorly healed, the epidermis gone, showing angry red, puckered skin. She grabbed his allcomm, looked it over for a moment, then spared him a quizzical glance. She confiscated it and backed away from him, still pointing the rifle at his face.

They were good, disciplined, and working together with militaristic precision.

A new figure emerged from the transport—a man, also shorn, but with no tattoo on his forehead. He wore a gold chain around his neck; the crisscrossed fabric across his chest was red instead of black. The lights cast his face in stark relief—a crooked nose, deep lines around his eyes that showed his age, and a trimmed goatee salted with gray. The rifle carriers gave him a wide berth, keeping their gazes and their rifles trained on Kane, Hal, and the rest.

The man stopped and looked over each of them in turn. His gaze lingered on Kane. He glanced at the burned woman, who nodded and produced the allcomm. He took it from her, examined it, and stuffed it in a pouch tied to his waist.

He pointed at Kane. "You."

His voice rang out with calm command, clear and deep.

Kane took a step forward, keeping his hands raised.

"You're not from Petra."

Kane shook his head.

"Can you speak?"

He cleared his throat. "Yes."

"And this vessel," the man said. "It's not Petran, either."

"No," Kane said. "It's mine."

The man's eyes widened at that, and Kane wondered if he had angered him.

But the man turned his attention toward the others. "These, however…" His lip curled as he looked over their tattered clothes and filthy appearances. "These are Petran."

"They're with me," Hal said. He lowered his arms, keeping his palms open and facing out. Two of the tattooed men stepped forward, weapons at the ready, but their leader stopped them with an upraised hand.

He approached Hal. In a low voice, he said, "Do you know who I am?"

Hal met the man's stare. He made no reply at first, and Kane knew he was considering his words. Finally, Hal said, "You're the one the painted men fear. You are Dur Kofny."

The man raised his chin and smiled. "You flew here from Mainland?"

"Yes."

Dur Kofny turned to his soldiers. "Did you hear that? They know my name all the way across the ocean!"

The soldiers cheered, some pumping fists in the air.

Dur Kofny looked over Kane, Hal, and the others again, then at the lander. "Very interesting. We need to discuss this. Bring them."

CHAPTER SEVENTEEN

After breakfast, Ankledge went to the infirmary to visit the prisoners.

A strong antiseptic smell hit him as soon as he entered. He had never seen so many occupied beds, though the place was no longer filled to capacity. Enough of the wounded had been patched up and discharged that the medics could start getting some rest. The staff here had had very few breaks since the explosion at the armory.

Ankledge's footfalls sounded flat on the white tile floor. The prisoners were held under armed guard in a partitioned-off section toward the rear of the infirmary. He walked past rows of beds separated by curtains, most filled with patients bearing severe burns, broken limbs, bloodstained bandages, or multiple contusions. Some of the curtains were drawn. A few of the wounded caught his gaze as he passed. He nodded at each of them. Those who weren't too badly sedated nodded back. One even attempted a feeble wave. Ankledge gave him a faint smile.

The staff at the horseshoe-shaped central medical station nudged each other and stood when they caught sight of him.

"Please, relax," he said to them. "Where's the senior med?"

A middle-aged man with a pockmarked face, dressed in blue scrubs, raised a hand.

"Walk with me."

The med stepped out of the station and joined him. His name badge identified him as Doctor Cabot.

"I'm here to see the prisoners," Ankledge said. "What's their condition?"

"We operated on the one with the chest wound. He lost fifty percent of a lung and suffered liver and kidney damage. We repaired what we could, but his blood loss was critical. He's in a coma."

"And the other one?"

"His leg will need surgery, too. At the moment, we don't have the resources. His injuries aren't life-threatening, but I'm not sure he'll walk again. We've given him painkillers for now."

"Is he lucid? I need to talk to him."

"He might be asleep."

"I'll need to wake him up for a few minutes."

Cabot nodded. "Shouldn't be a problem, Warden."

"Good."

They reached the partitioned area. Two guards in black stood to either side of the opening.

"Thanks, Doctor," Ankledge said. "I know you're busy. Get back to work."

Cabot inclined his head slightly and went back to his station.

The guards snapped to attention. "At ease," he said to them. "I'll just be a few minutes."

They stepped aside to let him pass. Beyond the partition were the two beds, side by side, with no curtain separating them. On the nearest lay the one in a coma. A respirator tube had been taped over his mouth; multiple IV lines snaked to his arms. The monitor nearest him showed depressed vitals—slow heart rate, shallow breathing, minimal EEG activity.

On the other bed, the inmate with the shattered femur lay asleep. A single IV proceeded from a wall dispenser to an arm—his painkillers, no doubt. The injured leg had been elevated and immobilized.

Ankledge leaned over him. Dark skin, the color of topsoil richer than Petra's, with long hair that lay in a braid over one shoulder. His mouth hung open; he snored softly.

Ankledge shook him by the shoulder. The inmate kept snoring. The warden shook again, harder this time. "Wake up. Now."

The man's eyes fluttered open. He focused on Ankledge with effort. His gaze dropped to take in the warden insignia on Ankledge's uniform, and his brow furrowed.

"That's right," Ankledge said. "You know me, scumbag. And I know you." Both prisoners had been scanned on his orders, and the data run against the biometrics in the inmate processing records. Ankledge had reviewed the results over breakfast. The one in the coma was Berian, a drug runner from Crystalline who'd killed three enforcers during a bust. He'd claimed the case against him had been manufactured, that he'd been ambushed by corrupt cops in the pay of a local crime lord whom he'd run afoul of.

This one, on the other hand… "Your name is Anton Roman, convicted of sedition on Nerylite. You are an avowed and unrepentant anarchist. Sentenced to life imprisonment on Petra four years ago."

Roman looked away.

Ankledge grabbed the man's jaw and forced his gaze back to him. "You want to listen when I talk. Got it?"

Roman's eyes blazed. His mouth moved sluggishly, as if gummed shut. "Nothing—" It came out as a clotted whisper. He cleared his throat and tried again: "Nothing to say to you."

"We'll see about that. But for now, you just pay attention." Ankledge released Roman's jaw. "Halleck Ellum is dead. They're all dead, but for you and Berian over there. It's over." He stepped back and allowed a few moments for the news to sink in.

"Lying sack of shit." But the fire went out of his eyes even as he spoke. The tone was more sullen than defiant.

Ankledge kept his face neutral. It was an easy bluff to run. He almost believed it himself, despite the negative results from the search parties so far. He leaned in again. "It's over, except for one thing. You never could have gotten this far on your own. You had inside help. And I want to know who they are."

"Don't know what you're talking about."

Ankledge smiled. "Yes, you do. And I'm inclined to be generous if you cooperate. We can fix up that leg of yours or maybe get you a fully functional prosthetic. We can take you back to Mainland, anywhere you like, with all the supplies you can carry. You can live out your days telling stories around the campfire about the glorious day you stormed Control. Or"—he straightened, still smiling—"we can slap a simple cast on the leg and drop you in the middle of Bone Tribe territory."

"Always knew you were a grade-A cocksucker, Warden."

"Glad we understand each other." Ankledge pulled up a plastic chair next to the bed and sat. "Look, I'll make it easy on you. Just give me a name. One name, and I'll let you get back to sleep."

Roman only looked at him.

"All right, I'll make it even easier. I'll give *you* a name. Emma Goring."

The inmate jumped as if goosed…then closed his eyes and shook his head, cursing himself under his breath.

That was all Ankledge needed. Chief Mehr's suspicions were confirmed. *She worked hard to keep Pythen from going to the armory*, he'd said. *She seemed very intent on keeping him away from it. Too intent, I think.*

Ankledge stood. "There. That wasn't so hard, was it? Thanks, scumbag. I'll take it from here."

He walked out of the infirmary without another word.

Mehr and Ankledge had developed a routine of meeting for lunch to discuss the day-to-day business of Control, usually in the private dining room where Ankledge had entertained Kane Pythen the night before last. At Mehr's request, they changed plans and met in Ankledge's office.

The warden had spent the rest of the morning touring the island, taking in first-hand the damage at the armory, landing field, and comm array. Functionaries gave nervous updates on the clean-up efforts. It was slow going, with personnel spread thin. The armory was the worst—a total loss, flattened. It would have to be rebuilt. The landing field had been cleared enough to allow for takeoffs and landings, but only search crews were flying; surveillance flights were suspended. They had neither the manpower nor the aircraft to spare. Work at the comm array, where the damage had been lightest, was the most encouraging. Full communications capacity would be restored by nightfall.

Mehr arrived at Ankledge's office direct from the cold site. He looked much better than he had yesterday, benefits of a night's rest and a crisp new uniform.

Lunch had already been delivered—cold sandwiches of thinly sliced bullo meat and fresh lettuce grown on the island. Bullo meat could be a bit tough and gamy, but was quite tolerable when salted and seasoned with the right blend of spices. The serving staff had arranged the place settings on the conference table, along with a pitcher of ice water and two glasses. Ankledge had already begun eating. He motioned Mehr over to the table.

"Sorry I'm late," Mehr said, taking his place.

Ankledge wiped his mouth. "Not to worry. How's the cold site?"

"Not so cold anymore. The power situation seems to have stabilized for now." He took a bite of his sandwich.

"But?"

Mehr chewed, swallowed. "But we're going to be down there a long time. It will take months to repair the damage in the Hub. The cold site doesn't have enough capacity to handle all of Control's functions for that long. We'll have to expand."

That would mean even more delays before the Hub could be rebuilt. "No matter. It has to be done."

"The signatories aren't going to appreciate the added cost."

"No, probably not." The mention of the signatories brought to mind his conversation with Mardell. His Portship had gone through early this morning, bearing its report back to Cassea. Ankledge poured himself a glass of water and drank. "You've reviewed the Cassean in-flight vids?"

Mehr nodded and pulled out his allcomm. "I've brought them along. They're cued up for playback."

"Go ahead."

The chief set the allcomm in the nearest dock. The blinds closed; lights dimmed. The projector in the center of the conference table lit; the in-flight images flickered into existence just above it.

The vids were difficult to watch, given the weather conditions and the speed of the aircraft. The first time through the loop, Ankledge could only resolve gray sky and the rapid passage over what appeared to be a forested ridge, made indistinct by the rain. Upon cresting the ridge, there was a bright flash in the lower right corner of the image, followed by a whitish blur streaking across the frame. The landscape tilted wildly as the bomber banked, coming about 180 degrees with dizzying speed. The ridge filled the frame again. Ankledge glimpsed something small and quick that vanished into the storm, trailing black smoke. And the vid ended. Ten seconds' worth of footage at most.

Similar images, from each of the Cassean bombers involved, played in succession, showing the same scenes from different angles. Ankledge picked up a little more detail with subsequent viewings: the flash was missile fire from the bombers; the whitish blur must have been the Jurisian lander. But that was the best he could make out.

He said, "What does this tell you?"

"It corroborates most of the Casseans' account. Here." Mehr worked a control on the front panel of the allcomm dock, and the video playback slowed to half speed. He pointed. "There's the lander, approaching from the left."

"I see it."

"And there"—Mehr paused the playback at a frame that showed a smaller flash near the blur of the lander, one that Ankledge had heretofore missed—"that's the missile hit, on the starboard side."

He advanced the playback again. The landscape rolled past as the bomber banked in slow motion. When the craft finished the turn, Mehr went to a frame-by-frame. "This is what I spent most of the morning analyzing." He pointed to the smoke trail and to the small shape of the retreating lander. "I cleaned up the image as best I could. Here." He touched another control. The hazy curtain of rain disappeared, the gray backdrop of cloud faded, and the outline of the lander came into sharper relief. "There's smoke, but not much. And we can't make out any flames at this distance." He was silent for the next several frames. The lander appeared to be wobbling in flight, but—

"They have structural integrity," Ankledge said.

"Yes, sir."

"So they couldn't have been hit very hard."

"A glancing blow, but enough to damage their starboard controls."

As Ankledge watched, the lander banked and disappeared into the clouds.

The playback froze. Ankledge stared at the final frame, mentally replaying what he had just seen. "That last turn…seemed deliberate."

"I think so, too. And another thing: I used the landmarks to calculate the lander's altitude throughout the vid and mapped it against the terrain. They had to *climb* to clear that ridge. They just barely made it. And the lander continues to climb afterward, all the way up to the moment we lost sight of it." Mehr removed the allcomm from its dock. The image vanished, and the blinds reopened.

"So," Ankledge said. "Your conclusions?"

Mehr took another bite of his sandwich. "I think the Casseans might have been a little optimistic. They wounded the lander for certain. But the last we saw of it, that ship was still flyable. It would have been a rough ride, I grant you—"

"What are you saying? You think they survived?"

Mehr took a breath and set down his sandwich. "It's possible. Not likely, but possible."

"They flew right into the storm."

"Yes, sir. And they might have done so deliberately, to throw off pursuit."

Ankledge pushed his plate away. He no longer wanted it.

Mehr continued: "The storm probably finished them off if they stayed in it for any length of time. It would have taken a hell of a pilot to bring them through it, given the damage they had taken."

"Kane Pythen flew combat missions on Cassea. He was decorated for it."

"Yes, sir."

Ankledge drummed his fingers on the blackwood tabletop. "You say the storm *probably* finished them off."

"Probably. But they may have gotten further than we supposed before they went down."

"So we should widen the search."

"Yes."

Doing so would stretch their resources even thinner. But Ankledge had to show the Casseans some wreckage, and soon, before they decided to involve the other signatories.

"Worst case scenario," Ankledge said. "Suppose they made it through the storm? Would they be able to launch?"

"I doubt it. They would need to repair those starboard controls first."

"Then they would need to land. Where?" Ankledge pulled out his own allcomm and accessed the maps stored in Control's network. Mehr did the same.

"Somewhere close," Mehr said.

"There isn't anything close. They were headed east when last seen." To the east was nothing but ocean, all the way to Southland. To the west was the rest of the island chain. Control was by far the largest of them; the others were little more than glorified rocks with thin skins of sandy soil.

"They could have doubled back, headed west. We wouldn't have been the wiser, not with the Hub destroyed."

"All right," Ankledge said. "We widen the search to include the rest of the islands. Let's get close satellite scans, too. And maybe we could review the tracking telemetry from the attack."

"We could," Mehr said, "but it might be a waste of time. All those ships flying around in such close proximity—it probably wouldn't tell us more than we already know."

He had a point. "Bring up the data, anyway. Have it ready in case we don't find them fast."

"Yes, sir." Mehr worked on the rest of his sandwich.

"One other thing. I spoke with the prisoner this morning. About that matter we'd discussed."

Mehr paused in his eating. "Emma?"

"She's one of them."

Mehr closed his eyes. His jaw muscles bulged. He opened his eyes and said, "Unbelievable. After all these years. How long has she been…?"

"No idea. It's moot at this point. The damage is done."

"I'll arrest her myself. Right now."

He started to get up, but Ankledge waved him back into his chair. "No, Tomas."

"We're not going to just let her—"

"Of course we won't. But she didn't do it all by herself. I doubt like hell she planted those charges at the armory."

Mehr considered. "I suppose not. She would have been too conspicuous there."

"But I'll bet she knows who did."

Mehr accepted this silently. His gaze was still hard. He tore into his sandwich as if attacking it.

"Tomas, it wasn't your fault. You know you have my every confidence."

"I let you down."

"No. *She* did. After lunch, I want you to send her up to this office." Ankledge reached over to put a hand on his arm. "And do it with your game face on. You need to be natural with her. No snapping or coldness. As far as she knows, she still has your total trust."

Some of the stiffness left Mehr's arm. "Understood."

"If she asks, you don't know what I want with her."

"Right."

They spent the rest of lunch discussing minor items, updates on other functional areas of Control, some small talk. As Mehr's mood eased a little, Ankledge said, "Listen, when this is over, maybe you should take a furlough. Some time for yourself. When was the last time you visited Land's End?"

Mehr sipped his ice water and chuckled. "A few years, I guess."

"It would do you some good, I think."

He tipped his glass Ankledge's way. "What about you, Rolf? When was the last time *you* were home?"

Ankledge allowed himself the faintest of smiles. "I haven't been to Land's End in decades. Petra is my home now."

The two sat in silence for long moments. Mehr broke it by pushing his chair away from the table and standing. "I'll coordinate the expanded search."

"Thanks, Tomas."

The chief walked out of the office. Ankledge paged the kitchen staff with his allcomm to let them know lunch was over. He got up and walked to his windows.

From this vantage point, none of the damage was visible. To the untrained eye, Control looked as it always had, year after year. But Ankledge knew better. The landing field should be busy with multiple takeoffs and launches. Instead, most of his skimmers and transports were looking for that damned Jurisian craft. The harbor, too, was empty, with a significant portion of the ships combing the search area for wreckage. Tramcars should be running over the rails, preparing the base for the next shipment of prisoners.

Of course, there was no telling when that schedule could be resumed. Even if the Casseans didn't alert the rest of the signatories, it would soon become obvious that something was very wrong on Petra. Routine requests for Portal transit were being shunted aside. Only the Jurisian Portship had a valid access code at this time, one that had been given upon arrival. A logjam was building. And nothing he did could mitigate the necessity for the supply ships that brought the raw materials and fuel Petra lacked.

The kitchen staff entered the office and cleared away the remains of lunch. Ankledge ignored them, standing at the window with his hands clasped behind his back, calculating how much time he had left, playing through various response scenarios.

Even under the best of circumstances, it was going to be a near thing. If it weren't for the Casseans and that Jurisian Portship, he might have had enough time to package this mess properly, make it tidy and free of loose ends, and present it all to the signatories with a pretty bow.

But it wasn't playing out that way. And he needed to be ready.

Rolf Ankledge held no romantic illusions about himself. Over the years, he had dispassionately catalogued the changes age wrought on the face in the mirror. He had noted with trepidation the first telltale aches and swellings of arthritis in his hands and knees. Strong painkillers and regular exercise kept him functional; not even Mehr knew. But its inexorable progress would eat away at him. Even with treatment, Ankledge figured he had perhaps another five years, at most, before age and infirmity forced him to step down as warden. Mehr would take over, of course, and would do a fine job—but Rolf Ankledge would become gradually more helpless, more irrelevant.

And when that happened, there would be no place waiting to take him in. As he had said over lunch, he had no home anymore but Petra. He could never return to Land's End. Indeed, as the keeper of Ported Space's dirtiest secrets, he would be welcome nowhere, not even on the signatory worlds. Mardell's attitude toward him, so typical in the warden's dealings with Compact members, was proof enough of that.

Ankledge intended to kill himself before then, before he became nothing more than an enfeebled exile. He had forged his destiny from the beginning; he would forge his own end, too. No one would decide it for him. Not the Casseans, nor the Jurisians, nor the signatories, nor the Halleck Ellums and Anton Romans that swarmed on Petra.

His allcomm beeped, rousing him from his musings. He glanced at the message on the display. Emma Goring was on her way up.

Ankledge composed himself and shut the blinds. He sat at his desk, waiting for her with his hands folded.

Ten minutes later, a knock sounded at his door. He let her in using the desk controls.

Emma peered around the door before entering. The petite redhead had been in his office before, but only on special occasions. As she crossed the space between the door and the desk, she looked around as if searching for others.

Ankledge didn't know her very well. She had worked exclusively for Mehr. She had a reputation for professionalism, efficiency, and discretion.

"Emma. Please have a seat."

"Thank you, Warden." She sat and crossed her legs.

"Thanks for coming on such short notice."

"Of course. I was a little curious—"

"Sure you are. Can I get you anything to drink?"

Her look of disbelief would have been comical in another context. "I-I'm fine, Warden."

"We'll just get started, then." Ankledge sat back in his chair, angling it so that he appeared to be looking past her. In truth, he watched her in his peripheral vision. "Emma, I don't think I need to explain to you how serious the situation here is."

"No, sir."

"We have a great deal of work to do, much damage to repair."

She kept silent and still.

"The casualties and property damage are bad enough. But even worse is the toll this raid has taken on morale." He swiveled his chair back to her, reestablishing eye contact. "These prisoners who attacked us didn't act alone. Everyone understands that."

She shifted in her chair, just enough for Ankledge to notice.

"Control can't function in an atmosphere of fear and mistrust. These...people, whoever they are, did more than aid and abet the prisoners. They destroyed the armory, killing two people in the process. That makes them murderers. They must be found. Rooted out."

She nodded, solemn.

"There is some good news, however. One of the wounded prisoners has agreed to help us. He has given us some names." He watched her for a reaction.

She only blinked. "I see."

"You realize that I'm telling you this in the strictest confidence."

"Yes, Warden. May I ask what the names are?"

"I have to keep that classified for now. This is a delicate matter; I'm proceeding as carefully as I can."

"Of course. But...are you sure this is good information? A man in his situation might be willing to say anything."

Oh, she was good. "We're comparing what's he's told us with our personnel records now," Ankledge said. "But yes, we believe it's solid." Let her make of that what she could.

Emma leaned to one side, resting her chin in her hand. "Sir, what is it you need from me?"

"For the moment, nothing. I'm just bringing essential staff into the loop. I'm doing this one person at a time, and only with those who have been cleared of suspicion." Ankledge smiled. "You were the first to make the list. I thought it was important to convey the message to you personally."

"I—thank you." A faint frown wrinkled her brow.

She was very good, showing nothing more than uncertainty. But then, she'd operated under Mehr's nose for God knew how long without arousing suspicion. She would have to be good to pull that off.

"The first arrests will take place as soon as we've corroborated the prisoner's story."

"*First* arrests?

"Oh, yes. This is just the beginning of the investigation, I'm afraid. It's going to be...well, very difficult for everyone on Control. You'll have to prepare yourself."

Her features smoothed. She straightened the front of her uniform. "I'll do my best."

"No doubt you will." He worked the desk controls again, opening the door. "That's all, Emma. I don't want to keep you. I know you're busy."

She stood and started to head for the exit, then turned back. "Warden, what about Kane Pythen? I've heard—"

"The search crews are looking. But given the storm..." Ankledge shook his head. "Too much to hope for. He's dead. So is everyone who was aboard that lander."

"Does his Portship know?"

"They've been contacted. They're awaiting confirmation."

"I see. Thank you, sir."

She left. Ankledge watched her go and closed the door behind her.

Using his allcomm, he composed a message to Security, ordering constant surveillance on Emma Goring. He wanted her every move documented, every communication monitored and traced. Sooner or later, she would attempt to warn her traitorous friends. Ankledge was curious how many of them there would turn out to be.

He had forged his destiny from the beginning. And he wasn't done yet. Not by a long way.

CHAPTER EIGHTEEN

By day, Kane got a better look at their prison.

Dur Kofny held court at a fort in the forest. The place had been constructed of logs, stone, and earth, dug into a hillside and sheltered from satellites and surveillance skimmers by a huge canopy of leaves and branches that had been erected over the entire structure. A palisade of sharpened stakes, three meters tall, formed the perimeter.

Kofny had given Kane permission to walk outside the wall, so long as he didn't stray out of sight of it. And why not? Kane had nowhere to run.

Small huts and tipis crowded around the fort, forming a ramshackle village of sorts. Campfires burned; the smell of cooking meat wafted through the chilly morning air. Kane's stomach rumbled. Men, women, and handfuls of small children clustered around the fires, all staring as Kane passed. Whispers and murmurs trailed in his wake.

The palisade encompassed a twenty-five-meter radius, to the best of Kane's estimation, proceeding from the base of the largest hill in the vicinity. Shorn soldiers bearing Dur Kofny's mark on their foreheads stood watch from platforms behind the wall. They kept their attention on the villagers, but Kane knew they would open fire on him if he attempted to bolt. Kofny had trained them well; they were all business, showing no signs of boredom. They did not joke among themselves, nor attempt to bully or impress the people they watched over. They barely spoke at all.

Kane craned his neck to examine the camouflage canopy. It wove its cunning way through the surrounding foliage, tied around tree trunks with fibrous strips of wood. As he watched, two of the soldiers, high in a tree, repaired a hole in the canopy with fresh twigs and leaves.

The fort was one of five such outposts under Dur Kofny's control—or so he had boasted when he had brought them here the previous night. Kofny had boasted of many things.

As they had ridden in the transport, bouncing and jostling over the rugged terrain, Kofny had expounded on the wonders of what he called his "empire." It stretched from the coast of Southland all the way to the highlands Kane had first spied from the air—about 130 kilometers, if his figuring was correct—and from the Killflood River in the north to the desert in the south, known simply as Wasteland. From his study of Petran maps, Kane estimated it was an equivalent distance.

They had traveled for about an hour before coming to a stop outside the fort. By night, the palisade had loomed black and ominous, firelit orange from within. The soldiers had escorted them through the gate and shown them to the sheltered wooden stalls, prisoner pens, where they had spent the night. The pens were lined with dried native grasses, like stables, and were just large enough to house four apiece. Kofny had provided them with some food, strips of dried meat and small packets of grainy seeds, and then retired inside the fort.

Kane had been stuck with Cromberg, Orem, and Raxel for the night. They had slept poorly in the cold, huddling next to each other under the grass for warmth.

As he walked, Kane found himself unable to stop thinking about the allcomm Dur Kofny had confiscated, residing in that pouch on his belt. Kane hoped against hope that Sason had tracked the signal he had sent, but he doubted it. She wouldn't have had time. And even if she had, she would only know the location of the wounded lander. If she sent another, it would never find him.

By Kane's reckoning, he couldn't be more than thirty kilometers from the coast—still within the allcomm's range. And with the lander's antenna now properly positioned, he could contact the Portship. If he could just get the allcomm back, send another signal…

Footsteps crackled in the undergrowth behind Kane—Cromberg, apparently also out for a morning constitutional. Kane shook away his musings and greeted him.

Cromberg grunted in reply. Remnants of grass hung in his hair and beard.

"Rough night," Kane said.

"I've had rougher. North of the Fracture on Mainland, nights can get mighty cold."

They meandered through the village, taking in the sights, such as they were.

"Quite the setup they have here," Kane said. "Do you have anything like it on Mainland?"

Cromberg shook his head. "Nothing this big. We make use of caves, mostly. This Dur Kofny, whoever the hell he is, knows a lot about construction. Knows about a lot of things, really."

"He's ex-military," Kane said. "That much is obvious."

"And totally bugfuck crazy. Got himself set up like some kind of god, here in the forest."

Kane, who had already come to the same conclusion, nodded as they walked.

Cromberg leaned in closer and lowered his voice: "If I get the chance, I'm gonna kill him. With my hands if I have to."

Kane stopped. "No. You can't just—"

Cromberg spoke through clenched teeth. "Yes, I *can*." He grabbed Kane's upper arm in an iron grip and moved him along. "Stop gawking; you're drawing attention."

Kane glanced at the villagers watching them, then looked back at the fort. The wall and its lookouts were still visible through the trees. He resumed walking.

Cromberg released his arm. "I'm not interested in waiting to find out what he's going to do with us. Good old Hal thinks he can talk his way out of this. He's full of shit."

"If Kofny wanted us dead, he would have killed us by now."

"Kofny's out of his fucking mind. If he wakes up today in a bad mood, he'll have his soldiers spit us on those stakes." Cromberg flicked a hand in the direction of the fort. "And if not today, then tomorrow, or the next day. I ain't waiting for that to happen. So if the opportunity presents itself, you just stay the hell out of my way."

"Cromberg, listen to me. Even if you *do* manage it, you would die moments later. Those soldiers of his are fanatics."

Cromberg looked straight ahead. "Yeah. I know."

"Then why—"

"There would be chaos afterward. And you can bet your ass I'll go down fighting. I'll take a few of them with me." He glanced sidelong at Kane. "Some of you might be able to make it out in the confusion."

"So you've made up your mind to die, is that it? A noble sacrifice for the rest of us?"

Cromberg nodded. "Something like that. Better than I deserve, probably, but I'll take it."

Kane slowed. Cromberg continued ahead of him, oblivious. "What do you mean by that?" Kane said.

Cromberg stopped and turned. "I ain't some revolutionary like Hal. For a while, I thought maybe I could be. But I see now that's never gonna happen. Fallon's dead, and we left Roman and Berian behind to die, too. They won't ever escape Petra, and they never should have been here in the first place." He trudged on.

Kane hurried to catch up with him. "And you deserve to be here, is that it?"

Cromberg spat. "I killed a man on Adriana, Pythen. It was just supposed to be a robbery, but he made a move for my gun…and I was high on 'Phoria. I blew his head off. Didn't feel anything at the time. Seemed like something that happened in a dream. I was so high I didn't even bother ditching my clothes; I was covered in the guy's blood." He paused and leaned against a tree. "Adriana enforcers caught me the next day. I was in the middle of a comedown from the 'Phoria. Cowered in a shivering little ball, drenched in sweat. Never even had a lawyer or a trial. Pleaded guilty and got shipped to Petra a month later." He took a deep breath, head back, eyes closed. "Guy was just a businessman working late, that's all. He had a wife, three kids. One of them was a newborn."

Kane stood, irresolute. His instinct was to put a hand on the man's shoulder and tell him he needed to let go of the past, but he thought of Tayla and Shamlyn and just couldn't do it.

"All the wrong people are dying," Cromberg said. "If anyone else should get left behind, it should be me."

They stood in silence. Kane bowed his head. The sounds of the forest—chittering of unseen animals, wind rustling the leaves, villagers calling to each other—swirled around them.

Crunching footfalls approached. Kane looked up.

Three of Dur Kofny's soldiers—very young, all of them, perhaps no older than Fallon had been—came upon them from behind. The tallest one said, "Back inside. He's ready for you now."

Kane and Cromberg faced each other. "Remember what I told you," Cromberg said. He headed toward the fort. Kofny's soldiers parted to let him pass, then looked to Kane. He started walking, too.

The soldiers led them into the fort proper, a set of interconnected, irregular chambers with earthen walls, supported by logs and stone. Squarish vents cut into the ceilings let in fresh air and some daylight, muted by the permanent shade of the camouflage canopy. Small torches mounted on the walls provided flickering illumination. No doors separated the chambers; Kane glanced inside several of them as he passed, noting sleeping soldiers, stacks of produce and bagged grain, stores of cloth, weapons, and unmarked containers he assumed had come from raids on transports.

They passed into a small tunnel, stooping to enter. The ground sloped as they proceeded; Kane had to step carefully to avoid slipping on the gravelly soil. They were going deep into the heart of the hill. The amount of time it must have taken to dig out all of this—impressive. Dur Kofny's boasts from the previous night seemed more plausible. And this was only one of five such places.

They emerged into a larger chamber, some ten meters across and half as high, lit by torchlight. Other entrance/exit holes, six in all, radiated in every direction. Hal, Miga, and the others sat on rows of log benches to Kane's right, guarded by some of Kofny's soldiers. Hal looked up as Kane and Cromberg entered.

Dur Kofny himself reposed at the far end, seated on a wooden chair upon a dais of solid stone, flanked by two more soldiers. These two wore strips of red crisscrossed fabric, like Kofny, but no gold chains. Their musculature bulged from their uniforms. Personal bodyguards, Kane figured.

The soldier escort shoved him and Cromberg toward the wooden benches. Cromberg glared at the one who pushed him. For a moment, Kane feared he was about to do something rash, but he sat. His gaze wandered about the chamber.

Kane sat with Hal and Miga on the first bench. The wood had

not been shaped or sanded; its knotty bark bit into his back and buttocks.

Dur Kofny raised his arms. "Now we can begin. Be it known that we are assembled here today to decide the matter of these defendants." He nodded toward the benches. "The boss of the Night Riders has arrived and will be heard first. Bring him in."

From an entrance hole behind Kofny's left shoulder, a figure stepped into the chamber—a bald man, his head and chest painted black, his nose crooked and swollen—the leader of the Southlanders that had attacked the lander. He moved stiffly, favoring his wounded hip, now bandaged. He bowed before Dur Kofny.

"Speak," Kofny said.

The Southlander cleared his throat. "General." He jabbed a finger at Kane, Hal, and the others. "They came into Ferrum without our say-so. They tried to move in on our territory. They fired on us. Sixteen dead, and bullos, too."

"Yes, so you told me," Kofny said. "What is it you want?"

"We pay our tribute to you every month. We never miss. That's the law. And we want what the law says—blood for blood."

"Don't lecture me on the law." Kofny spoke as if reprimanding a child. "When I'm in chambers, I *am* the law."

"Blood for blood. We pay our tribute." The Southlander bowed again and stepped aside.

Kane discerned some of the social structure. *Boss...territory...tribute.* The painted man led a gang, not a tribe—an outfit calling themselves the Night Riders. They got their own little piece of Kofny's "empire" in exchange for regular payments, in whatever passed for currency on Petra—food and supplies, most likely. A giant protection racket, typical prison society. Kane wondered how many other gangs paid tribute to Kofny.

Silence fell in the chamber as Kofny considered, glancing from the Night Rider to Hal and his people. His gaze came to rest on Kane. "You," he said, and pointed. "You will speak for all of them."

Kane sat, nonplussed. To his right, Hal rose. "Wait, General. I lead these—"

Kofny cut him off with an upraised hand. The soldier nearest to Hal slammed the butt of an assault rifle into his stomach. He doubled over, gasping.

Cromberg, Miga, and the others came to their feet. The soldiers raised their weapons to fire.

"No!" Kane stood, spreading his arms as if he could stop Hal's people from rushing. For a wonder, they held their places. "All right. I'll speak for them."

Hal, still doubled over, unable to talk, nodded. He sat, pulling two of the others down with him.

Slowly, the rest of the Mainlanders resumed their places on the benches. The soldiers kept their weapons raised. Kane extended his hands in front of him, palms up to show they were empty, and stepped toward the center of the chamber. He faced Kofny and bowed as he had seen the black-painted "boss" do. "General, we—"

"Is it true?" Dur Kofny said. "Or are you going to call one of my bosses a liar?"

"We had to make an emergency landing at Ferrum. We're not after anyone's territory. When the…when the Night Riders attacked, we only defended ourselves."

The boss bared his teeth at this, but held his ground.

Dur Kofny raised an eyebrow, smiling. "You're pleading self-defense? That doesn't happen much here."

"We—"

"The Night Riders lost sixteen. How many did you lose?"

"They had arrows and spears. We had—"

"*How many*?" Kofny's voice reverberated in the chamber.

Kane swallowed hard. "Three, General."

Kofny nodded, lips pursed. "Only three. Well. Seems to me that sixteen of theirs was a bit…excessive."

Kane realized how silly he sounded, trying to defend himself and the others in this kangaroo court. All of this was just a show, a way for Kofny to fire up his soldiers and intimidate his prisoners. He wanted something. The sooner Kane played along, the sooner he would find out what it was.

If he wakes up today in a bad mood, he'll have his soldiers spit us on those stakes. And if not today, then tomorrow, or the next day.

Kofny said, "I rule from the ocean to the highlands, from the Killflood to Wasteland."

His soldiers murmured their assent.

Kofny pointed at Hal. "You knew my name, all the way across the ocean. If you know who I am, then you *must* have known that you can't waltz through my empire without permission. The Night Riders pay tribute for my protection. I can't just allow you to land here and start gunning them down. You have paid no tribute at all."

Hal opened his mouth to speak, then closed it. He seemed to be catching on.

Kane saw where this was going. He recalled the way Kofny had ogled the lander. The man had a liking for technology. Kane glanced at the Mainlanders. They were all watching him, waiting. He faced Kofny again. "What tribute can we offer you, General? Would our ship be sufficient?" It would never fly again, anyway. Kane only needed the comm array one more time. He would worry about that later.

A slow smile spread over Dur Kofny's face. Kane got the distinct impression the man was toying with them. The air in the chamber seemed to thicken, redolent with the smell of earth, burning torches, and body odor.

"You can start by telling me the truth."

"I have."

Kofny's smile vanished, replaced by a scowl. He leaned forward in his chair. "Look at me, man. Look long and hard. Do I present the appearance of a fool? Of a dolt?"

"I…no, General."

"You're standing in my chambers. You're only alive because I suffer it. You would do well to stop playing games with me and answer my fucking questions." The scowl smoothed out, and Kofny reclined once more. "Now then. You didn't swim across the ocean to get here. You flew in that lander of yours, carrying that raggedy bunch of Petrans sitting behind you."

Cromberg muttered something unintelligible and was shushed. Kane ignored it; at this juncture, he didn't want to risk looking over his shoulder.

Kofny's gaze remained focused on him. "You have already admitted you're not Petran. And you're certainly not from Control. If memory serves, the markings on your lander are…Jurisian?"

Kane nodded.

"Speak up, if you want to keep your tongue."

"Yes, General."

"I've spent most of the night trying to figure out, first, what a Jurisian is doing on Petra, second, why he's ferrying around a group of heavily armed Mainlanders, and third, how they managed to crash on my land. I'm an educated man, but I confess you have me stumped." Kofny took a breath and adjusted the strips of red cloth crisscrossed over his chest. "You asked what tribute you can offer. I'll say it one last time: you can start by telling me the truth. Who are you, and what are you doing here?"

Silence stretched as Kane considered his answer. He saw little point in lying. In fact, doing so could be disastrous. Dur Kofny was a megalomaniac, but that didn't preclude shrewdness. And Kane was far out of his element, thrust into this madman's circus and operating on limited sleep. He doubted he could weave a convincing story that would hold up to any kind of cross-examination. If Kofny caught him in a lie, they were all dead.

He told the truth, starting with his name, then recapping the events of the past two days: the purpose of the trip to Petra, the raid on Control, Hal's plan for escape, the abortive attempt at launching in the storm. Throughout, Kofny remained impassive; Kane could not tell if he believed a word of it.

Kane finished, and silence fell again. Kofny looked over the Mainlanders, considering each of them in turn, before focusing again on Kane. "Fugitives. That much I figured. The rest I doubt I would have ever guessed. So tell me, Kane Pythen of Juris, are the skies over Southland about to be filled with Control ships hunting for you?"

"Not if they think we died in the storm."

Kofny shook his head. His shoulders shook with silent, mirthless laughter. "I'm not a fool, Pythen, but I think you might be if you believe they won't figure it out." He glanced upward with a vague wave. "The skies belong to Control. Their satellites will spot that lander sooner or later—if they haven't already. And when they do, the bombings will begin again. They'll blast the highlands to rubble, burn the forests flat, then scour the ashes until they find your bones. You've done much worse than trespass and kill a few Night Riders. You may very well have doomed us all."

Kane's insides sank as if leaden. He held himself rigid, telling himself that all this was just a show, a mere thumping of the chest, intended to frighten them. None of that changed the fact that Kofny had an excellent grasp of the situation. If he was trying to scare them, he was succeeding.

An angry buzz rose from Kofny's soldiers. Even his two bodyguards, stoic to this point, glowered at Kane.

Kofny stood and made a cutting motion with one hand. "*Quiet!*"

The buzz stopped. His bodyguards snapped to attention.

Dur Kofny stepped off the dais, advancing. Kane held his ground, but kept his eyes averted. Kofny got near enough for Kane to smell the man's rotten breath. "I don't know," Kofny said. "Maybe the smartest thing for me to do is light a signal fire, bring Control here myself…and turn you over to them. Yes, that seems safest. They might even be grateful."

The general paused as if awaiting a response, some attempt to dissuade him—or perhaps anticipating a plea for mercy.

Maybe Cromberg was right about the man. If that were the case, Kane had nothing left to lose. He took a step closer to Kofny, speaking so that only he could hear: "Is that all you are, then? Rolf Ankledge's lackey?"

Kofny backhanded him across the face. The force of it drove Kane to the ground. His cheek stung; the salt taste of his own blood flooded his mouth. He wiped a surprising quantity of it from his split lip. Kofny stood over him, hand raised for another blow.

Still on all fours, Kane looked up. He raised his voice: "What are you going to say to him? Will you ask him not to bomb you this time? Or will you beg?"

Kofny's face twisted with rage. He kicked Kane in the ribs. Kane collapsed, his wind gone.

"*You're* the one who should be begging, if you knew what was good for you!"

Kane heard scuffling in the rear of the chamber. He rolled over so he could see. Cromberg was on his feet; Hal, Orem, and some of the others were restraining him. Hal had hold of one arm; Orem had lowered a shoulder into Cromberg's chest. Every weapon in the place was now trained on him. The soldiers kept their cool, but if he got free, he would be dead before he took his first step.

Kane dragged in wheezing breaths and raised himself to all fours again, then to his knees. Kofny watched him, hands on hips, eyes wide and wild.

With a mighty effort, Kane summoned the strength to stand. He swayed on his feet, fighting to breathe. The sticky warmth of his blood trickled down his chin.

"Anything else to say?" Kofny said.

Shoulders heaving, Kane worked to get his wind back. Oddly enough, he felt more in control of the situation now. That Kofny hadn't killed him for his insubordination was all the proof he needed that this was indeed a show. And as poor as his bargaining position was, he might still have something to offer.

"General," he said, and wiped blood from his chin again. "Consider this: if we get off Petra, the warden is finished. Control is finished. That means no more bombings. No more skimmers. No more surveillance. Ever."

Kofny turned away, disgusted, and returned to his chair. Kane risked a glance back at Cromberg. The others succeeded in easing him back to the bench.

"A bit optimistic of you," Kofny said.

Kane brought his eyes front.

Kofny flexed the fingers of both hands as he spoke. "Even if what you say is true, what would stop a new warden from moving in?"

"The Petra Compact would fail."

"Someone would fill the void, sooner or later."

"Maybe so, but in the interim, you'd have time to fortify your position here."

"Hmpf." Kofny's mouth twitched, but no smile was forthcoming this time. "Military man, are you, Kane Pythen?"

"Years ago."

"That's where you learned to fly?"

"Yes." A horrid suspicion dawned in Kane's mind.

"Well. I'll say this for you: fool you may be, but it takes real courage to shoot off your mouth to me in my chambers. Especially when you and your friends are on trial for your lives." He nodded, as if confirming his words to himself. "But even if you were by some miracle to get offworld, I'm not so romantic as to believe that any of these *Mainlanders*"—he sneered the word—"would give one rat's ass about Petra. I think they'd scatter to the farthest corners of Ported Space and spend the rest of their miserable lives in hiding. And you, Pythen, with your position of privilege and comfort back on Juris, would never be willing to take on the entire Petra Compact yourself. You have the air of a man with too much to lose."

I'm not interested in joining the revolution. I just want to go home. I'll help you get off Petra, but after that, you're on your own. Kane's own words, back on Control. He couldn't deny them.

"So idealistic as your suggestion may be, I think I have a better idea." Kofny lifted his chin. "I've decided."

Kane waited. He knew what was coming, what the entire charade had been about.

"I'll take your lander, Pythen—as *part* of the tribute you owe me. We'll hide it in the forest so Control will never know it was here." He paused. "For the rest of your tribute, you will stay here, and teach my soldiers how to fly."

Kane closed his eyes.

"We have ways of bringing down Control's aircraft, and even of turning them to our use, as you have seen. Most of them, unlike your lander, are still flight-worthy."

Kane opened his eyes at that.

"Yes," Kofny said, "my people noticed the damage on the starboard side. Rather hard not to, really." He dismissed it with a shake of his head. "Now, I was never a pilot, and neither were any of my soldiers. In truth, before they came to Petra, few of them knew little more than thieving, rape, and murder."

Kane rubbed at his ribcage, where Kofny had kicked him. His lip still stung.

Kofny was looking past him now, his gaze distant. "But they can be trained. The proof is all around you. I will supply you with my best, my smartest. You will instruct them in combat flight technique. And then no one in Southland will even dream of opposing me, ever again. The other warlords will crawl to this chamber in tears. Someday, I might even have a fleet to match Control's."

The soldiers erupted with raucous cheers, making Kane start.

When they subsided, Kane said, "General, Control still owns the skies. They have their satellites. If they spot unauthorized ships flying, they'll—"

Kofny looked at Kane. "Petra's a big world. They can't watch every meter of it every minute. And they don't have many eyes on my lands. Already, they fear to fly here. They've altered their flight patterns. They've stopped making drops.

"You'll avoid detection. And when the time is right, we'll *let* them see us flying. Once they realize they've lost their monopoly on air power…" His face softened; his voice dropped to a whisper. "It'll be glorious."

Kane could not mistake the finality in Kofny's words. The man's delusions of grandeur only cemented the deal.

The Night Rider boss, who had been standing to one side,

stepped forward. "And what about us? Sixteen dead! What do we pay our fuckin' tribute for?"

Kofny sighed theatrically. "Oh, calm yourself. I haven't forgotten why we're here. Stand down."

The boss fidgeted for a moment, shifting his weight from foot to foot, before resuming his place.

Facing the Mainlanders, Kofny extended a hand to the painted boss. "The Night Rider speaks the truth. They pay tribute for a reason. The law is clear: blood for blood. You killed sixteen Night Riders under my protection. They killed three of yours. That leaves you thirteen lives short. Tomorrow at dawn, you will settle up."

Kane expected Cromberg to lunge again, but he only sat, shaking his head. Hal, on the other hand, was on his feet. "You can't—"

Kofny's soldiers, already primed by the previous outburst, wasted no time. Two of them got in front of Hal, jabbing the barrels of their weapons at his chest.

Kofny said, "Unless you care to do it now?"

Anguish and anger warred across Hal's face.

"Hal, stop!" Kane extended his arms in opposite directions, as if directing ground traffic. "Wait a minute here. Just wait." He faced Kofny again. "General, they were only defending themselves. Don't—"

"I've heard both sides of the story, and I've decided." Kofny looked bored. "I'm not in the habit of repeating myself, Pythen."

"If you hurt these people, I won't teach your soldiers to fly."

"Then you'll die at dawn, too." Kofny said it easily, matter-of-factly. "No need for such drama. Besides, by my count, there will still be"—he made a show of looking over the Mainlanders—"three of your friends left."

"If you kill me, you can kiss your dreams of commanding a fleet goodbye."

Kofny chuckled. A genuine smile appeared. "I'm a patient man. If we can't fly now, we'll fly later. Maybe the next time we down a skimmer, we'll take the pilots prisoner instead of killing them." He shrugged. "Your choice, Pythen."

Kane ran out of words. He looked back. Hal was still on his feet, but all the fight had gone out of his stance. He stepped back, his face expressionless.

Kofny stood and crossed to Hal. The soldiers that had interposed themselves parted to let him pass. "I'll give you the day to decide which ones will pay the tribute. Draw straws, pick numbers—I don't care how you choose. You say you lead this little gang of Mainlanders. Let's see just what kind of leader you are." He paused. "If you were a true general, you would be willing to lay down your life for your people. Something to think about while you're deciding."

Dur Kofny exited the chamber through the same hole he'd used to enter. His bodyguards trailed him, followed by the Night Rider boss, who gloated as he left.

CHAPTER NINETEEN

As the soldiers led them out of the central chamber and back to the prisoner pens, Miga caught Cromberg's gaze. He nodded in her direction. She made certain she walked next to him so they could get in the same pen.

She had paid scant attention to the "trial." It felt to her like an abstraction, an event happening to someone else, and she was just observing. And she had been wrestling too much with her own mind to care.

She kept getting dispatches from the blind spots in her memory. Just flashes, but they left impressions, afterimages. And they had become more frequent since landing in Southland, since the attack that had killed Fallon.

The bullo-riding gang weren't like the Bone Tribes—more sophisticated weaponry, for one thing. And no Bone Tribesman would bother with domesticating bullos. Nonetheless, the Night Riders' painted faces and bodies and their predilection for tropograss were a little too familiar.

Various parts of her body ached with each memory flash, recollections of old wounds. A gash in her shoulder burned as she glimpsed a bone knife stabbing at her. The Night Rider boss's gloating smile as he'd exited the chamber called to mind a Bone Tribesman's painted face hanging over her, teeth gritted, and the noise of guttural growls; her crotch stung as she thought of it. As they emerged from the fort and were escorted to their pens, she could hear from over the wall the sounds of children playing in the "village;" their cries and catcalls mingled with shrieks from the past and images of splattering blood and crushed skulls. Her stomach roiled.

Taken singly, the flashes meant nothing. But as a whole, they began to form coherent pictures. She checked her hands as she walked. They trembled, just a little. Her control was slipping.

They arrived at the pens. She went in the furthest one on the left, with Cromberg and a couple of the others behind her. She turned in time to see Hal and Kane attempting to get into the same pen, but the soldiers shoved them into the next one. Good.

The wooden door closed—a flimsy thing, like the pens themselves, comprised of bundled branches and scrap lumber lashed together with vines. Daylight shone through numerous gaps. As cells went, they were far from secure, but they weren't meant to be. Even if a prisoner got out, Kofny still had his soldiers and the fort wall, which only had one gate, and that well guarded.

Initials and hash marks had been carved into the wood here and there, evidence that the pens had been used many times.

Cromberg whispered, "We're getting out of here. By dawn, we'll be gone."

Miga nodded. Gone, or dead trying.

Another flash, this one of a much more current memory—sitting at a workstation in the Hub on Control. These were the worst of all, though she could not say why. Rage surged in her. She put it down, yet again. The effort it took was tiring.

Memories from only a few days ago were beginning to affect her as badly as those phantom moments from her before-time. Worse, even. She feared that if she lost control now, she would never get it back, that her sanity would shred like ancient paper, become scattered and lost.

She went to a corner of the pen and sat, hugging her knees. It helped still the trembling in her hands.

Black.

She shook all over. No, correction: someone was shaking her. She came back to herself.

Cromberg had her by the shoulders. "Miga!" he whispered. "Hey. What's wrong with you?"

"Get your hands off me right now."

Cromberg released her and stepped back. Orem and the other

Mainlander in the stall—Varley, Miga thought her name was, gray-haired but sinewy and tough—regarded her warily.

Annoyed, she said, "What's the matter with you?"

"We've been talking for the last five minutes," Cromberg said. "Did you hear a word of it?"

"I—" Oh, no. Not blackouts again. Not now. Her head ached. "Just…just say it again."

Cromberg glanced over his shoulder, looking at the wall. Through the gaps in the branches, Miga discerned shapes moving on the other side. Hal was in that pen, as was Kane Pythen. She could hear their muffled voices, but could not make out anything they said.

"Hatching a brilliant plan, do you think?" Cromberg kept his voice low.

"We can get out of this," Miga said.

"Yeah. And we will. Before Hal decides which of us get to die tomorrow."

"He wouldn't do that," Orem said.

"Yeah? You sure?" Cromberg motioned for him to come closer. Orem shuffled through the piled grass and crouched at his side. Cromberg whispered, barely audible: "You don't know Hal like I do. This isn't just about escape for him; it never was. He's got his damned revolution to start. He's got to get his fucking *message* out. He's already sacrificed Roman and Berian. What makes you think he won't offer up all of us next?"

Orem ran a hand through his white hair and turned away.

"He had no choice with Roman and Berian," Miga said. "You know that." She defended Hal out of habit, but her confidence in him *had* been shaken of late. Or was that simply a function of her unraveling sanity? She couldn't tell.

"And he might think he has no choice now. Come on, Miga, you understand him better than any of us."

"Yeah, I do. He was the one who let you join us when you first came to Petra. Remember that? I voted to keep you out."

He winced. "That…that was different."

"We've all saved each other's lives. A couple of times over, in a few cases."

"I'm telling you, that was different." Cromberg rubbed his bearded face, hard enough to stretch the skin. "Sure, he'll want all of us to make it out of here. But can you honestly sit there and tell me he wouldn't give us all up if it meant *he* could get off Petra? He's got that messiah-of-the-masses bullshit going. You know that in his heart, he's thinking if anyone survives this, it has to be *him*. None of us could do his work."

Miga's headache worsened, throbbing. The hell of it was, she couldn't argue with him. Some of the same thoughts had crossed her mind. "What are you saying?"

He flipped a hand in the direction of the next pen, where Hal and Kane were still speaking in low, urgent voices. "We don't wait for him to decide anymore. We make our own plans. And we watch our backs."

Orem sat in the grass with his head resting against the door. "Oh, man. This is fucked."

"Tell me about it," Cromberg said, keeping his gaze on Miga. "So are you with me?"

She put a hand up in a warding gesture. Oh, it was so hard to think straight. Her head was bad, and getting worse. "If anyone's going to sell us out, it'll be Pythen."

Cromberg grumbled. "Yeah. He's a problem, too."

"Miga? Cromberg?"

It was Hal's voice, whispering. Miga could make out his shape in the next pen.

Cromberg pointed at her. "Think about it. If nothing else, watch your back." He looked to Varley and Orem. "You two. Keep an eye out for those soldiers. Yell if they get close enough to overhear."

Orem peered through the gaps in the door. Varley moved past Cromberg and Miga, looking out through the back of the pen.

Cromberg spoke over his shoulder: "What?"

"We're gonna get out of here," Hal said. "You know that, right?"

Cromberg shot Miga an *I-told-you-so* glance.

She crawled to the other side of the pen. "What do you have in mind?"

"These stalls are easy enough to get out of. The trick will be getting outside the wall."

Cromberg inched closer to Miga. "Yeah, we've thought of all that, Hal. Thanks."

Hal was silent for a moment. Taken aback, maybe. "Listen, we—"

"I'll get you out, Hal. Leave it to me. I'll get us all out. You trust me, right?" He looked meaningfully at Miga.

Again, Hal took several moments before replying. "Of course. But whatever we do, it has to be quiet."

A grim smile came to Cromberg's face. "No, I don't think so."

"I—what did you say?

"It's not gonna be quiet, Hal."

"No!"

Orem and Varley turned at Hal's outburst. "*Pipe down,*" Orem whispered. "Jesus."

Hal lowered his voice. "Cromberg, damn it, you're not going to pull some crazy stunt. That's an order. We're *sneaking* out of here. We need to put as much distance between us and them as possible before they discover we're gone."

Fading, fading. A cascade of images, sounds, sensations flashed through Miga's mind: blood, screams, the salty taste of cold, raw flesh, force-fed to her. Penned—in shelters even more crude than this one—like an animal with the other women, raped daily. And of sitting at a workstation in the Hub. The memories rolled past her eyes, a long-delayed tide finally coming in. She was powerless to stop it.

"All right, Hal," Cromberg said. "Whatever you say." But he shook his head slowly as he spoke. "And what do we do once we get out of here?"

"That's up to Kane. He—"

Black.

"...wait for dark."

Miga blinked several times in succession. Hal was still talking, Cromberg was still listening. No one appeared to have noticed the lapse. It couldn't have been very long. A minute or two, perhaps.

Deep breaths. Still the trembling. Focus. But the tide was coming in.

"Right," Cromberg said. "After dark."

Orem looked up from his peephole. "Someone's coming."

The whispers dried up. Outside the pen, soft footfalls sounded. Shadows cut off the light coming in through the gaps in the door. The figure on the other side lingered, silent.

Whoever it was moved on, and light shone through the door again. A collective exhale filled the stall.

That ended the discussion. No one spoke. Shifting and rustling noises from the adjacent pen told Miga that Hal had moved away from the wall. Orem and Varley gave up on their lookout duties.

Good.

Cromberg took her by the arm and urged her back toward the far corner. Exhausted, she allowed it.

"You heard that, right?" Cromberg said. She nodded vaguely. He was going away, becoming unimportant.

"He wants it quiet. Right. I'll bet he does. But that ain't gonna—"

Fading, fading. From far away, she caught snatches of his voice, gravelly even in a whisper: *knows so much…chaos…burn…*

Black.

CHAPTER TWENTY

Dur Kofny's soldiers let them out of the pens, one at a time, to use what passed for the fort's latrines—a row of covered benches over dug-out pits beyond the shoulder of the hill, north of the gate. Hal was grateful for that. He had feared they would force them to piss and shit in the grass of their pens. Thank God for small favors.

It also allowed him to get a better feel for the layout of the place and the positions of the guards. He had instructed the others to take mental notes every time they were let out. Probably they didn't need to be told, but now wasn't the time to overlook the details.

He took another trip to the latrines after the midday meal—more dried meats and seeds, washed down with some swallows of gritty water. Two guards escorted him to the benches and back, never taking their eyes off him. One of them was the woman with the burned jaw and neck, disconcerting to look at. And Hal had seen a lot of wounds. By contrast, the familiar stench of the latrines was just a fact of life, something he'd gotten used to in his fifteen years on Petra. In another life, it would have gagged him and made urination impossible. These days, his piss came easily in such places. He wondered if he'd even be able to adapt to polite society again, if he ever got out of here.

Then again, *polite society* had put him here in the first place.

The palisade hugged the contours of the hill and terminated at the shoulder, curving until it met a wall of exposed brown rock. A lookout post protected the fort's flank. Hal had no doubt there would be a similar setup on the other side. The sentries could also watch him piss, if they wanted, but evinced no interest once they saw his escorts.

A shit detail for those sentries—literally. Hal smiled at the thought.

He wondered what Kofny did when these pits filled up. Someone would have to empty them periodically, take the waste somewhere beyond the wall, well away from any water supplies, and perhaps burn it. Another shit detail, one with which he was not unfamiliar.

He finished his business and let them lead him back to the pens. Seeing the sun through the camouflage canopy was difficult, but the slant of the shadows told him the time was around midafternoon.

Cam and Ellis, who had been part of Hal's settlement on Mainland since its founding a decade ago, were taking the opportunity to catch some sleep before nightfall. Only Kane remained awake in their pen, standing at the door as the guards ushered Hal back in. "I have a request," Kane said to them. "Please tell General Kofny I'd like to talk to him."

The burned woman said, "Why?"

"I need to make arrangements with him. For the training."

She laughed. "The general talks when he pleases, comes when he pleases, and goes when he pleases."

"If you'll just tell him, I'll be grateful."

"I'll be sure to do that." She shoved Hal into the pen and shut and barred the door.

When the guards had walked on, Hal said, "Do you think she'll do it?"

Kane shrugged. "Probably. Maybe. I don't know."

"You have to get to Kofny before the rest of us can move."

"You make a habit out of repeating yourself?"

He was right. Hal had told him that at least twice already. Make that three times. He squatted, then sat in the grass, away from Cam's and Ellis's sleeping forms. "Sorry," he said in a low voice. "It's something I picked up. A lot of my people—well, there aren't many inmates on Petra with advanced educations, you understand."

Kane settled into the grass. He matched Hal's undertone: "Do you think this can work?"

"It has to work."

"That's not an answer."

"Best one I have for you right now."

Kane gave him a *give me a break* look.

"What do you want me to say?" Hal said. "A lot will depend on how good Kofny's soldiers actually are."

Kane spread his arms. "Take a look at this place. He didn't build it himself. I'm willing to bet they're pretty good."

"Yeah, well, so are we. Kofny will find that out soon enough."

But they weren't going up against Bone Tribesmen this time, nor even the raiding parties Hal had spent his days fighting on Mainland. These soldiers were another order of magnitude, at least as well trained as his own people—and better equipped.

Still, what he'd said to Kane had been the literal truth. It had to work.

Kane said, "You have to figure out a way to keep Cromberg in line. He has a death wish, you know."

"I know." Hal rested his head against the back of the pen and closed his eyes. "He's a good man to have at your side in a fight. But when he gets like this..." He let the thought dangle, opened his eyes. "Kane, everyone who volunteered for this mission knew the risks. They knew that a significant percentage of them wouldn't make it." He dropped his voice to a whisper. "I wish I could save them all, but"—he shook his head—"I'm realistic enough about our chances here. We're going to lose more, whether we wait for sunrise or not."

Some very dark thoughts popped unbidden into his mind, as they had when Dur Kofny had pronounced sentence. It was possible, however unlikely, that Kofny was a man of his word, that he would only execute thirteen of their number. He, Miga, and Cromberg could still come out of this and be allowed to go on their way.

Draw straws. Pick numbers.

Kofny's "blood for blood" law made a certain twisted sense in this environment. Killing Hal would profit Kofny nothing, and he would have no cause to fear retribution afterward. So it was quite plausible that Hal could walk out of this fort unharmed.

That wouldn't stop the Night Rider gang from setting upon them as soon as they walked out of the fort, perhaps, but it was a consideration.

He was dismayed by how tempting such thoughts had become.

No. These were his people. They had bled with him, even *for* him, too many times. As much as his long-suppressed sense of justice screamed at him to wreak holy vengeance upon Juris and the fetid, corrupt mass of the Petra Compact, he could not abandon what had become his extended family. The firebrand revolutionary that had been shipped to Petra fifteen years ago might have done it. But not the man he had become.

Besides, they would get nowhere unless Kane escaped, too. So one way or another, Hal had no choice but to incur Dur Kofny's wrath. The thought made him smile.

"Something funny?" Kane said.

"Not really. I need you to do something for me, Kane." Hal faced him. "If I don't make it out of here, I need you to carry on for me."

Kane leaned back, away from him. "What do you mean?"

"I know what you said about not joining the revolution. But, Kane—" A blockage formed in his throat. He cleared it as best he could. "If I die here, don't let it be for nothing. Not after all this. Please"—he put both hands on Kane's shoulders—"tell someone that Hal Ellum died on Petra."

In the ensuing silence, a cool breeze whistled through gaps in the walls.

"Don't talk like that," Kane said.

"Don't let it be for nothing. If not for me, then for everyone else here who shouldn't be." He recalled their conversation in the ship, just before landing in Ferrum. "Suppose you're right about Farside? Can you just let that go?"

Kane pushed Hal's hands off his shoulders. "All right, enough."

"Please, Kane."

Kane put up a hand, looking away. "Stop. Just stop, Hal. I hear you, all right? It won't be for nothing."

"Is that a promise? You give me your word?"

Kane let his hand drop and hung his head. "Yeah. My word."

"Look at me, Kane."

He did. His features seemed to sag as if weighted. But he kept his gaze steady. "My word on it, Hal. It won't be for nothing."

"Thank you."

Kane pushed some of the grass around, lay down in it, and closed his eyes. Hal remained sitting. He should try to sleep, he knew, but his emotions roiled within him. Better to take this time to get some measure of control over himself, to be ready when the time came.

An hour passed in silence, broken only by the whistling of a breeze or the sounds of soldiers walking past the pens, engaged in low-voiced conversation. Hal's inner storm subsided. He felt centered again.

Footfalls approached the pen. The door was unbarred and swung open, letting in late afternoon light. The burned woman stood there, weapon drawn. She stepped into the pen, gazing down at Kane, asleep on his side. She kicked him in the thigh, just hard enough to startle him awake.

He scrambled to a sitting position, blinking and squinting.

"Get up," she said. "The general wants you."

Cam and Ellis stirred. The burned woman backed out of the pen, keeping the barrel trained on Kane. He got to his feet.

"See you later," Hal said.

Kane acknowledged with a brief nod and walked out of the pen.

CHAPTER TWENTY-ONE

The vow he'd made to Hal still rang in Kane's ears as the burned woman brought him to a southern section of the palisade. Dur Kofny was conducting an inspection there, squatting, running a hand over the stakes, pushing against them. When he saw Kane and the burned woman approaching, he straightened and dismissed the soldier with a wave. She departed.

When she had gone, Kofny set hands on hips. "Weren't you paying attention in chambers? Are you still unclear as to the chain of command around here? How many more beatings will it take for you to understand?" He jabbed a finger into Kane's chest. "You don't give me orders. You don't summon me. If I see you, it's because I choose to suffer your presence."

"My apologies, General. I didn't intend to appear like I was summoning you. I know you're a busy man." Kane tried to speak with what he hoped was an appropriate balance of deference and confidence. Kofny seemed like a man who tolerated neither cowardice nor impudence.

The general remained stern. "What the hell do you want?"

"I'd like to see the aircraft I'll be training on. If that's possible."

It turned out to be the right thing to say. Dur Kofny's scowl evaporated. "I think we can arrange that. Wait here. This will only take a few minutes."

He satisfied himself that this section of the palisade was secure, then led Kane to the main gate. The sentries saw them coming and opened it as they arrived. Kofny favored each of them with a clenched right fist, held shoulder-high. The sentries returned the salute.

Once outside the wall, Kofny showed him to the transports, three in all, wings retracted, parked in a line in a large clearing along the northern shoulder of the hill. If Kane's orientation was correct, the latrines were just on the other side of the palisade. They were upwind of it, thank goodness.

The clearing had not occurred naturally. Tree stumps level with the ground dotted the area, and the forest's thick underbrush had been cut away, leaving only wispy grasses. The camouflage canopy stretched overhead, hiding the vehicles from prying eyes.

The nearest guards were a couple of sentries watching from a post on the other side of the palisade. That surprised Kane until he thought about it. What would a bunch of ragtag forest dwellers want with transports, anyway? They certainly couldn't eat them.

He walked around the vessels, checking for signs of damage or neglect. Blackened blast marks—from assault rifles, Kane guessed—peppered them. Rust stained the hulls at the seams, but nothing serious. Some of the viewports were cracked. He bent to inspect the wheels. Other than minor gouges and scuff marks, they appeared to be in good repair.

"You took all of these in raids?" Kane said.

"No one leaves them by the side of the road, Pythen."

"No, but…I'm just amazed at the condition they're in. They're all airworthy, you say?"

"As far as we can tell."

"I'd have thought they would have taken more damage."

Kofny smiled, arms crossed. "Some of them have. Those are broken up for scrap. Any excess fuel is siphoned off and stored, too."

Fuel. Kane hadn't considered it, but that had to be a major issue. "How many flyable craft do you have, General?"

Kofny looked into the woods for a moment, pondering. "Ten."

"Jesus." No wonder Control was afraid to fly here. "What kind of weapons do you have? Anti-aircraft batteries?"

"The transports have to land in order to disgorge new prisoners. That's when they're most vulnerable." Kofny ran a hand along the hull of the nearest ship. "Control tried everything to stop us—increased security, touch and go landings—but we adapted."

"Ten transports. How do you plan to keep them fueled and maintained? You can't scavenge forever."

Kofny gestured toward the woods. "You saw that settlement where you crashed?"

"Ferrum?"

"Call it whatever you like. It's dust now."

Kane recalled how picked clean the place had appeared, no structures left standing. "It had a fuel depot, didn't it?"

"And lubricants. And spare parts. So did a lot of settlements. We have more than you think, Pythen. And we're quite frugal with it. Don't you worry; we've done quite well with scavenging. It'll carry us a good long way. But"—he clucked his tongue—"you're right. Sooner or later, the fuel will run out. Especially since Control has stopped landing here."

Kane caught the way Kofny was looking at him. "That's why you want flight training. So you can range farther."

"I'm building a fleet here, Pythen. One day, when I have enough firepower, I'm going to lead a raid on Control. And when I do, I'll reduce it"—he pounded a fist on the lander's hull—"to rubble." He looked at Kane with a flinty expression.

Kane thought Kofny's fleet, if he ever assembled one, wouldn't make it halfway across the ocean before Rolf Ankledge's missiles rained down on them. But pointing that out to Kofny wouldn't get the allcomm back.

As Kane continued his bogus inspection of the ships, inside and out, Kofny went on. He boasted of the raids in which he'd acquired this or that transport. He spoke of the camouflaged trails they used to wind such unwieldy craft through the woods, and of how they moved mostly at night to avoid detection. He told gloating tales of other warlords' abortive attempts to steal transports of their own. The man's ego seemed as boundless as the ocean.

So it went for the rest of the afternoon and into the evening. Kane accompanied Kofny on his rounds through the village and to various sentry posts in and around the fort. He couldn't help stealing occasional glances at the pouch on Kofny's belt that bulged with the squarish outlines of Kane's allcomm.

As night fell, the general invited Kane to dinner in his quarters. Kane silently gave thanks; at last, some privacy in which he might be able to act.

It was the second time in three days he had dined with a power-hungry madman.

The accommodations weren't as luxurious as Ankledge's dining room, and the food was nowhere near as varied or as well prepared. But at least it was authentic Petran.

They ate in Kofny's private quarters—roughly hemispherical, about half the size of the chamber where the "trial" had been held. Illumination came from a short torch standing on a wide base, set in the hollow in the wall. Strips of dried leaves served as a curtain in the entryway. Woven mats, made from the same fibers that tied down the camouflage canopy, covered the earthen floors. A pile of grasses in an alcove marked Dur Kofny's bed—no better than those in the prisoner pens, except that Kofny got it all to himself.

The meal, served on square wooden dishes, was bullo meat on the bone—freshly cooked, not dried—and an assortment of small, hard fruits the size of large marbles, red and yellow and green. Their tastes ranged from sweet to outright bitter. Kane ate them, anyway. It was the closest he'd come to a decent meal since Control. He washed down the bitterness with water in carved wooden cups. It tasted flat, devoid of any grittiness. It must have been strained and boiled.

Kofny tore into his meat with gusto. For once, he spoke little.

Kane glanced at the pouch again. He did not trust in his skills as a pickpocket. The best he could hope for was that the man would doff his belt at some point, or perhaps drift off to sleep. Failing that, Kane would have to at least knock Kofny unconscious. He didn't have any kind of weapon—not yet, anyway. But Hal's plan to sneak out wouldn't be put into motion until after midnight. That gave him several hours.

Over dinner, Kofny grilled him for details of a training schedule. Kane improvised, drawing on his own training. "First, I'll have to get familiar with these craft. And your pilots will need to know every single onboard system before they leave the ground. The people you pick will need excellent memories." Kane could not help feeling amused as he talked. He had been required to study volumes of instruction manuals and had logged hundreds of hours in simulators before he'd first flown. The very notion that he could train pilots in these primitive surroundings was laughable. He had to be careful to keep his amusement from showing in his expression or his voice.

Kofny absorbed it all with nods, sometimes asking questions, as if he were a base CO—which, Kane supposed, the man probably had been at one point.

"Bottom line, Pythen: how long before they can fly solo?"

"At least a year."

"No." Kofny licked his fingers, which glistened with grease from the bullo meat. "No, that won't do. Six months."

"General, I don't think—"

"I don't give a shit what you *think*. If you can't do it in six months, you can't do it."

Kane made a show of pondering the deadline. He warned himself to be careful not to overplay it: power-mad Kofny might be, but he hadn't gotten this far by being stupid. "I suppose they don't need to be experts in dogfighting right away. I might be able to get them up in six months."

Kofny set down the haunch of meat he'd picked up. "No. No *mights*, Pythen. You'll either do it or you won't."

Kane bit into another of the hard fruits—bitter again. "I'll do it."

Kofny fixed him with another of his stares, then went back to his food.

They finished dinner. Kofny pushed their empty plates aside and swigged the water from his cup, draining it.

He finished with a satisfied *ahhh* and set the cup with the plates. "I don't have many vices, Pythen, but a general is entitled to a few perks." He pulled one of the pouches from his belt—not the one with allcomm, but another—and opened it. He removed what looked like a homemade cigarette—small, wrapped in a brown leaf. He lit it from the torch and took a long drag. Its end glowed red-orange, and it gave off a smell both sharp and sweet. Kofny closed his eyes and rocked his head back.

"Tropograss," he said. "We don't have the makings for fine wine here, so this will have to do." He held the cigarette out to Kane.

He knew better than to refuse. A token puff or two should suffice. He took the cigarette and dragged on it. The taste was strongly herbal. Heat seared his lungs. He held the smoke as long as he could before bursting into a fit of coughs.

Kofny smiled, took the cigarette back, and held it up. "Like gold around here. I pass it out to the troops on special occasions, and to the gang bosses, too. Good for morale." He chuckled. "Never let it be said I'm not a benevolent leader."

Even as the coughing fit subsided, the stuff began fogging Kane's senses. It was stronger than he'd supposed. He would have to be careful, or he'd end up sleeping through the night and missing his opportunity.

Kofny sat with his legs crossed, serene. "You're the first actual military man I've had in my camp, Pythen. I have high hopes for you. These others"—he waved in the direction of the curtained entryway—"career criminals, most of them. They can be trained as soldiers, but none of them are fit for command. But as a pilot and an officer, maybe you can understand what it takes to be a leader."

The high began to creep into Kane's awareness—not a manic one, thank God, but a slow pulse of endorphins. And that was only from one drag. No wonder it was so popular.

To Kane's relief, Kofny didn't offer more. He took another drag, stubbed out the cigarette on the floor, and returned it to the pouch. "That's enough for tonight, I think." He ran a hand over his bald pate, his gaze distant. "A leader, Pythen. A man who commands respect, a man who can make the hard choices. You follow?"

The general's voice seemed to be coming from kilometers away. Kane bit the insides of his cheeks, hard, trying to clear some of the fog. The injury from the crash bled afresh, but the tropograss blunted much of the pain. "Yes, sir," he said.

"On Grace-of-God, I ordered the deaths of a hundred and fifty-four civilians. Do you think that was easy? I assure you, it was not."

"Grace-of-God?" The name pricked Kane's memory. Grace-of-God had no trade or diplomatic relations with Juris, so news from there was sporadic. But he associated it with— "The Roseday Massacre?"

The words popped out before he could stop them.

Kofny's eyes widened—whether with anger or curiosity, Kane could not say. "You've heard of it, then."

"Only very little." It was the truth. Kane hadn't recognized the name Dur Kofny, and he knew only a few details about the incident. "Some kind of counter-terrorist operation gone wrong, wasn't it?"

Kofny became sullen, gazing at the floor. "Never trust what you hear and see in the media. You've been in combat, Pythen?"

"Yes."

"Then you know what it's like in the field. Nothing went wrong on Roseday. It was a conscious choice. My men had to patrol neighborhoods known to harbor terrorists. We had suffered two attacks in the previous week, attacks that had killed thirty of my soldiers. There were no leads. No one was helping us. We had to help ourselves. I saw what had to be done, and I gave the order." Kofny shook his head as if to clear it. "And it worked. That was the last time my soldiers came under attack. Terrorist activity dropped to zero."

He sighed. "But of course the media got hold of it. And that scared the politicians. And after that, there was no talking sense to any of them. The trial was nothing more than a publicity stunt, a chance for everyone to grandstand. The verdict was a foregone conclusion. I never even bothered testifying."

Kane edged away from him. Kofny paid no mind, lost in his recollections. "I'd do it again," he said. "It was worth it, if only to show the world how to do what needs to be done."

He looked at Kane. "Maybe you can understand that. Not now, of course. But someday."

Kofny stopped. He seemed to be awaiting a reply. Kane could not think of one.

"Shocked, are you? Well. Perhaps that's to be expected. But I have faith, Pythen. I have an instinct about you. I've always had a great admiration for Juris."

Rolf Ankledge had said much the same thing. Both of them had more respect for Kane's homeworld than he did.

"It's because I feel this...this..." Kofny's hands made circular motions in the air. "This *kinship*, I suppose. Anyway, it's why I've decided to save you from yourself."

The tropograss made comprehension difficult for Kane. He took several seconds to realize that Kofny had said something strange. "From myself?"

Kofny uncrossed his legs and stretched them. "Yes, of course. That plan you and your friends had for escape—it won't work. It will only get them killed."

Kane sat up a little straighter, frowning. "Wait...I—"

Kofny spoke in tones of a gentle scolding: "Did you really think I wouldn't expect something like this from you? That you would just let thirteen of your number be executed? No, I expected you to make a break for it. In the dead of night, correct? Maybe take out one or two of my soldiers by stealth, then make a run for the wall? Eh?"

Kane went cold. His stomach churned. He wondered how Kofny's men could have overheard them.

Kofny said, "Not difficult to figure out, really. I'll have some guards pulling extra shifts overnight, watching the pens. Any mass outbreak, however quiet, will be noticed. And the Night Riders will get their blood-for-blood a little sooner than expected."

Kane understood the reason for the tropograss now—to keep him impaired, even sedated. He bit the inside of his cheek again, cutting through the haze. "General, don't…don't do this."

Kofny put up a hand. "No, no. Don't beg. The law is the law." He pulled the pouch containing the allcomm off his belt and removed the device. "You're interested in this, of course." He held it up, examining it from several angles. "You've been staring at it all day. I should smash it, right here, right now. What would you do then?"

Again, Kane got the sense of being toyed with. Kofny wouldn't smash it, surely. He could make use of allcomms if his "empire" was as far-ranging as he claimed. Kane opted for silence. There was no good answer.

Kofny tucked the allcomm back into its pouch. "Well, when you're ready, Pythen, make your move for it. We'll see what happens." He picked up the plates and cups and stood. "For now, I'm going to get some more water. Tropograss makes me thirsty." Looking down, he said, "You'll spend the night in here, away from those friends of yours. The next few hours will be unpleasant for you, but you'll come through. And in the morning, you can start thinking about how you want to spend the rest of your days."

He went out. The leafy curtains rustled in his wake.

CHAPTER TWENTY-TWO

Miga sat in the darkness, grateful for it. She huddled in a corner of the stall, trembling uncontrollably.

Orem and Varley were snoozing. Cromberg was awake but silent, a shadow sitting across from her.

The tide had come in, bringing with it a flood of memories long suppressed. It was all she could do to keep from screaming and clawing at her skin until the blood ran thick. The sleeping demon that had occasionally showed its face in the past was awake now, straining for release.

Cromberg had noticed. He had tried asking her what was wrong, but had given up in the face of her silence. She doubted she was capable of coherent speech, anyway.

Out of nowhere, he said, "All right, to hell with it. We're gonna go. Hang on, Miga. Just a little bit longer." He nudged Orem and Varley. "Wake up." He went to the door and raised his voice: "Guard!"

Moments later, a shape, silhouetted by torchlight, appeared outside the stall.

"Need the latrine," Cromberg said.

The guard muttered something under his breath, but he unbarred the door and opened it. "All right, come on."

It was hard to tell in the darkness, but she thought Cromberg gave her a look over his shoulder before going out. The door closed. Orem and Varley stirred and sat up.

The tide…

The flashes from her memory stretched into longer glimpses, bringing with them some sense of chronology, a narrative structure. And she understood much that had gone before.

Those flashes from the Hub, for instance. They were showing her things she hadn't seen when they had been holed up there. And then there was the ease with which she had navigated Control's security systems and the way she had walked those corridors without consulting maps or diagrams.

She recalled faces that didn't belong to any of her comrades, faces of people she *knew*. A red-headed woman about her age, wearing a Petran uniform, stood out. A friend…a colleague.

Miga Bronn knew how that uniform could sometimes itch, how it felt stiff at the collar. She had worn it for many years.

"God," she whispered. "Oh, God. Oh, God. Oh, God."

She had come to loathe the job. She and her red-headed colleague—or was she a superior?—had learned what was going on here and been repulsed. They—and others—had decided to take action.

It would have been a simple matter to request termination of her contract, to go back home to her life on Adriana, with Willem and the boys. It would have hurt financially, but they could have worked through that.

Willem…the boys…

But those were mere concepts, abstractions. She couldn't recall Willem's face, nor bring to mind the boys' names. Her shattered consciousness still would not allow her to know those things. Or perhaps those memories were gone, wiped out by Petra and the choices she had made.

The knowledge that she had participated in this planet-sized travesty of justice, that she was guilty as an accessory to the wrongful imprisonment on Petra of untold thousands—unsupportable. She couldn't walk away.

She had spent months secretly gathering records from the archives, volumes of classified material damaging to every member of the Compact. Maybe she had left an e-trail that had led them to her. Or maybe her private messages attempting to establish a media contact, sent via Portship back to Adriana, had been intercepted. Or maybe—and this she thought most probable—

someone had ratted her out. Whatever the case, she had been discovered.

Imprisoned in the Holding Area.

Interrogated.

And on an unscheduled night flight, dropped off in the middle of Bone Tribe territory to die.

In a sense, she had. The woman Miga Bronn had been was annihilated on the southern plains of Mainland, destroyed by daily rapes, force-feeding of human flesh, and the sight of brutalities she could not remember, even now. The ghost of that dead woman had slept within Miga—until Hal Ellum had hatched his mad scheme to escape the inescapable.

It would have been better if he had never brought her on this mission, better still he hadn't let her join his settlement the day she'd stumbled upon it out of the wilderness, after having escaped the Bone Tribes.

The mindless shelter of her blackouts was gone. She rocked herself, shivering, silent tears streaming down her cheeks, helpless in the grip of surging emotions—anger, terror, despair, by turns homicidal and suicidal.

Oh, what they had done, what they had done to her. All of them.

Raised voices outside the pen roused her from her hellish memories. Shouts. The sounds of running feet. She caught only snatches:

"Hurry! Get..."

"...the hell is going..."

"Man down! Man..."

"...on the loose! Don't..."

Unsteady, Miga got to her feet. Orem and Varley were already standing, peering through gaps, their faces pressed against the door.

She came up behind them. "What do you see?"

"Not a damned thing," Orem said without turning around. "Some kind of commotion."

"Cromberg," she said.

"Gotta be."

"Cromberg?" That was Hal, speaking from the adjacent pen. "What are you talking about over there? Where's Cromberg?"

"Out there," Miga said.

The commotion intensified. And the night breeze brought with it a new smell—a horrible burnt stench unlike that of the woodsy aroma of campfires. Some of the soldiers outside were calling for water.

The wall between their pen and Hal's rattled. He was pounding on it from the other side. "Goddamn it, Miga! We agreed on a plan! It was supposed to be quiet!"

"I guess Cromberg decided something different."

"He'll get us all killed!"

Orem said, "Better that than to let them execute us at dawn. I'd rather go down fighting."

"I wasn't going to let that happen. Damn it, we had a *plan*!"

His voice grated on Miga. Through gritted teeth, she said, "Now we have a new plan."

That quieted him. Thank God. She recalled what Cromberg had said about Hal, something about him selling them out to Dur Kofny. And she wondered, not just about Hal, but about Kane Pythen.

Someone unbarred the door; it fell open, revealing chaos inside the fort. Yelling soldiers ran past, oblivious. The shadowy figure that had released them moved quickly to the next pen, and the next, and the next. Cromberg.

The prisoners emerged from their pens, gaping at the scene, glancing at each other.

Orem turned to her. "What now?"

"Get outside the wall."

Cromberg was already urging the others in that direction, working his way back to where she stood. They started running.

Hal had stepped out of his pen, along with Cam and Ellis, and was yelling something at Cromberg. Miga couldn't make it out. She looked across the expanse of the compound, toward the dug-out hillside, and spotted one of Kofny's soldiers pointing in their direction, also yelling. A moment later, assault rifle fire erupted. Clods of earth exploded in front of Miga. Blasts hit the pens, sending splinters flying.

Everyone scattered, ducking as they ran. Varley dropped, a smoking hole in her chest. Orem collapsed, clutching a leg and screaming, until another shot exploded his skull.

Weapons fire rained down on them from all directions. Miga ran on instinct, expecting to be hit any moment. The gate was too far away, and there was no cover between here and there. She headed instead toward the hillside, weaving and dodging among running soldiers. One of them, apparently quicker-minded than his compatriots, made a grab for her. Miga had a full head of steam by then; she lowered a shoulder and bulled through him, knocking him aside. She found an entrance in the hill and ducked inside.

She was in a tunnel. Before proceeding, she risked a backward glance. No one had given chase. The soldier she'd run through scrabbled to his feet, looking around. The chaos and the darkness of the entrance hid her.

She glimpsed the pens she'd just escaped. The bodies of her friends littered the ground all around them. The rifle fire had stopped. Many of the soldiers ran toward the northern side of the fort. An orange glow came from that direction. And that horrid stench had grown stronger. She recognized it then, an uncommon but hardly unheard-of smell on Petra—burning shit. Cromberg had set fire to the latrines, probably with a torch taken from an overpowered guard. And the fire was spreading, urged on by the breeze.

Someone charged into her from behind and ran on, into the confusion, oblivious to her.

A group of soldiers with weapons raised approached the pens, waving aside those running toward the fire, intent on the bodies on the ground.

Miga went further in, feeling her way along the wall. A few meters along, she found a recessed area, some kind of dug-out chamber. As she stepped into it, she tripped and fell onto a pile of something that smelled and felt leathery. A few moments of groping and fumbling in the darkness told her that she had stumbled onto a storeroom of bagged grains.

More soldiers ran past the storeroom and into the night. Miga sat on the bags, breathing hard, feeling over her arms, legs, and torso for any wounds. She hadn't been hit.

But plenty of the others had.

Another figure stumbled into the opening. Her breath stopped.

"Miga? Miga!"

Cromberg. His gravelly voice was unmistakable.

"Here," she said.

"I thought I saw you headed this way." He stepped into the storeroom and crouched. "Are you hit?"

She shook her head, then realized the futility of the gesture. "No."

"Bastards got me in the shoulder."

"Which one?"

"The left."

She reached for his shoulder. He sucked in a breath at her touch. Her hand came away sticky with blood. "You need a tourniquet."

He tore off a strip from the bottom of his shirt. Outside the storage area, someone ran past carrying a torch, briefly illuminating them. She caught the pained expression on Cromberg's face, the clenched teeth, before darkness descended again.

He put the cloth into her hands. "Here. Tie it."

She did the best she could without light, looping the strip around his armpit, tying it, and tightening until Cromberg grunted. Years of practice kept her hands steady.

"Thanks," he said. "Come on. We need to find Pythen before this whole place goes up in flames."

"The others?"

He was silent for a moment, breathing hard. "Gunned down, most of them. Thanks to Hal."

"Hal?"

"I took my escort out very quietly. He never got a chance to cry out. And the fire should have given us more time than it did. They knew what we were going to do, Miga. They were ready for it. Hal sold us out."

"Sold us…" That didn't seem right, but she couldn't say why. Her thoughts were too jumbled and scattered. "Hal—"

"Just like I said. He sacrificed us to save his precious fucking hide."

"It couldn't have been Hal. He's been penned up with us all day."

"Not during his trips to the latrine."

She supposed it was possible. But a more plausible suspect came to mind. "Pythen. He's been gone all day."

"Yeah, him, too. Maybe he's acting as Hal's messenger boy. Fucker."

"Did Hal get shot with the others?"

"I couldn't tell. Come on." He took her arm and guided her to her feet. "Pythen's in here somewhere. If he won't fly us out of here, he's gonna at least answer some questions before he dies."

"But…" She frowned, struggling to concentrate. "If Hal got shot, then he couldn't have been in on—"

"If we find him alive and unharmed, we'll know, won't we? Come *on.*"

He pulled her along, leading her deeper into the tunnels. The burnt smell intensified. Smoke stung her eyes.

CHAPTER TWENTY-THREE

It occurred to Kane that Dur Kofny had been gone a good while. He had claimed to be stepping out for some water. Meanwhile, a commotion seemed to be growing outside. And a strange smell filtered back to him.

He stood, swaying a little, and grabbed the torch standing in its hollow. The tropograss might have been wearing off a bit; he'd only taken one drag, after all. Or maybe he was beginning to adapt to it. He went out through the exit, careful to keep the torch from igniting the leafy curtain.

The tunnel from Kofny's private chamber stretched ahead of Kane, sloping a bit as it went. It was empty, but he could hear shouts echoing from somewhere and everywhere. They were difficult to pinpoint.

He started walking, trying to recall how he had gotten here. For all the work that had gone into it, the interior of the fort seemed small and straightforward. He didn't believe he would get lost. Ahead was the large chamber where Kofny had held court. Unless Kane's recall was faulty, the tunnel that led toward the entrance would be directly across from him when he got there.

As he proceeded, the strange smell strengthened. Something was burning, something other than torches.

He reached the large chamber. It, too, was empty, but the shouts were louder, easier to make out. He heard cries of *fire* and *evacuate*.

And something else, something that sounded an awful lot like his name.

He smacked himself in the face, hard. Then again. And again. Some of the tropograss fog receded. But he still heard someone calling: *Kane…Kane…*

Before he could stop himself, he stepped to the center of the room and raised his voice: "Hal? Hal?" He turned as he called out, sending his voice down the other tunnels.

Above the other shouts: "Kane! Where are you?"

Hal's voice seemed a little louder, but Kane still couldn't pinpoint a direction.

"Here! In the—" He paused, wondering what to call the chamber, anyway. His gaze lighted on the chair on its dais, where Kofny had pronounced sentence. "The throne room."

"Stay where you are; I'll come to you! Keep talking!"

Kane kept turning in a circle. "Here! I'm here! Hurry up, Hal! I think there's a fire somewhere!"

"No shit."

Kane whirled. The Night Rider boss, his black face paint smeared and running down his bare chest, entered through a tunnel to Kane's right. Teeth bared, the man brandished a crude knife fashioned from bone. Kane backed away, holding the torch in front of him.

The Night Rider advanced, shifting the knife from hand to hand. "You can burn it down. But you won't get away. Blood for blood. You gonna die now." And he charged.

Kane backed into the dais, stumbled, but somehow kept his balance. He swung the torch at the Night Rider. The man stopped short, dodging the flame, thrusting the knife. A crazed smile appeared on his face. He feinted left, right, left. "Scared? Huh? You scared yet? Boo!" He punctuated each sentence with another thrust. The torch held him at bay.

The Night Rider feinted again, then came straight at him.

Kane swung the torch, but the Night Rider batted it aside, hard enough to send it flying from Kane's hand. It skidded across the earthen floor. Kane spun left. The blade tore his shirt, its point just grazing his skin. The Night Rider crashed into the dais, knocking over the throne.

Kane ran for the guttering torch. The Night Rider recovered and charged again, snarling. Kane got to the torch just as the painted man leaped, tackling him from behind. Kane twisted as he fell, landing on his side. The knife blade gashed his right bicep. The pain dispelled the tropograss fog. He bucked and squirmed, supine, as the Night Rider straddled him. The man's muscled legs held him in place. The Night Rider raised the knife for a killing stroke.

"Kane!"

Hal's voice. He burst into the chamber from an entrance hole to the left, holding an assault rifle. The boss hesitated, the knife held high. Kane thrust the torch into his face.

The boss screamed and fell backward. Kane scrabbled away from him. The Night Rider sat up, his face burning. The flames spread with amazing speed, covering his head and chest in seconds, as if he'd been doused in oil. The body paint, Kane guessed.

The Night Rider boss's screams modulated to shrieks. He staggered to his feet, stumbled, and fell again, writhing and making sounds no longer identifiable as human.

Kane couldn't help gaping. He'd flown missions beyond count on Cassea, but he'd never before killed a man hand-to-hand. Horror suffused him, mingled with an unmistakable sense of triumph. It had been easier at the controls of a bomber.

Hal grabbed him and hauled him to his feet. The Night Rider stopped writhing and screaming; he became a flaming heap. The chamber grew hot and filled with the smell of burning flesh, at once sweet like pork and harsh like coal. Kane's stomach soured.

"Let's go," Hal said, and pushed him toward the hole leading outside. "Move!"

Numb, Kane moved, resisting the urge to cast away the torch. He and Hal ducked into the hole and scrabbled upward.

From behind him, Hal said, "Where's Kofny?"

The afterimage of the burning man hung in Kane's vision. The smell seemed caught in his nostrils. "I-I don't know. We have to find him. We need the allcomm."

They came to a series of irregular chambers that Kane recognized—storage areas, places for soldiers to bed down. He knew the way now and moved faster. "Where'd you get that rifle?"

"I grabbed it from a weapons stockpile. I don't even know if it's loaded."

"Where are—"

He stopped. They had rounded a final bend and stood in the exit. Flames engulfed the area beyond.

The stake wall burned in half a dozen places. Fire and hot ash from the camouflage canopy rained on the scene. Soldiers ran, carrying large skins of water and dumping them on the worst blazes, but to little effect. The gate hung open, unguarded, allowing Kane to see some of the forest beyond the wall. Some of the trees were catching.

In the center of the grassy clearing between the wall and the hill, Dur Kofny stood, bellowing orders.

Hal and Kane exchanged glances. Hal raised his rifle and took aim.

A yelling figure ran at Dur Kofny from behind and jumped on his back—Cromberg. Kofny collapsed, Cromberg on top of him. He grabbed for Kofny's head, trying to snap his neck.

"Shit," Hal said.

The two rolled and wrestled. Some of the soldiers spotted the fracas. They dropped their waterskin loads and ran for their leader. Hal opened fire on them. The rifle discharged cleanly, dropping two soldiers in their tracks. The others—three in all—turned toward him and Kane. Hal took them out before they could bring their weapons to bear. "Come on!" He ran for Cromberg and Kofny. Kane followed, shielding his head from the hot ash as best he could with one arm.

The fort was in complete uproar. Soldiers shouted conflicting orders, while some of their fellows ran for the gate. Baking heat filled the compound, accompanied by the roar of the flames.

Kofny and Cromberg clawed and flailed at each other. Kofny landed a blow on Cromberg's face; Kane heard the crack of bone from where he stood. Cromberg responded with an elbow to Kofny's throat, drawing a gurgling snarl. Kane flung the useless torch aside and grabbed for one of Kofny's arms before he had a chance to strike again. Hal got hold of the other. Together, they strained and hauled Kofny off Cromberg. Kane's wounded arm screamed in protest. Kofny thrashed, tearing free from their grasp, and drove a punch into Kane's midsection, knocking the wind from him. Kane fell, gasping in hot air. Kofny, on all fours, grabbed an ankle and pulled Kane toward him.

In spite of the din, Kane quite clearly heard Hal say, "Blood for blood." The rifle discharged, and half of Kofny's skull exploded. Blood sprayed Kane's face. Kofny's body thudded as it hit the ground.

Hal, Kane, and Cromberg froze in tableau. Cromberg regarded Hal with something like wonder.

"Put it down, Hal! Now!"

Kane took a moment to recognize the voice as Miga Bronn's.

She stood three meters away, holding a pulse emitter. She stood over the limp form of a soldier she had apparently just disarmed.

Hal, breathing hard, stared at her, his face a mask of incomprehension. "Miga…what—"

"You sold us out, just like Cromberg said. You son of a bitch."

Kane caught the expression on her scarred face—or rather, the lack of it. Her eyes were vacant, unseeing. Kane had no idea what she was talking about, but he doubted she had even noticed that Hal had just saved Cromberg's life.

Cromberg, his nose broken and bleeding, stretched a hand toward her. "Miga, don't. It's not—"

She swung the emitter toward him. "*Keep the fuck away from me*!" Spittle flew from her lips.

Cromberg cringed.

"All right." Hal set the rifle on the ground and straightened, palms out. "There. Now let's—"

She spun toward Kane. "And *you*. Carried Hal's message to Dur Kofny, did you? Just like always." She advanced on him. Kane scrabbled away. "Fuckers like you. Just sit and watch, never get involved, never risk your necks. You let Petra happen." She raised the emitter, sighting down the barrel. "*You let it happen! Do you know what they did to me*?"

"Miga! Stop!" Hal ran for her.

He'd taken two steps when Miga swiveled toward him. The emitter crackled, spitting blue sparks that hit him in the chest. His back arched; his arms flew wide. He fell a moment later.

"*No*!" Kane crawled over to Hal's motionless form. His mouth and eyes were still wide open in a gruesomely comical expression of surprise. Star-shaped burn marks blackened his shirt. Kane felt for a pulse at his neck with a shaking hand. He could discern none.

Cromberg screamed Miga's name. She remained still, the emitter aimed where Hal had been. Her lips moved soundlessly.

Somewhere, assault rifle fire boomed. Miga took a hit in the side, hard enough to spin her around. Another shot blew open her chest. She collapsed in a heap.

Cromberg grabbed Hal's rifle and returned fire in the general direction of the shots, toward the hill. Kane couldn't tell if he was hitting anyone, but the incoming fire ceased.

The air had become searing hot. Flames continued to rain all around them. Dur Kofny's soldiers were losing their fight with it. Kane spotted several of them running away, carrying armloads of supplies. Cromberg, kneeling next to Miga's body, bellowed at the sky.

Too many shocks at once, threatening to tear Kane's mind loose from its moorings. The sight of Kofny's body brought him some focus. He crawled toward it—on his belly, in case there were any more true believers left in the fort. With effort, he managed to roll the corpse over so that he could get at the allcomm.

He grabbed it and scrabbled over to Cromberg, who was still baying inarticulate rage and grief. Kane screamed in his ear: "Get up! Get moving!"

Cromberg swung a wild punch at Kane, but he ducked it and grabbed the bigger man by the shoulders. "You can die later if you want! But we're leaving *now*."

Cromberg looked from Miga's body to Kane, his face an agonized rictus.

Kane tried to haul him to his feet, but Cromberg would not be budged. "Come *on*. Don't let her die for nothing. *Move*."

At last Cromberg moved. They ran.

PART THREE

NOT FOR NOTHING

CHAPTER TWENTY-FOUR

Rolf Ankledge stood in the partitioned-off corner of the infirmary, gazing in disbelief at the corpses of the prisoners, Roman and Berian.

Cabot, the senior med, the man with the pockmarked face whom the warden had spoken with the previous day, stood between the two beds, shaking his head.

"This one I can understand," Ankledge said, nodding toward Berian's body. "He wasn't expected to survive. But damn it, I spoke with *this* one." He hit Roman's sheet-covered leg with the back of a hand. "He was fine. And you said his injuries weren't life-threatening."

"Warden, I'm as baffled as you. He just…slipped away. Maybe he had some medical condition we were unaware of, something that exacerbated his injuries."

Ankledge scratched behind an ear. "And do you suppose you'd care to tell me how a man with some mystery condition could have survived on Mainland for years with no access to medical care beyond rudimentary first aid? I'm no med, but that seems a little hard to believe."

Cabot tapped his chin, supporting the elbow with his other arm. "We'll know more after the autopsy."

"The man had a *broken leg*, for Christ's sake."

"Yes, Warden."

The man's manner grated on Ankledge—too unconcerned about

what had happened, too unfazed by Ankledge's obvious displeasure. Almost insolent, even.

No. It was more than insolence. This doctor was lying to him.

Traitors. Snakes. Emma Goring was just one of many. Control crawled with them. Of course they wouldn't sit still while Ankledge had two prisoners in custody capable of ratting them out.

As if the day hadn't been difficult enough already. The search teams had turned up nothing. As the hours had worn on with no reports of success, Ankledge could think only of how this would look on the other side of the Portal. News of its closure would be spreading. The backlog would be growing. Questions would be asked. Every passing moment increased the likelihood of leaks to the media. Mardell's report would be generating all kinds of heat on Cassea, discomfort that would soon become contagious.

And now this.

Ankledge's hands clenched and unclenched. He stepped closer to Cabot and spoke in a low voice: "Doctor, are you happy here on Petra?"

Cabot stopped tapping his chin and folded his arms. "Now, why wouldn't I be happy here, Warden? Is there some reason I shouldn't be happy?"

"Watch your tone, Doctor. If I give the word, you'd be in the Holding Area in a matter of minutes."

"The Holding Area. For what? Am I being accused of something?"

They dueled eye-to-eye for long moments. Ankledge had to give him credit: for a doctor, even a Petran doctor, the craggy-faced man stood his ground well.

"The autopsies will be completed tonight." Ankledge cocked a thumb at his chest. "And *I'll* pick the examiner."

"Suit yourself, sir."

Ankledge's allcomm chirped. He snatched it off his belt and answered it.

Chief Mehr was on the line. "We have her."

Ankledge frowned at the doctor. "Disappear."

Cabot obliged, leaving him alone with the two corpses.

Ankledge spoke into the allcomm. "What the hell are you talking about?"

"We took her, Warden. We have her in the Holding Area. You need to get down here right away."

"Goddamn it, Tomas, I told you that no one moves on the woman until—"

"I've just sent you an audio intercept that we've traced to her. Listen to it, and meet me in the Holding Area. Now." He disconnected.

Ankledge stared at the allcomm as if it had come alive in his hand. The display showed the audio file Mehr had just sent him. He activated it.

The time stamp indicated the transmission had been initiated less than half an hour ago. The intercept cut in on a woman's voice in mid-sentence: "...did this come from? And who are you?"

He couldn't place the voice, but he thought he'd heard it somewhere before. The second voice, however, he recognized—Emma Goring's:

"I can't tell you that. Not now."

"If you don't tell me, I'm terminating this transmission."

"No, don't! I have information for you about Kane Pythen. Things they're not telling you about what happened down here."

Goring went on to recap the takeover of the Hub, the ensuing standoff, and the bombing of the landing field. The other woman remained silent, but the context made clear who she was—that damnable, prickly captain of the Jurisian Portship. And the traitorous bitch was telling her everything.

"God *damn* her!" Ankledge got moving, letting the audio play on. Outside the partition, he paused long enough to say to the guards, "No one sees those bodies until I get back. Understood? No one. Not any of the med staff, no one in command—I don't care how many stripes they wear—*no one* but me. Shoot anyone who tries to get past you."

Wide-eyed, the guards acknowledged.

Ankledge bolted from the infirmary, headed for a tram that would take him to the Holding Area, listening to the intercept all the while. Staff saw him coming and hurried to get out of his way.

Goring had finished her recitation. "They're searching the islands for wreckage. They presume everyone on board was killed."

The Portship captain—Hemly, her name was—was silent. Ankledge thought for a moment that she had ended the transmission, as she'd threatened. Then she spoke again, her voice dry, businesslike: "What is this you've uploaded to me?"

"Records from our archives. Assembled by…by a friend of mine. This is highly classified information, data from Portal transits and prisoner drops that never officially took place."

"Then why are there records of them at all?"

"Blackmail material, in case any Compact members step out of line. I'm sure the signatory governments have copies of the same records, for the same reason."

Ankledge, nearing a tram platform, slowed, gaping at his allcomm.

Goring went on: "It's vitally important to get this information off Petra. I had planned to give it to Kane Pythen, but with him dead, you're the best hope we have. Please believe me. Review some of the data yourself."

Again, Hemly was silent for long moments. Ankledge came to a complete stop.

Hemly said, "Why would you do something like this? Do you know how much trouble you could get into? How much trouble you're getting *me* into? Me, my ship, my crew?"

"You're already in danger. The longer you stay here, the greater security risk you become." Goring paused. "I don't have time to explain all this right now. But as for me…I've been waiting for years for the chance to expose the truth of this place. This opportunity won't come again—not in my lifetime."

Ankledge closed his eyes, cursing Emma Goring's name. No wonder Mehr had acted.

"Kane Pythen isn't dead," Hemly said.

Ankledge's eyes snapped open.

"He isn't?" Goring said.

"I got a brief transmission from him twenty-seven hours ago. He was cut off, and I haven't been able to raise him since."

"What did he say?"

"Very little. I only know that he's in trouble down there. Before we could trace the signal, we lost him. But according to our data, we think he's—"

Goring cut her off. "Stop. I hear someone coming. I—"

The transmission ended abruptly. Ankledge tapped some keys on the allcomm, thinking it had perhaps locked up. But the display indicated there was nothing more to the intercept. Either Mehr's men had taken her at that point, or she'd broken the connection herself.

Ankledge sprinted for the tramcar platform.

Emma Goring stood silent before the warden.

Her Petran uniform, complete with the rock-and-eagle insignia Ankledge himself had designed, was rumpled and untucked. Her face was pale and haggard. She had struggled when apprehended, Mehr had said. But she stood before Ankledge with her hands behind her back, unbowed, her gaze straight ahead.

They were in an empty cell in the Holding Area, bare concrete walls and floor, cot bolted to the wall, toilet in one corner. Chief Mehr and the two surveillance officers that had apprehended her waited outside.

Ankledge worked to appear as calm as she did. Rage wouldn't get the job done, tempting though it was. He cleared his throat. "I can't tell you how sorry I am to see you in here, Emma. I'd ask you why, but I suppose there really isn't any point, is there?"

She didn't reply. He hadn't expected her to. A disgrace to that uniform she wore, but she clung to the disciplines, anyway—acting as if she were a damned prisoner of war.

"No," Ankledge said, answering his own question. "So let me tell you what's going to happen. I'm going to give you my allcomm. You're going to reestablish contact with the Jurisian Portship. You're going to get that captain talking. It sounds like she may have an idea where Pythen is. We want to know what she knows."

He held the allcomm out to her. She glanced at it, but made no reply.

"Emma, it's not too late. The data you've illegally transmitted can be explained away. It's just names and dates, after all. Without outside corroboration, I'm not sure anyone would believe it, anyway. We can tell Captain Hemly that one of our senior staff members has had a mental breakdown. In light of recent events, that would seem more plausible than the paranoid story you're trying to tell."

He walked in a slow circle around her as he spoke. Her gaze remained focused straight ahead.

"What I'm trying to say, Emma, is that there's still a chance to pull back from the abyss. We can undo the damage you've caused, and no permanent harm done. You'll be fired, of course, but I don't think you'll consider that any great loss. You can return to your home on Adriana, get the professional counseling you need. And we can forget about all this unpleasantness." He paused, standing at her right shoulder, then leaned in, speaking confidentially: "But you have to help us first. Without your assistance, we can't move forward."

Of course, he had no intention of letting this woman ever see Adriana, or any other world in Ported Space, ever again. If she were intelligent, she would see through the ruse. But he had to try.

She shook her head, the slightest of movements, as if to herself.

Ankledge came back around to face her. "Beg pardon? Are you saying you won't cooperate? I don't think—"

"You don't understand, Warden."

Her voice surprised him. He had expected her to wait him out in silence. That was how he'd do it. Maybe there was some hope he could get her talking. "What don't I understand?"

"How pointless all of this has become." And she smiled. "Petra is finished, and so are you. I never thought I'd live to see it happen, much less play a role in it."

An urge to belt her stole over him. He controlled it.

The situation bore a resemblance to an earlier security breach, several years ago. A Hub staffer had tried smuggling out damaging records from the archives. What had her name been? The details escaped him. He couldn't even recall the woman's face. When this was over, he would investigate whether the two incidents were in any way related.

"That's all I have to say, Warden," Goring said. "Do whatever you want to me. It doesn't matter anymore." Her smile vanished, and she went back to staring straight ahead, unseeing.

"Emma, despite what you know—or rather, what you think you know—I believe *you're* the one who doesn't understand." He stepped back, spreading his arms. "Petra is far from finished. Too many powerful people have vested interests here. They'll make certain nothing comes of this…little rebellion of yours. Outside of some highly placed individuals in the Compact, no one in Ported Space will know the last few days ever happened." He took two quick steps toward her, getting close enough that his face would fill her entire field of vision. "You know what that means? It means your attempt at noble sacrifice is for nothing. Do you get that? *Nothing.*" He kept his face in front of hers. She would not meet his gaze.

He eased back. "You might just be intelligent enough to recognize the truth when you hear it. I think you should reconsider your decision."

Emma Goring held her silence.

Ankledge's allcomm chirped. Annoyed, he snatched it off his belt. It could only be Chief Mehr; all other calls had been blocked. And Tomas knew better than to disturb him with something trivial at the moment.

It was a text message from Mehr, three simple words: *Southland is burning.*

As Ankledge entered the cold site, the staff snapped to attention. Ankledge ignored them, his attention drawn to the red indicators flashing on workstation monitors throughout the room.

Mehr took over at the security station. The functionaries manning it stepped aside. The chief worked the keys with practiced fluidity, while Ankledge watched over his shoulder.

"There," Mehr said. The monitor displayed a satellite image of Southland—though at this hour, most of the image was dark, impossible to see. The land contours were outlined in yellow on the screen; without them, Ankledge would have had no idea what he was looking at.

Dark, except for pinpricks of impossible light near the western coast, north of the desert. Mehr zoomed the image. At this magnification, the pinpricks became blotches of yellow-orange light. If he hadn't known better, Ankledge would have assumed they indicated a cluster of small cities lit against the night. Ankledge counted three of them.

"Forest fire," Mehr said. "Big one."

"Have there been any storms in the area? Lightning strikes?"

Mehr shook his head. "It's been dry for the last week. That's just going to make it worse. As for the cause—we're not sure. It could be a campfire gone out of control. The area's heavily populated."

Yes, and that part of Southland had become damned dangerous of late. Control had lost an alarming number of ships in the region. Some of the survivors had come back telling tales of sophisticated guerilla attacks far beyond the skills of the usual gangs and warlords.

Someone down there had gotten careless. Well, good. That would set them back, whoever they were. And with some of the brush cleared, Control might be able to get a better look at what was happening in that forest.

"A campfire," Ankledge said.

"Maybe. Or maybe not." Mehr's fingers flew over the keys. The monitor switched to a tracking satellite view—long-range, showing Mainland, Control, and Southland. "After I saw this, I took a chance on that telemetry of the attack. We thought it wouldn't be of much use, remember?"

Ankledge nodded. "I take it you found something?"

Mehr hit a key. A set of blips displayed over Control—the ships from Farside and the Jurisian lander. It was impossible to tell from the display which was which. Then the blips went in motion, their trajectories marked by dashed lines that quickly became a hopeless tangle—the bombers looping over the island again and again. As they'd feared, not much use.

Except...

As the telemetry played on, one of the blips broke off from the pack and headed east, over the ocean. And kept going.

Mehr sped up the playback. The blip turned southeast. As Ankledge watched, it made its inexorable way to Southland.

Ankledge's breathing slowed. "Unbelievable."

"I never thought they'd go that far, either," Mehr said. "But they had a full fuel load at takeoff." He brought up another display mode, infrared this time, and zoomed in on the coastline of Southland—graduated grays, outlined by the stark black of the ocean. The remains of a settlement came into view—a small grid of streets. Any structures would be nothing but rubble by this time. "Ferrum," Mehr said. "Long deserted."

He zoomed again and pointed to a strange shape just north of the settlement. The outline of a winged craft. A lander, not Petran.

Mehr looked back at the warden. "This is live data. That's where they are right now." He switched back to normal satellite view and zoomed out again, until the glow of the forest fire showed on the monitor. "I don't know what they're doing, but all of this can't be coincidence."

An alert clarion began wailing, coming from across the room, in the direction of the tracking station.

"Launch detection, sir!" It was a staffer's raised voice. "Warden, we have a launch detection!"

Ankledge called back: "From Southland?"

"No, sir! From orbit. From the Jurisian Portship. Looks like a lander."

A strange calm dropped over Ankledge. Pieces falling into place, courses of action becoming clear. "Heading?"

"Just a moment, sir, calculating…"

Ankledge waited, already guessing the answer.

"Sir, it's on a reentry trajectory. Projections show the destination…somewhere in Southland."

"Initiate emergency procedures. Put the entire base on escape alert."

Warning tones sounded over the PA system, echoing throughout the cold site.

Mehr said, "It would take hours for us to reach Southland."

"We don't have to," Ankledge said. The escape alert had already armed the orbiting missile platforms. Any launch detections on the surface would be targeted and fired upon. "That new lander will be able to touch down, but it will never lift off. And that Portship captain will be none the wiser."

Ankledge's allcomm chirped again. He glanced down, baffled. The only person on the island currently authorized to contact his allcomm was Chief Mehr, and he was standing right behind him. No one else could override the block, except—

"No," Ankledge said. "Oh, no."

He answered the call.

Colonel Mardell's voice came on the line before Ankledge could even frame a greeting: "Warden, I see that an escape alert has been issued—again. What are you doing?"

Of course. It had been a courtesy arrangement worked out when the Casseans had first set up their black ops on Farside: in the event of such an emergency, an automated message was beamed to them so that they wouldn't inadvertently fly into any crossfire. It was how they had been able to respond so quickly to the takeover of the Hub. The escape alert had already warned them that something serious had happened on Control; they'd had the bombers prepped by the time they'd gotten Mehr's call.

Ankledge was amazed at the speed with which Mardell had spotted the alert. He must have been watching for it. And it was the middle of the day on Farside—no chance of catching them asleep.

"Damn it, Mardell, I have an emergency situation on my hands right now. Let me—"

"Have you located the Jurisian and the other escapees? Meaning they're alive?"

Ankledge gritted his teeth. "Yes, no thanks to you. They're trapped on Southland. But there's another lander on its way down to them right now. If you'll let me do my job, I'll have this situation resolved tonight." He moved to cut off the call.

"Another lander?" Mardell said. "How did that happen?"

Ankledge's calm was slipping. Rising anger made his hands tremble. "There was a brief communication."

"The escapees managed to contact the Jurisian Portship?"

"Colonel, when this is over, I promise you'll be fully briefed. At the moment, I have to—"

"Answer me, Warden. That's what you have to do."

Ankledge's eyes widened in astonishment. For a moment, he forgot about Southland, Kane Pythen, and the lander on its way to rescue him. The rest of the cold site had gone silent. Ankledge glanced around; everyone in the room had heard the exchange. They all stared at him, their expressions mirror images of shock.

He cleared his throat. "Colonel Mardell, I think you forget yourself."

"No, I believe *you* do. You said it yourself, Warden. You're accountable to the signatories of the Petra Compact. I don't work for you, sir. It's the other way around. Now answer me: did they contact the Portship?"

Ankledge's chest heaved, as if he'd run a race. He licked his lips. When this was over, he and this pissant colonel were going to have a conversation. No, better yet, he would speak with this pissant's superiors on Cassea—after which, Mardell's black ops experiment on Petra would be terminated.

But that would have to wait. He said, "Yes, Colonel. As I indicated, there was a brief communication from the surface to the Portship."

The allcomm line was silent. Ankledge glared at the unit in his hand.

At last Mardell spoke again. "All right. It pains me to say this, Warden, but that Portship cannot leave Petra."

"Jesus!" Ankledge activated the earpiece and put it in. "Colonel, I'm in my temporary command center at the moment. This isn't the best place for this conversation."

"No time for niceties now. Your entire plan was based on convincing everyone, including the Jurisians, that their envoy was already dead. They now know otherwise. Who can tell what else they know? And whatever they've learned, they'll report as soon as they get back to Juris." Mardell paused. "Your plan has failed, Warden. That Portship must be destroyed."

Ankledge waved an arm angrily at the staring staffers, a *get-back-to-work* gesture. They obeyed, returning their attention to their workstations. Ankledge lowered his voice: "Do you have any idea what the consequences will be?"

"No. And neither do you. But I have a fair idea what *will* happen if that Portship leaves the system. I prefer the devil I don't know. I'm sure we can devise a cover story later."

"Colonel, you have to listen to me. I can handle the Portship. I can handle this entire situation, if you'll just—"

"No." Mardell's voice was firm. "No, I'm afraid I've lost faith in your ability to get this under control. We've tried it your way, Warden. Now we'll try mine. You either destroy that Portship, or I will."

The bastard was giving Ankledge orders—and incredibly stupid and dangerous orders, at that. The warden's head throbbed with his accelerated heart rate. His pulse pounded in his ears. He rubbed his scalp with his free hand. "You can't possibly mean it."

"You forget: I've already fired on one Jurisian vessel this week."

Ankledge pictured Mardell as he had last seen him: overweight, bespectacled, officious...soft. All of this could be a bluff. "Colonel, if you do this, you're doing it on your own authority, and against my strong recommendation. You alone will be answerable for it. I'm not even sure the Petra Compact will be able to help you. Are you sure you want to put Cassea in that position?"

Incredibly, Mardell laughed. "Everyone in the Compact has too much to lose here. They won't let Cassea stand alone, Warden, don't worry. I do appreciate your concern, though. Now, if you'd be so kind, deactivate that damned missile system of yours. I have to initiate an emergency launch, and I don't want any of my ships shot down by mistake. Are we clear?"

Ankledge caught furtive glances cast his way from workers at nearby stations. First the doctor in the infirmary, then Emma Goring, and now this. He was being balked at every turn. The uncomfortable feeling of being cornered stole over him. He hadn't felt that way in a long, long time.

"Warden? Do you hear me?"

A bitter taste flooded Ankledge's mouth. "I read you, Colonel." He worked the keys, bringing up the executive menu and disarming the platforms. "It's done."

"Be certain of it, Warden. Any *accidental* firing on Cassean craft, and we'll finish the job we started a few days ago."

Ankledge fumed, but held his tongue. He kept his mouth clamped shut.

"I'll inform you when it's finished," Mardell said. "If you like, you can get to work on a plausible cover story."

He disconnected.

Ankledge kept the earpiece in, staring at the floor, not seeing it.

Mehr said, "That idiot will destroy us all."

The warden's hands ached. Ankledge looked at them, flexing the fingers, noting the lines there, the faint swelling. Arthritic pain flared in the joints.

He recalled Emma Goring's words: *Petra is finished. And so are you.*

"Finished," Ankledge said under his breath.

"Sir?" Mehr said.

No. Not by a long way. He had forged his destiny from the beginning, had created Petra from the remains of a failed colonization. He and he alone would decide when he was finished—not some officious bastard like Mardell, haunted by the things he'd done, lacking the courage of his convictions, the will to do what was needed.

Moving with deliberation, he removed the earpiece, stowed it in its slot on the allcomm, and replaced the allcomm on his belt. "Tomas. Take over at the next workstation." He nodded toward it, currently manned by a white-haired woman watching the progress of the forest fire. "Bring up satellite tracking. I need two views: surface on Southland, and in orbit. I want to know where the lander is at all times. And as soon as the Cassean ships come into range, I'll want to see them, too."

Mehr nodded and moved to obey.

Ankledge turned back to the workstation in front of him. He still had the executive functions open. He scanned the options, thinking through the steps he would need to take to recalibrate the missile platforms. It had been a while since he'd done it. But he should have enough time.

"Not finished yet," he said to himself. "Not yet."

CHAPTER TWENTY-FIVE

Kane drove the stolen transport as fast as he dared, forward lights illuminating a trail of twin ruts through a maze of trees. Flying back to the coast was out of the question—he saw nothing approaching an airstrip, and he wasn't familiar enough with the controls—so he kept the wings retracted and the throttle open. The forest fire, a swiftly advancing wall of flame urged on by dry winds, raged behind. Eddies of sparks and hot ash blew past the viewport—reminders, as if he needed them, that the blaze was still back there. Even sealed up inside the transport, he could smell the smoke.

Cromberg kept watch out one of the rear viewports, watching not for the fire, but for signs of pursuit. Somewhere behind them was another transport, crewed by the burned woman and a handful of her comrades-in-arms, hellbent on vengeance, if nothing else. As Cromberg and he had made their escape in the commandeered transport, the soldiers had opened fire on them. The vehicle's armor and blast-resistant viewports had withstood the impacts. Oblivious to the surrounding chaos, the burned woman had slung her weapon and gestured to the others, motioning them toward one of the other landers.

Kane had no way of knowing how far back they were—assuming the conflagration hadn't swallowed them yet. If they got within visual range, they'd be able to open fire. The artillery would be enough to at least disable the vehicle he drove, if not worse.

He used his allcomm to guide him, homing in on the crippled lander back at Ferrum—the rendezvous point.

The "road" system Dur Kofny had cleared through the woods was simple enough to follow, swerving around hills or gullies but always returning to a rough westerly track, toward the coast. He had seen only one intersection, running north-south, which he had duly ignored. The bright spot in one corner of his allcomm screen, representing the lander, steadily advanced toward the center of the display.

Though the instruments of this transport were foreign to him, he'd been able to deduce, even as the fort had burned, how to start the engines and work the driving controls. Much of the interior had been torn and gashed. The *X* that marked the foreheads of Dur Kofny's soldiers had been drawn in some tar-like substance on the bulkheads and exit hatches.

The trail turned north, running along the edge of a steep embankment. The forest to the east glowed a hellish orange. Kane kept glancing in that direction, unhealthily fascinated. He hoped he'd be able to head westward again soon.

He pulled out his allcomm, setting it to home in on the lander, and sent a transmission to the Portship, praying the lander's antenna was still aligned.

It was. Sason Hemly came on the line. "Kane? *Kane*? Talk to me!"

Emotion surged over Kane. He shoved it aside. "Captain, you don't know how glad I am to hear your voice."

"Likewise. Are you hurt?"

"Not yet. But this is an emergency. I need you to send the other lander down to me on remote, *right now*. Forget about diagnostics and flight protocols. Just send the damned thing. Trace this signal and use it to guide the ship. It will take you to a coastal settlement on Southland. I'm on my way there now. I'm about"—he checked the range on the allcomm's display—"twenty kilometers away. But I'm traveling overland, so it'll probably be longer than that."

To his immense gratitude, she didn't ask any questions. "The lander is already prepped for launch. After your last transmission, I thought you might need it. Just a second, Kane, we're tracing the signal...got it. Coast of Southland, twenty-five degrees south latitude."

He opened the throttle a little; the going was relatively smooth—as long as he didn't swerve onto the embankment on his left. Twenty kilometers between him and freedom. Fierce determination rose in him. They were going to get there; nothing would keep him from it now. Nothing. He'd drive the damned transport through stone if he had to.

"One other thing," he said. "There's a forest fire raging down here. I don't know how far it'll spread, but it's moving damned fast. Just in case you pick it up on your instruments."

"Is it blocking your way?"

The trail still led northward; the orange glow in the east seemed brighter. Or he might have been imagining it. "Not at the moment."

"Keep moving, then. We're launching the lander in five minutes."

Kane ran some quick calculations in his head. Assuming the road to the coast wasn't too convoluted, the transport would get there before the lander did. But not by much.

"Captain, before you launch, will you plot a return course for me? It will save me some time."

"Good idea." A pause. "One of my crew is doing it now."

"Excellent." It had been a long time since he'd gotten anything resembling good news.

"Kane…I know you don't have time to explain everything that's happened, but I need to tell you about a strange communication I got from Control. Someone sent us a bunch of archived data. A woman. I didn't get her name. She said she intended it for you. I've glanced through some of the files. They appear to be prisoner records."

Emma Goring. Had to be. He remembered Hal telling him that they had gained access to the archives, about a million years ago.

Thinking of Hal made his heart hurt.

"She said it was vitally important," Sason said.

"It is. It will come in handy when we get out of here." Kane glanced back at Cromberg, who had turned away from the rear viewport and was listening to their conversation.

Sason's sigh of relief was audible even over the allcomm. "Thank God. I thought she sounded like someone on your side. But, Kane, I have to tell you, I think she's in trouble. She got cut off."

Kane sobered. "We're all in trouble, Sason."

"Funny. That's what she said. Kane, we're almost ready to launch here. I need to—"

"Go ahead. I have some driving to do."

"I'll leave the channel open."

"Thanks, Captain. I mean it. I can't thank you enough."

"Thank me in person. When we're through the Portal."

"That's a deal."

The line went silent.

Kane took a deep breath and glanced again at Cromberg. "You heard? We're getting out of here."

Cromberg nodded. His eyes were downcast.

Kane alternated between watching the trail and looking over his shoulder. "Hey. Don't quit on me. Not now. You're not allowed to die yet."

Cromberg mumbled something inaudible, still studying the deck.

"What did you say?"

He raised his head and spoke up: "I said, I killed them. Hal and Miga and Orem and Varley…all of them. They're dead. Because of me."

"No," Kane said. "No. Cromberg, listen to me. Dur Kofny knew what Hal was planning. He figured that Hal would try to sneak away in the dead of night. He was ready for it. If it hadn't been for you, no one would have gotten out of there. Understand? We wouldn't be having this conversation." He risked slowing the lander so he wouldn't drive off the trail. "Cromberg? You hear me?"

Cromberg shook his head slowly. "All the wrong people are dying."

Kane braked the lander hard, stopping it.

Cromberg was on his feet. "What the fuck are you doing?"

Kane turned the chair around so he could face him. "You know, you might want to consider that maybe you aren't the person you were when you came here. Maybe you don't deserve to die, Cromberg. Maybe you're one of the *right* people now."

Cromberg stood there, gaping.

"Something for you to think about. Now would you mind watching our backs?"

The moment froze in tableau. Cromberg's beard quivered. At last, he turned back to the rear viewport.

Kane faced forward and throttled up again.

Fuckers like you. Just sit and watch, never get involved, never risk your necks. You let Petra happen.

"No," he whispered.

What have they turned you into, Kane?

The embankment to the left smoothed out. The trail again turned west.

It continued on a more or less straight track, descending as it came out of the hills. Kane decelerated a little, letting gravity do some of the work for him, leery of losing control and crashing into a tree.

The smoke in the air cast a haze in the glow of the transport's forward lights. He glimpsed small creatures charging through the underbrush, following the road, running from the inferno behind them. He expected to see people fleeing, too—villagers, soldiers, painted gang members—but the woods seemed devoid of human habitation. The transport had outpaced them all. The thought disturbed Kane. He and Cromberg were just ahead of the fire. Anyone further back, on foot, was doomed. He wondered how many of them there were.

"What's the matter?" Cromberg asked.

"Huh?" Kane shook himself. "Nothing. Why?"

"You're slowing down."

Kane looked over the instruments. Cromberg was right. Kane throttled up again.

A lot of people were dying on Petra tonight. As Cromberg had already observed, not all of them were the right ones.

At last, the forest thinned out. He thought he glimpsed patches of night sky, though the glow from the fire blotted out any view of the stars. The allcomm told him he was only a few kilometers away.

The trees thinned further, and rolling grassland took over. Kane accelerated again. The ride became considerably rougher, pulverizing his insides. He leaned forward in his seat, *willing* the transport on, steering it around the larger rocks in the way. Some came up too quickly for him to avoid. The transport crashed over them, jolting the frame hard enough to pull taut the restraints keeping Kane in the chair. The craft was not an all-terrain vehicle. Kane was past the point of caring. He would drive until the wheels came off the thing.

The last of the hills smoothed out, and the ground became sandier. Ahead lay an expanse of blackness that could only be the ocean. He checked the allcomm; they had emerged from the woods a little north of the lander. He swung the transport south, searching the sky in vain for any sign of the rescue ship.

Dark, indistinct shapes loomed in the near distance—the ruins of Ferrum, he guessed. They would come to the landing field soon.

He spoke into the allcomm: "Sason, this is Kane. We're at the rendezvous. What's the status?"

The allcomm was silent in response; he feared he'd lost the signal. Then she came on the line: "We're through the ionization blackout. I'm bringing it down as fast as I can. It's gonna come screaming in, Kane."

"Good. I'm watching for it." He turned back to Cromberg. "Any sign of them?"

Cromberg shook his head.

The ruins were just ahead now. The ground became stony. Kane slowed, but kept moving, peering into the darkness for familiar landmarks. He saw what might have been the flat expanse that marked the remains of the landing field, but he couldn't yet discern the shape of the lander. Maybe he had—

There. The forward lights picked out the canted wings and fuselage of the lander, still stuck in its ditch, off to the right, maybe fifty meters distant. He steered toward it.

A stuttering flash of white light in his peripheral vision. He turned toward it—just as a pair of explosions hit, sending up gouts of rock and soil, just ahead and to the left. Right where the transport would have been had Kane not steered for the lander.

The second transport charged out from behind a hill, lights blazing.

"Christ!" Kane said.

He jerked the transport hard right and accelerated. Its rear end spun out. Kane wrestled with the wheel to bring the ship back under control. The ocean to the west was a dead end. He brought the transport around to the north.

From aft, Cromberg cursed. The sudden maneuver had sent him crashing to the deck.

"Where the hell did they come from?" Kane said. "You were watching the whole time." He opened the throttle all the way. Under better conditions, he could have taken off. But he was too unfamiliar with the instruments—and despite Kofny's boasts, Kane had no way of knowing whether the craft was airworthy. In any case, the transport couldn't get him to the Portship.

Cromberg scrambled to the forward controls, groping seats along the way for balance. "They couldn't have gotten ahead of us."

"How do we know? They're more familiar with the woods than we are. Maybe we took the long way around."

A third explosion sounded behind them. Another near miss.

Cromberg pulled himself into the copilot seat next to Kane. "What are you doing?"

"What does it look like? Putting some distance between us."

"Turn us around."

"What?"

"Now! We have artillery, too." Cromberg reached overhead, pulled down the combat targeting array, and pressed his face against the scope. He gripped the side handles, his finger poised over the triggers.

And of course he was right. The second lander was on its way, defenseless. It would be demolished as soon as it touched down unless Cromberg and he could destroy the destroyers first.

Kane braked and spun the transport around. Another shell burst, just overhead. Shrapnel fell in a rain, pelting the transport.

The pursuers were there, twenty meters ahead, their forward lights blinding. Cromberg depressed the trigger. Guns mounted on either side of the transport discharged. The other ship swerved right; the shells detonated harmlessly, chewing up more earth. The two vehicles roared past each other.

"She's got good reflexes," Cromberg said. "Bring us back around."

Kane did his best. The damned thing steered with maddening sluggishness. His only comfort was that the odds were even.

The transport cut a laborious semicircle. The vehicle's frame groaned under the strain. Kane opened the throttle again. The transport sprang forward.

The other ship had already completed its turn and was bearing down on them, maybe fifty meters out. Muzzle flashes flared from its guns. A moment later, Kane's retracted port wing exploded. The force of the blast threw Cromberg out of his seat. Kane, strapped in, felt the impact in his bones.

Cromberg pulled himself into his seat again. Blood from a scalp wound streamed down his face, into his matted beard. "Fuck!"

"Don't worry about it." Kane jockeyed with the lander's controls, keeping them on course. "This thing's flying days are long past."

Alert indicators flashed red on the instrument panel. Kane ignored them. He still had the engines and most of his maneuverability, such as it was. He started bringing the transport around again.

Another blast hit them midships, knocking the craft sideways. The roar was deafening, making Kane's ears ring, but the vehicle's armor held…for the moment. It must have been a glancing blow.

"No *way* they could have turned that fast," Kane said. "What the hell?" His arms and shoulders ached with the effort it took to keep the transport from rolling. His wounded bicep sent throbbing heat down his forearm. He straightened their course and throttled up again.

"These things have more than one set of guns," Cromberg said. "And there are more people on that ship than this one."

The odds weren't as even as he'd first thought. "Great. If we stay out here, they'll pick us apart. We have to run." He hunched over the steering column, pushing the transport for all she had. The other ship would have to turn back around if Kofny's people wanted to keep him in range. That should give him time to put some distance between the two vehicles.

It occurred to him how comical this would have appeared had he not been in the middle of it—two military-style transports, both earthbound, charging and banging away at each other like gigantic jousters, until one of them turned tail.

"We can't run forever," Cromberg said.

"Let me worry about that. You get back to the rear portal and tell me where the hell they are."

Cursing, Cromberg got up and staggered aft, again groping at seats to keep his balance. The rough ride made the transport shake as if caught in a moderate quake.

They were heading south now, toward Ferrum, jostling over uneven landscape. To port stood the darkness of the forest from which they had just emerged, silhouetted by a faint orange glow. The fire might reach the coast, after all.

Kane risked a backward glance. Cromberg reached the portal and peered out. "You see them?" Kane asked.

"Hell, yes, I see them. They're about a hundred meters back."

"Are they gaining?"

"Doesn't look like it. But we can't run for—"

"Hang on!" On impulse, Kane steered for the forest, not braking. Again, the frame screeched. He expected to hear the thump of

Cromberg's body hitting the deck, followed by more profanity, but heard only a strained groan instead. Cromberg's reflexes weren't too bad, either.

"What the fuck are you *doing* up there?"

"We need cover. We're going back into the woods."

"You mean the woods that are on fire?"

"Where's that transport?"

A pause. "Still chasing. Might have gained a little. They—shit. Incoming!"

A muffled detonation sounded aft. Kane held his breath, but the transport continued its run for the forest without taking another hit.

"Came up short," Cromberg said. "We're out of range."

"They don't want us going in there."

"*I* don't want us going in there."

"Get to an exit hatch and open it. Then hold on!"

"What are you—"

"Just *do* it. Now!"

The land began rising again, the black wall of the forest filling the forward view. Kane glimpsed distant flames topping trees and gulped.

There was no road to mark the way, nor even a trail cleared by Kofny's soldiers. He could not hope to get very far—not that he wanted to. But he should be able to find what he was looking for before he got to the forest proper.

Smaller trees, the outliers of the woods, began to close in. Kane nudged the transport left, right, left, slaloming among them without slowing. Further along, such moves would become difficult, then impossible.

A clunk sounded behind him, followed by the rush of wind. Night air filled the cabin. Cromberg had gotten the hatch open.

The transport plowed through thickening undergrowth. A line of trees stood just ahead. Kane jockeyed around them, scraped against another tree on the right. The way became claustrophobic as the ship topped a rise.

His instincts told him it was as good as he would get. He raised his voice: "Hang on! This is gonna be rough!"

On the downhill side of the rise, he slammed the brakes and throttled all the way back. The transport's wheels screamed and locked. The ship bucked and slewed. He fought it, barely aware that he and Cromberg were both yelling, incoherent. The transport slammed into a tree and caromed left, skidding sideways. It hit something hard and jolted to a stop.

The cabin's interior lights went out; the instrument panel spat sparks and flame. The forward viewports cracked. Warning sirens blared. The acrid smell of fuel and hydraulic fluids filled the air.

The force of the crash knocked the wind out of Kane. Unable to speak, he flapped an arm at Cromberg, indicating he should get out. In the dim illumination of the emergency lighting, Kane thought he could see Cromberg's form limping through the open hatch.

His body screaming protest, breath rasping in his throat, Kane groped for the harness release, found it. With bare seconds remaining, he hit what he prayed was the emergency evac toggle, just above the remains of the shattered instrument panel. Explosive bolts blew, and the forward viewports fell away. Kane crawled out, flopped onto the nose of the aircraft, and fell into scratchy brush.

His breath came in tearing gasps. The transport had hit a huge tree hard enough to make it lean. He flailed, grabbed a low-lying branch, and pulled himself to his feet just as the forward lights from the other transport crested the rise.

Kane ran. His lungs burned.

The pursuing transport went into a skid as it tried in vain to stop. Kane heard the screech of its wheels and kept running.

Impact. The crash of armored hulls, followed by an explosion as his stolen transport's leaking fuel ignited.

Concussion knocked Kane flat. A rush of hot air surged over him. He covered his head with his arms.

When it passed, he peered out. Flame engulfed both landers, giving off baking heat. Burning shrapnel fell all around him, starting miniature blazes of their own.

Ironic, he thought, to have fled one forest fire only to start another.

Kane got to his feet and scrambled away from the wreckage, looking around in vain for Cromberg. He would have called out, but his lungs wouldn't let him pull in enough breath. He headed up the hill, back the way he had come. Muscles throughout his body ached, especially around his ribcage and shoulders, which had taken the brunt of the crash.

He reached the top of the rise and collapsed, unable to go on, at least until his lungs began cooperating again.

A hand grabbed his shoulder.

He started, flailed. A dark figure filled his vision, backlit by the fire. It had wild hair and a very strong grip. Cromberg. Kane calmed himself.

"Are you injured?" Cromberg said.

Kane shook his head. His breath was coming back to him, slowly.

"Jesus, man. You drive even worse than you fly."

Kane would have laughed if his body would have allowed it.

"Come on." Cromberg hauled him to his feet.

Kane leaned on him as they walked west. Cromberg urged him along, but running was beyond him. At times, Kane's feet left the ground. Cromberg was all but carrying him.

At least the going was easy—grassy and downhill. Kane spared a look behind him; the tips of the flames from the crash were just visible over the crest of the rise. The wind carried the smoke toward them. Kane turned around and trudged on.

Another explosion, like a burst of thunder, shattered the night. It came from above. Kane cringed, sure that Control had found them.

A large shadow swooped across the sky—impossibly fast, moving north to south. An aircraft, engines roaring, less than a kilometer up. It flew over the ruins of Ferrum and banked, descending. Even in the darkness, Kane recognized its shape and the sound of its engines.

The lander.

Cromberg stopped and stared. "Is that…?"

"That's it. Thank God."

He could walk on his own now. He picked up his pace, without bothering to watch where he was going, his gaze riveted on the lander the entire way. It described a 270-degree arc, heading out over the ocean before returning, working its way down. It would be descending on automatic, he knew. It was sophisticated enough to land itself as long as conditions weren't too dicey.

He began to run, ignoring the protests from his body. Cromberg joined him. It made little sense; the ship wouldn't leave without them. But Kane couldn't have stopped himself even if he'd wanted to.

As they ran, the ship came down in the remains of the airfield, its landing lights illuminating it in blue, red, and white. It touched down with far more grace and control than Kane had managed. It braked hard, decelerating to a full stop and then waiting, looking quite at home there, as if landing in the ruins of a deserted settlement on a prison planet were part of its daily routine.

Kane and Cromberg were about three hundred meters away, still running, when a strange sound carried over the wind—a keening noise. Kane slowed, stopped, panting and cocking his head.

Cromberg paused a few paces ahead of him and looked back. "What?"

Kane held up a hand. "Quiet for a second." He concentrated on the sound—high-pitched, distant, like a cry…human.

Cromberg's eyes widened. He looked past Kane, pointed.

Kane whirled.

The burning forest gave off just enough illumination for him to see two figures chasing them, a hundred and fifty meters distant. One of them seemed to be carrying something in both hands, something like a weapon.

"Who—"

"Kofny's soldiers," Cromberg said. "From the crash. Some of them must have gotten out." He grabbed Kane's arm and tugged. "Move!"

Kane moved. But his legs felt weighted. The muscles had already been pushed to the limits of their endurance. Petra would not let them go.

He sighted on the waiting lander. Some of the weight lifted; he ran faster. Cromberg, on a full-out sprint, opened a large lead. He looked back at Kane, who only waved him on. "Don't wait…for me!" he said between breaths.

Kane didn't dare look back over the last hundred meters. He could be shot at any moment. He could die within sight of freedom, the waiting lander the last thing he would see.

They reached the broken expanse of the landing field. Even as they approached, the ship deployed its debarkation ramp. Thank Christ Sason had thought of it. Kane's allcomm had been destroyed in the crash.

Cromberg stopped at the ramp and gestured at Kane. "Come on! Come on!"

Kane reached the lander and ran up the ramp without breaking stride. Cromberg followed.

As he stepped aboard the lander, Kane hit the switch just inside the hatch that would retract the ramp, then ran for the forward controls.

The cabin was well lit and impeccably neat. It smelled of cleaning solvents and new upholstery. It smelled—ah, God, it smelled of Juris.

Kane and Cromberg strapped in. All the readouts and instrument panels were green—except for the fuel indicator, which hovered at just below half. The ship had used up a lot to descend so quickly. But it would be enough to get them back.

Kane activated the comm. "Sason, do you read?"

"Right here, Kane. Where are you?"

"On board."

"Thank God. That forest fire is huge, and it's closing in on you. We can see it from orbit."

Kane chuckled. "Yeah. We're aware of it."

"Cut the fucking chitchat," Cromberg said, pointing out the viewport.

The lander had come down facing east, toward the hills and the forest. The prisoners chasing them had closed to within twenty meters. One of them was indeed carrying an assault rifle—the woman with the burned face. She raised it to her shoulder and took aim.

Kane engaged the drive before she could take out the wheels. The lander jerked forward. An indicator on the instrument panel lit, warning him that the exit hatch had not yet sealed. The debarkation ramp was still retracting.

A rifle blast slammed the viewport. Kane and Cromberg both flinched. Impact resistant, the viewport held without cracking. The burned woman sighted again, aiming lower.

Kane started turning the lander. The craft was less maneuverable than the transports, and was revving up from a dead stop. More shots peppered its body, dull thuds Kane felt in the soles of his feet. They did minimal damage to the hull; landers were not only airworthy but spaceworthy. One of the shots hit a wheel—number five, according to the instruments.

"We'll be all right," Kane said to Cromberg. "She'd have to hit a few more to—"

"My God, look at them," Cromberg said, something akin to wonder in his voice.

Kane looked out the viewport and saw.

Cromberg wasn't referring to Kofny's soldiers. Emerging from the hills, momentarily illuminated by the lander's forward lights as it continued its turn, were hundreds of figures—some riding bullos, many more on foot—all running full bore toward them. They were too distant for Kane to make out distinct features.

Not just members of the Night Rider gang; there were too many of them for that. They had to be refugees from the forest fire. And they had seen the lander come down.

Even the assault rifle barrage stopped. The soldiers must have seen them, too.

The lander completed its laborious turn, and Kane throttled up. The afterimage of those prisoners running for his ship, running for a chance at freedom, hung in his vision.

The roar of the engines swelled in his ears. The broken runway hurtled beneath the lander's wheels. The familiar force of takeoff acceleration pushed Kane into the cushions of his seat. It felt heavenly, even euphoric.

The wheels left the ground. The lander lifted away, climbing as it headed over the black expanse of ocean, leaving Southland behind.

It occurred to Kane that, at any moment, they could be blasted out of the air by a missile from Rolf Ankledge's damned defense system. He could only hope that Ankledge still thought him dead and that Control's surveillance systems were too damaged to pick up the lander's launch from the Portship. Given everything he had been through in the last two days, he thought it not unreasonable to pray for a modicum of good luck.

"Sason," Kane said into the comm, "we're on our way."

"Thank God. Kane, you need to hurry."

"We're coming as fast as we can."

"I mean it, Kane. We've just picked up the approach of unknown ships. They're leaving atmosphere and appear to be on an intercept course with us."

A chill settled over Kane. Cromberg frowned at the comm.

"Control?" Kane said.

"I don't think so. In fact, they seem to be…Kane, this is impossible. It looks like they launched from Farside."

CHAPTER TWENTY-SIX

"Clear the room," Rolf Ankledge said.

Mehr looked up from his workstation. "Beg pardon, sir?"

"You heard me." His voice was calm, steady, resonant with years of command. Good.

The system was ready. And so was he.

No one else knew what he had done, not even Tomas. Everyone had been too busy tracking the lander as it had descended to Southland. They had clustered around the monitors displaying the satellite data, silent, waiting to see if the Jurisian vessel would take off again. Ankledge hadn't bothered watching; he'd assumed Pythen would get the thing off the ground. And he'd been right. The lander had been on the ground less than twenty minutes. Throughout, Ankledge had kept working.

And then the Casseans came into tracking range, on an intercept course with the Portship.

It would be very close. But he still had time.

He smiled at Tomas Mehr's quizzical expression. "Go ahead, Tomas. Clear the room."

Some of those working nearby overheard. Hushed words rippled through the cold site.

Chief Mehr stood and raised his voice: "All right, everyone clear out of here. Let's move."

They began filing out, casting dubious stares at the warden.

"Now!" Mehr's voice rang off the concrete walls.

The staff double-timed out of the cold site. The room emptied in seconds.

"Good," Ankledge said. "You, too, Tomas."

"Sir?"

"You don't want to be around for this."

The chief glanced at Ankledge's workstation. His mouth opened as if he were about to speak again, then closed with a snap. "Warden, what are you doing?"

"What needs to be done."

Mehr inhaled sharply. "No. You don't have to do this."

"They think I'm finished. The Casseans, the Jurisians, even the traitors on this island. They think it's over. They think this body"—Ankledge slapped his chest—"is just a walking corpse. Already, they're lining up to pick me apart. The rest of the Compact plans to join them soon." He shook his head. "But this corpse has one move left."

Mehr's face drained of color. A touch of pity tweaked Ankledge. Even for Tomas, whose loyalty had been steadfast through the worst of storms, this was asking a great deal.

"Go ahead. I think I need to do this alone."

"No!" Mehr grabbed Ankledge's arm. "There are other ways. You have plenty of leverage with the Compact. We have options. But if you do this, we won't get a chance to use them."

Ankledge pulled his arm out of the chief's grasp and turned back to the workstation. "Go on. It will be over soon."

"Call the Casseans. Get them to back down. You can do that much."

Ankledge glanced at Mehr's workstation, which displayed the tracking data from orbit. Graphics marked the relative positions of the Portal and the Portship. Curved yellow lines indicated the tracks of the lander and the Cassean craft. He supposed there might barely be time. If he even wanted to bother.

"I'll think about it. Go, Tomas."

The lander's navigation system calculated the launch point and initiated the countdown. Even at max speed and optimal ascent, the ETA was ten minutes. Then the upper atmosphere launch engines would fire, taking Kane and Cromberg to the Portship.

The Cassean ships—they could be nothing else—had the jump on the lander. They would reach their launch points and be in orbit first. He could only hope that his own launch point would put him closer to the Portship, give him a fighting chance to get there before they did.

Sason's voice was tense, clipped: "Kane, we've got the ship prepped for Portal transit. The *second* you're aboard, we go."

Kane was too focused on his instruments to reply. He pulled back more on the wheel, hoping against hope to nudge the craft along just a little faster, get it to altitude just a little sooner.

Already, Petra was a vast blackness below them. The night sky was cloudless, but the winds aloft were easterly and strong, making the ascent choppy. Stars bejeweled the heavens. If Kane craned his neck, he could see the Portal, a pinprick of brilliant white light, the brightest object in the Petran sky. The Portship was not visible.

"Kane," Sason said, "what do those ships want with us?"

"They're Cassean."

"What? How can that be? They—"

"Just trust me, Captain. Those are Cassean ships. And they're hostile."

"Would they really fire on a Jurisian vessel?"

Kane and Cromberg exchanged glances. "They already have," Kane said.

Sason had no reply to that.

"Hey," Cromberg said. "Are we gonna make it?"

Muscles tensed in Kane's arms, chest, and jaw. He spoke through clenched teeth: "I don't know." He concentrated, brainstorming for any ideas that might get them to the launch point sooner. Nothing came.

"Kane," Sason said, "I'm getting a transmission from Control."

Running a little late, perhaps, but not out of the game. It would be good to pick up any hints about what Ankledge knew. "Put it through," Kane said. "I want to hear it."

A moment later, the Warden's voice came over the comm: "...speaking. I repeat, this is Warden Rolf Ankledge speaking. I'm addressing the Cassean craft that just went into orbit. I'm also speaking to the Jurisian Portship. I am hereby giving you—all of you—your last chance to stand down. You are both attempting maneuvers that are prohibited in Petran space. Captain Hemly, you are in receipt of classified records that have been transmitted to you illegally. Delete those records now, and I won't press charges. I can send a detail to your ship to verify your compliance.

"Furthermore, the lander you sent to the surface was not cleared by Control—a direct contravention of Petra security protocols. That craft must be sent to Control for impoundment and inspection."

So Ankledge knew about the lander. Not so late to the game, after all. At least he wasn't wasting time attempting to give Kane orders, even though he had to know Kane was piloting the ship.

"As for the Cassean craft—I know you launched under Colonel Mardell's orders."

Mardell—the name meant nothing to Kane.

Ankledge continued: "Be advised that your commander does not have the authority to give those orders. No member of the Petra Compact may initiate hostile activity here. *I* am the only one who may authorize military engagements. And this is a direct order: stand down immediately.

"I'm afraid the repercussions of any further unauthorized actions will be swift and severe. You have a single chance to avert certain disaster. I will not warn you again."

The comm went silent.

Kane glanced at the countdown display—five minutes to the launch point. If he overrode the system now, hit the primaries early…but no. They could find themselves in the wrong orbit, which would take both time and extra fuel to correct.

So Control was up and running, at least enough to have satellite tracking. Were the missile platforms active, too? The system was automated, Ankledge had said, meaning it would fire on those Cassean ships as surely as his own. The Warden hadn't done anything drastic—yet. But he sounded like he was about to.

Don't let it be for nothing. Tell someone that Hal Ellum died on Petra.

But the only two people who knew about Hal Ellum were on board this lander.

No. Others knew. Emma Goring, for instance. And she had sent Sason records from the prisoner archives. Those records were aboard the Portship, right now.

Fuckers like you. Just sit and watch, never get involved, never risk your necks. You let Petra happen.

What have they turned you into, Kane?

There was another way.

Kane's breathing slowed. "Ah, God," he said under his breath. "God, no."

Cromberg leaned closer to him. "What did you say?"

Don't let it be for nothing.

"No." Kane's voice dropped to a whisper. "Please."

He was out of time. Whatever he did had to happen *now.*

He cleared his throat. "Sason, are those Cassean ships still coming?"

"Yes. If they're planning to attack us, they'll be in range in the next few minutes."

A few minutes. He might still make it…but the chances were vanishingly small. And he knew in that moment that something much more important than his escape was at stake.

"Sason," he said, voice cracking. "Go."

Cromberg gaped at him.

"Kane, I'm sorry, I didn't get your last."

He cleared his throat again. "Go through the Portal. Go back to Juris. Share those prisoner records with the media. Spread the word. If you do it right, all of Ported Space will know. And then…have them send someone back for me."

"Kane, that's insane. I won't—"

"If you don't Port right now, you and everyone on board will die. Goddamn it, Sason, *go*!"

"I—"

"Tell my wife I love her. Tell her…tell her I'm sorry I made her wait so long." His voice cracked on the last few words. He leveled out the lander, effectively aborting the launch.

"*No*!"

Cromberg glared at the comm. "Damn it all, will you just do it? Those Casseans are going to blow you out of the sky!"

Sason fell silent, but the comm picked up raised voices in the background, other members of the Portship's crew, all talking at once. Kane could make out only snatches:

"…just accelerated! They're…"

"Captain, we have to…"

"…attack trajectory…"

Sason overrode them: "All right! Quiet! Stations!"

The chatter ceased.

Kane held his breath, mouthing the words: *Hurry, Sason. Hurry. Get out, before I lose my nerve.* If he reversed himself, if he told her to wait for him, she'd do it—and doom them all.

"Kane," she said, "I'll come back for you. I swear it."

He closed his eyes.

The comm went dead, without so much as even the faint hiss of an open line.

Kane Pythen hung his head and uttered a long, guttural cry. His body shook with the force of it.

Ankledge saw the Portship disappear from the satellite tracking and knew at once what had happened.

He sat alone in the cold site. Mehr had gone away, as ordered. Ankledge's finger hovered above the final keystroke, the one that would execute the launch command.

Data scrolled across the tracking monitors, telling him what he already knew: the Jurisian ship had Ported, leaving the lander and Kane Pythen behind.

Cowards. Bailing out just to save themselves. Perhaps Jurisians weren't as strong-willed as he'd thought. He supposed he shouldn't have been surprised. When you came right down to it, even some from Land's End—Chief Mehr for instance—lacked the essential drive to do what had to be done.

The tracking data showed Mardell's ships still closing on the place where the Portship had been, their pilots unaware of the futility of their mission. That would be a nasty surprise for them, but they were in for a worse one yet.

He would show them all the true meaning of *will.*

"Sorry, Tomas," he said to the empty room. And he pressed the final key.

Kane flew the lander in silence. Cromberg stared out the viewport, his expression blank.

The storm of grief and rage that had seized Kane had passed—for the moment. The core of him felt empty, hollowed out, spent. Deep weariness settled over him.

And he had no idea what to do next. He had nowhere left to go.

Cromberg stirred in his seat and pivoted it toward Kane. "They'll come back for you."

"Maybe," Kane said, hoarse. "If they're allowed to."

"You can—"

He stopped. Kane glanced at him.

Cromberg had leaned forward, looking out the viewport, gazing upward. From outside the lander, a brightening light illuminated his astonished face.

Kane looked up, too—just in time to see a false dawn blaze forth in the night sky over Petra.

Rolf Ankledge retired to his quarters, at peace.

He stood on his bedroom balcony, watching the fading glow overhead, the remains of the Portal. From here, his view was quite good.

What had been painfully bright to look at had become little more than a fuzzy patch of light just north of the celestial horizon. It could almost be mistaken for a distant galaxy—one that hadn't been there only hours before. Soon, of course, it would be gone, washed out by the dawn. By the next sunset, no sign of it would remain—gone, as if it had never been there.

Strong breezes blew from the west, warm, invigorating. The night air of Control smelled of the mingled sweetness from the jungle and the salt tang from the ocean. If he closed his eyes, Ankledge could imagine himself back on Land's End.

But he could not look away from the fading spectacle in the sky. Everyone on the night side of Petra would be similarly rapt, he figured.

He had walked out of the cold site to the sight of Chief Mehr standing in the corridor, ashen faced.

"You did it, didn't you?" Mehr had said.

Ankledge had placed a hand on his shoulder. "Thank you, Tomas. For everything. You were loyal right up to the end. I want you to know how much that means to me."

Mehr backed away, shaking his head. "We…this…this can't be…"

"One last thing, if you please," Ankledge said. "Control will have some visitors soon. Let all personnel know, will you? They can take shelter if they want. The Holding Area worked well enough last time, I think."

Mehr backed into the concrete wall, staring at Ankledge's feet. "This...madness..."

Ankledge had left him there. Perhaps, he had reflected as he'd left the cold site for the last time, all this had been for the best. Mehr was a good man, the best Ankledge had ever had under his command, but even he wouldn't have been able to take over Control. Perhaps no one in Ported Space would have been equal to the task. Petra had been Rolf Ankledge's dream made real, and now the dream had ended.

Well. All things pass. And he was only one man, after all. If there had been others like him, perhaps Petra would never have fallen.

On his balcony, gazing up at the embers of the Portal, Ankledge contented himself with the knowledge that he had performed his duty—no, it was more than that. He had done what he was born to do. Not many lived who could make that claim in good conscience.

The Casseans would be here soon, to wreak their vengeance. It was all Mardell had left, all he could do. He would send everything he had. With Control's defenses already weakened, Ankledge knew the base would not long withstand the onslaught.

They were coming soon, very soon. Ankledge fancied he could feel their approach, a kind of electricity in the night air.

Many—most—of his people would be huddling for their lives in the Holding Area. Such was the nature of sheep. Let them cower there. For his part, Ankledge would not deign to breathe the same air as that bitch Emma Goring, Doctor Cabot, or any of the other snakes that had betrayed everything Petra stood for. He preferred the air here.

He inhaled deeply, letting it fill him.

He waited, at peace.

They flew on.

Kane had long since given up staring at the sky. Every time he looked, it only confirmed what he had previously seen. There was no wishing it away. And it was a sight he doubted he would ever forget.

He felt disconnected from reality, as if he were watching from outside himself. He supposed he was in shock.

Still, they flew on. With nothing but water beneath them, Kane had no better ideas.

Cromberg said, "So how long does it take to build a Portal?"

Kane spoke in a monotone: "The actual assembly only takes about a standard year. But first they have to get the parts here. And from the nearest Portal to Petra, at sublight speeds…" He shook his head "I don't know. It would be a while. And that's assuming anyone wants to go to the trouble. They might…" Kane sighed. "They might decide everyone would be better off just sweeping this under the rug. That may be the easiest way for them to go now."

"They'll come. It might take years, but they'll come."

Kane spared him a weak smile. Whether Cromberg was sincere or merely trying to be reassuring, he could not tell.

"One good thing that will come out of this," Cromberg said. "Control won't last long without supplies. No new fuel. No new ships."

Kane nodded. "Control is done for. Ankledge must have known that even before he launched those missiles. He must have felt he had no other choice. I imagine the Casseans will take care of him, out of vengeance, if nothing else."

"So in a way, Hal got what he wanted. Petra is finished as a prison. We're free."

At the word, a stab of pain pierced Kane's heart. "I suppose. If you want to call it that."

Cromberg took a deep breath, exhaling in what sounded like a long, low growl. "We'd be welcome back on Mainland. It's not an easy life down there, but it'll be better for not having to worry about skimmer flights, satellite surveillance, and bombing runs. We have something started down there. And we could use someone like you to help us out."

Rising emotion closed his throat for a moment. Kane swallowed and said, "You mean you don't want to die anymore?"

They stared at each other for long moments. Finally, Cromberg said, "There's no point in me dying now. You, neither."

Kane went back to gazing out the viewport, though there was nothing to see but the stars. He considered Cromberg's words. "I'm not sure we have the fuel to reach Mainland."

"You still have enough to launch this thing into orbit, don't you?"

Kane looked over his instruments. He supposed Cromberg was

right. Once in orbit, they could come around to appropriate reentry coordinates in under an hour, then use whatever remaining fuel they had to land. They might be running on vapors by then, but Kane could at least make certain they came down somewhere over Mainland, rather than the ocean. And he didn't need a precise landing. If they got in the vicinity of Hal's people on Mainland, they could always walk. They had the time.

Tayla and Shamlyn were still out there. Though separated from them, he was not dead yet, and neither were they. There was a slim chance—perhaps infinitesimal—he might yet see them again.

And there had been a fleeting moment, not so long ago, when he had almost felt he liked this place. "All right," he said. "You can show me around your little piece of paradise."

Cromberg chuckled.

With one hand, Kane set the nav system to calculate a new launch point.

They flew on.

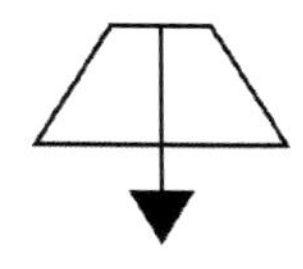

If you would like to be notified about new releases and other news of interest from Matthew S. Rotundo, please sign up for his mailing list at http://www.matthewsrotundo.com. Your email address will never be shared and you can unsubscribe at any time.

Word of mouth is critical to any writer's success. If you enjoyed this book, please consider leaving a brief review wherever you purchased it.

For a sneak preview of *Petra Released*, the next book in The Prison World Revolt series, please turn the page.

EXCERPT

Petra Released

CHAPTER ONE

He had become a teacher, here in this most unlikely of places.

He let Winter do most of the flying this time. She was his most promising pupil. She had a deft touch with the skimmer controls, in some ways even better than his. But then, he'd had precious little experience with repulsor-powered craft in his former life—before he'd come to the prison world of Petra on a fool's errand, and had wound up stranded because of it.

Kane Pythen brushed the thought away. It was easier to do when he kept his attention occupied.

Winter took the skimmer south, altitude two kilometers. The craft was easily capable of flying much higher—it had been built for surveillance, after all—but this was only a training flight. The hilly and treed terrain below became grassy, then more rocky and jagged, a harbinger of what lay ahead—the continent-spanning chasm known as the Fracture, a remnant of Petra's tectonically violent past.

Kane had let Winter pick their direction. He smiled. "Got a destination in mind, do you?"

"Quiet. I'm trying to fly here." But an answering smile tugged at the corners of her mouth. The word at Haven was that Winter had developed an attraction to a certain young man named Malkin. He had been on lookout duty at Alpha Post for the past two days.

Winter was a small thing, but muscular. She wore a simple top made of bullo skin, sleeveless to allow for free movement. Her biceps showed clear definition. She kept her dark hair tied back and out of her face when she flew. At only nineteen, her features were already weathered and hard. Petra-born, as was Malkin.

The day was overcast and cold, with northerly winds that jostled the skimmer. When he'd awakened this morning, Kane had felt the unmistakable bite of the frigid temperatures soon to come. The season Winter had been named after was on its way to Mainland. While the two of them flew, the rest of Haven busied themselves with the harvest.

She worked the twin handles on the control board before her, trying to keep the orientation true, but struggling with the wind. That was good. Kane wanted to stretch her, challenge her a bit. Loren had let him know in no uncertain terms that she expected competent flyers as soon as possible.

"Use your instruments," Kane said. "Don't try to guess what the wind's going to do."

She nodded impatiently, frowning a little.

It could be hard for green pilots to pull their attention away from the viewport—as if the aircraft would immediately crash if they weren't watching. He remembered the feeling from his early days of training. But he'd been brought along more slowly. At least a skimmer was nowhere near as complicated to fly as a bomber.

"You're doing fine," he said.

The craft was only five meters long and three wide, squarish and wingless—typical for a repulsor-driven ship. Its hull was painted black, but the gold rock-and-eagle insignia of Petra had been scraped and sanded off. The thrum of its generators was a constant vibration Kane felt in his feet, legs, and back. The interior consisted of a two-seater cockpit, a surveillance console starboard, where a third crew member would normally monitor incoming data, with some storage lockers and a cramped head aft.

Skimmers had rechargeable photovoltaic power cells that gave them incredible range but limited their size and hauling capacity. But since the fall of Control and the destruction of the orbiting Portal that had connected Petra to the rest of Ported Space, fuel was in extremely short supply. Skimmers were the only practical way to fly.

And the inhabitants of Haven, a settlement situated in the northern part of Mainland, Petra's largest continent, happened to have one—the same craft that Halleck Ellum and a small band of prisoners had lured into a trap just over five months ago.

Control was likely little more than a heap of smoking ashes by now, Kane knew. There would be no more surveillance flights, no more new prisoner drops, no more retaliatory bombings. As far as he knew, this skimmer was the only one in the air, anywhere on Petra. The notion both pleased and disquieted him.

Winter managed to smooth out their flight, her gaze shifting from the viewport to her instruments, her hands making minute movements, almost of their own accord, with the handles that controlled the repulsors.

"Good," Kane said. "Much better." He struggled to stay focused; the image of Tayla's and Shamlyn's faces tried to surface in his mind. If that happened, he would be of no use to Winter.

"I'll be flying circles around *you* soon."

"Probably."

The land rose; the terrain became more rugged. Broken rock formations, striated gray, red, black, and brown, jutted skyward. Side canyons that fed into the Fracture opened beneath them.

Thirty kilometers separated Haven from Alpha Post, perched near the Fracture's northern rim—a long day's hike on foot, a matter of minutes at a skimmer's top speed. But this was a training flight; Kane had Winter take it slow. They covered the distance in about half an hour.

The Fracture came into view up ahead, a great gash in the world, averaging some fifteen kilometers across and a kilometer deep. The jagged rock of the cliffs on the far side formed a huge wall. The bottom of the canyon, not visible from the skimmer's current position, coursed with raging rivers and falls, and lands that rarely saw the sun.

Alpha Post afforded the best vantage point to spot any unfriendlies attempting to approach from the south. Lookout posts were always manned; every able-bodied person in Haven took turns filling three-day shifts, working in pairs. The shelters were small, built of rock and/or wood, and camouflaged as well as possible. The broken land of the Fracture afforded plenty of hiding places; it was easy enough to make a shelter resemble a heap of broken stones.

Kane had already stood two watches since he'd come to Haven, including one at Alpha. Despite the spectacle of the Fracture, it was one of the loneliest places he'd ever known. The howl of the constant winds through the canyons haunted the nights—nights he had spent pining for his wife and daughter, impossibly distant from him now that the Portal was gone.

No. He could not afford such thoughts now. "How are you feeling?" he said. "Comfortable?"

"Getting there, yeah."

"Care to take a stab at landing this thing?"

Winter glanced at him, eyes widening a little, before turning her attention back to flying. "You think I'm ready?"

"More important, do *you* think you're ready?"

The skimmer had autoland capability, of course, but Kane didn't want her getting dependent on it. She had practiced putting the craft on the ground from heights of up to thirty meters. The first few attempts had been…rough, even with the skimmer's padded seating. But she had shown improvement in the last week.

"I guess. Sure."

"You don't sound very confident."

She rolled her eyes. "Yeah. Yeah, I'm ready. But make sure you're strapped in tight."

"It'll give you and Malkin something to talk about."

"Would you the post a call? Let them know we're coming?"

"Do it yourself."

"Come on, Kane, I'm kinda busy at the—"

"Multitask. Real pilots do it without thinking."

"Crap." She slowed and activated the skimmer's comm. "Alpha Post, it's Winter. Malkin, you read? A little surprise visit for ya."

The post had an allcomm of its own, one of a handful the Havenites had managed to scavenge over the years. But with no new prisoner drops, no more incoming transports to raid for supplies, Kane was hard pressed to imagine where they would get new batteries when the ones they had ran out.

"Malkin, come in. It's Winter. You read?"

The line was silent.

"Damn it," she said. "Probably taking a piss or something."

"Both of them? Who's he paired with?"

"Shaido, I think. They get careless sometimes. You know how it is out here. They better hope Loren doesn't catch them." Loren

Roman, the leader of Haven now that Hal Ellum was dead, brooked zero fooling around on lookout duty.

They reached the rim of the Fracture. Kane spared a glance toward the dizzying depths, for the moment hidden in a dense fog.

Winter brought the skimmer around, nearing Alpha's distinctive promontory. Kane leaned forward, peering at it, trying to discern signs of activity. He saw nothing but the stones of the shelter, not even the telltale smoke of a campfire—which would have been forbidden in daylight, anyway.

Winter came in over the promontory and went into a hover at a hundred meters, just as she'd been taught. The hum of the repulsors went up in pitch. "Here goes." She began to ease the skimmer down, slowly at first, then a little faster as she gained confidence.

Kane should have been concentrating on her landing, ready to take over at a moment's notice should something go wrong, but he was too busy craning his neck to get a look at the post. It became impossible; they were practically on top of it. He gave up the effort, sitting back in his seat. But unease nibbled at him.

The readouts showed the altitude as fifty meters. Forty. Thirty.

"Okay, slow your descent."

Even as he said it, Winter cranked the right control handle. The repulsors thrummed a little higher, and the skimmer slowed.

They came down a little harder than Kane would have preferred, jarring him in his seat, but quite passable for a beginner. She grinned at him, but he unbuckled and went to the top hatch without acknowledging her. Malkin and Shaido could be careless, true, but not *that* careless. He could only hope their allcomm battery had failed.

He opened the clamps holding the folding ladder in place and opened it. The top hatch was a quirk of the skimmer's ultracompact design—the only place left for an exit. Kane was too preoccupied to be annoyed with the inconvenience.

Winter turned in her seat. "Hey. Not too bad, don't you think?"

"Yes." He scaled the ladder and unsealed the hatch. It popped open with a hiss. Cold air blew in. "Come on."

He poked his head out and looked around, ready to duck back inside at the slightest unexpected noise or movement. Five meters to the right, the shelter stood silent. The wind was the only sound.

Neither he nor Winter had bothered to arm themselves for this little jaunt, other than the knife she kept strapped to one leg. There was nothing for it now. He clambered out of the hatch and reached down to help her up.

She had donned an extra skin against the wind. Scowling, she ignored his outstretched hand. "Nice job, Winter," she said as she climbed. "Really? Thanks, that's nice of you."

Kane stood atop the skimmer and took another look around, seeing nothing but the abyss of the Fracture. He shook his head.

Winter must have caught the expression on his face. She quit griping. The two of them climbed to the ground using the rungs set into the skimmer's black hull. She stood next to him, drew her knife. Slowly, they advanced on the shelter.

It nestled in a rocky depression some six meters wide, open toward the Fracture. Carefully selected stones formed a wall with a couple of holes that served as windows looking out at the chasm. Crude posts hewn with stone axes helped support it from the inside, Kane knew. The entrance faced east, away from the two of them, in a hollow hidden by an upthrust rock formation.

Winter called out as they approached: "Malkin? Shaido! Hey!"

Kane peered into one of the windows, but the shelter's interior was too dark.

Winter raised her voice: "Malkin! Shaido! Sound off!" Any echoes from the Fracture were snatched away by the wind.

They went around to the east side. Winter took point, knife at the ready. She and Kane scrabbled over the rock formation and dropped into the hollow on the other side.

A body lay prone in the entrance, pooled in dark blood, surrounded by a small flock of black, skeletal creatures with oversize beaks and membranous wings. Rockhors, they were called—inhabitants of the Fracture, carrion eaters. They ignored Winter and Kane, poking at the body and gulping down gobbets of flesh.

Winter picked up a nearby stone and hurled it at them, striking one in the back. It uttered a sound that was part croak, part screech. As one, the rockhors took wing and scattered. Screech/croaks filled the air. More emerged from the interior of the shelter; Kane and Winter had to duck to avoid them. They flew out of the hollow and were gone.

Winter knelt by the body and rolled it over. The face was a pulpy, unrecognizable mess. The arms had been gouged by the pecking of the rockhors. The torso had been torn open; viscera spilled out with a sickening plop. The stench of rotting flesh filled the hollow.

Kane's gorge rose; he fought it down. He'd faced up-close death since coming to Petra—as opposed to his days as a bomber pilot during the war with Cassea, where the bodies seen from the air had been something of an abstraction. He figured he should be somewhat bit inured to it by now.

But this was pretty bad.

He distracted himself by glancing around the hollow for any sign of whoever or whatever did this—not that he expected to see anything. The presence of the rockhors told him that the perpetrators were long gone. Still, no point in getting careless.

The body had something around its neck—a crystalline pendant on a length of silvery chain, now spattered with gore. Winter held the bloody pendant in one hand, her face grim.

"Malkin," she said.

"You're sure?"

"Necklace used be his mother's. The only thing he had to remember her by."

Winter's hand clenched around the pendant. She tugged once, hard. The chain broke easily. She stood and stuffed the necklace into a pouch on her belt.

Kane checked her demeanor. She carried herself stiffly but steadily, with no sign of trembling or breaking down at the sight of her lover's mutilated corpse—whether due to shock or a life spent on Petra, he could not say.

They found Shaido's body was inside the shelter, in a condition similar to Malkin's. The place was a shambles.

"What—" Winter cleared her throat. "What do you think? Heelocat?"

Kane called on his military training to maintain some clinical detachment. He shook his head. "A heelocat wouldn't leave so much for the rockhors. This wound"—he pointed to an abdominal slash across Shaido's belly, a twin of the one Malkin bore—"isn't a claw mark. It was done with knives." He glanced around. His eyes had adjusted to the shelter's dim interior. He spied the shattered remnants of electronic components. "And a heelocat wouldn't go to the trouble of smashing an allcomm."

"That could have happened in the attack."

"Possibly. But I doubt it."

"Yeah. Me, too." She shook herself. "I need to get out of here." She exited the shelter, stepping over Malkin's body.

She had the right idea. Kane followed her. They stood in the hollow, Winter still clutching her knife and glancing around, much as he had.

Kane shuddered. Though they were sheltered from the wind, it was still damned cold out here. He braced himself with one hand against the rock and closed his eyes, trying to think. He said, "They would have checked in last night, wouldn't they?"

Winter didn't respond. Eyes still closed, Kane raised his voice: "Wouldn't they?"

"Yeah. If they hadn't checked in, Loren would have sent you out here last night."

"So they've been dead for—" He opened his eyes and looked skyward. The overcast still hid the sun. "Maybe twelve hours, at most."

"Kane, who did this?"

His gut already had an answer. Hers probably did, too. But he wanted to think it through before jumping to conclusions. "Who's closest?"

"There aren't any settlements near here. Too close to the Fracture. And we're not fighting with anyone right now."

"Then could it have been one of our own people? Someone who had a grudge? Someone they'd quarreled with?"

She looked aghast at the thought, but she considered. "Maybe. I suppose. But—" She glanced over her shoulder at the shelter.

He finished for her: "But why leave the bodies for the next watch to discover? Why not hide them? Or better yet, throw them into the Fracture? A search could take days, even weeks. By then, there wouldn't be much left to find." He took some deep breaths. The smell was awful. "No, this looks like Bone Tribe work."

He waited for her to contradict him, to tell him he was crazy. After all, he'd only been here five months. She was Petra-born; she would be a better judge of a Bone Tribe attack than he.

Instead of vehement denial, she only frowned. "The Bone Tribes are all south of the Fracture."

"Yes, and the Bone Tribes are why this lookout post is here in the first place. In case they ever got the idea to come across."

Some adventurous souls had tried it in years past, according talk from old-timers in campfire conversations. But that had been decades ago.

"Why would they do that? Do you know how hard it would be cross the Fracture? Why go to all that trouble? And why didn't Malkin and Shaido spot them? Like you said, that's what this lookout is *for*."

The more he considered, the more certain he became. "The Fracture's not impassable. If you wanted to cross it badly enough, you could. And if you didn't want to be seen, there are plenty of hiding places." Kane leaned against the rock outcropping, arms crossed. "But that would mean they knew this post was here. That they were trying to avoid detection." And there was something else, too, something he didn't want to say to her: the Bone Tribes didn't kill for territory, or for fun. They killed for meat. Like the heelocats, they wouldn't have left so much for the rockhors.

Unless…

The two of them looked at each other at the same moment. "Twelve hours," Winter said.

Kane nodded. "At most."

"Jesus."

As one, they scrabbled over the rock outcropping, leaving behind the gruesome remains of Malkin and Shaido, and sprinted for the skimmer.

Some of the rockhors had settled on the craft. They scattered, protesting, as Kane and Winter climbed the ladder to the hatch.

Once inside, he went straight to the control board, while Winter secured the hatch. He powered up the repulsors; they responded with a satisfying hum. Over his shoulder, he said, "Strap in. Now. I'm driving."

She was in her seat moments later. Without being told, she got on the comm: "Haven, this is Winter. Copy? Emergency!"

Kane cranked the control handles. The skimmer shot skyward, banked hard, and barreled northward as fast he could push it.

"Haven, damn it, come in! Anybody on the frigging allcomm? Emergency!"

Loren Roman's voice came on the line, all business: "Copy you, Winter. Go."

"You have trouble coming, any minute now. Full alert. Get the weapons. They're coming out of the south. Kane and I will be there in"—she bent over the control board, scanning the readouts—"about ten minutes." She looked at Kane. "Right?"

"Sooner than that, if I can help it." He stared straight ahead, focused on the horizon. He flew low, only about two hundred meters, knowing he wouldn't have time for a graceful, textbook landing. The landscape below them became a blur. The first trees stood just ahead.

Loren said, "How many? Who are they?"

"Bone Tribes. We don't know how many."

The line went silent for a long moment. "Bone Tribes? Are you sure?"

Winter banged the control board. "I'm positive! They'll be there any goddamned minute!"

"All right," Loren said. "Acknowledged, Winter. You two get back as quick as you can."

Kane had the repulsors at max power. He had never pushed a skimmer so hard before. The vibration in the hull became pronounced, but the engine readouts, near redline, appeared capable of handling the load—at least for the short trip back to Haven.

"Oh, God," Winter said. She pointed out the viewport.

Kane followed her finger, looking again toward the horizon, and saw it—black smoke rising into the gray sky.

"Damn them," he said. He hunched over the board, pushing down on the control handles, as if the force of it could propel the skimmer faster.

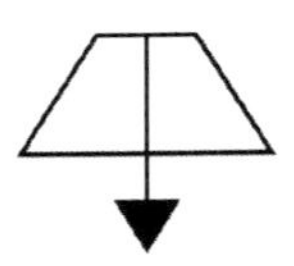

If you'd like to read the rest, look for *Petra Released*, coming soon.

ABOUT THE AUTHOR

Matthew S. Rotundo is an award-winning author whose short fiction has appeared in *Alembical 3*, *Orson Scott Card's Intergalactic Medicine Show*, and *Writers of the Future Volume XXV*. He is a 1998 graduate of the Odyssey Writing Workshop.

Matt lives in Nebraska.

Visit Matt's website at www.matthewsrotundo.com.

31812077R00151

Made in the USA
San Bernardino, CA
20 March 2016